UNEXPECTED
RETURN

by

PAMELA KNOWLES

**Grosvenor House
Publishing Limited**

This book is published by
Grosvenor House Publishing Ltd
Link House
140 The Broadway, Tolworth, Surrey, KT6 7HT.
www.grosvenorhousepublishing.co.uk

This book is a work of fiction. Any resemblance to
people or events, past or present, is purely coincidental.

A CIP record for this book
is available from the British Library

Paperback ISBN 978-1-80381-377-6
Hardback ISBN 978-1-80381-378-3
eBook ISBN 978-1-80381-379-0

ACKNOWLEDGMENT

I would like to thank Judi and Ken for editing this book and for their encouragement while I was writing it.

CHAPTER 1

THE SURPRISE

"What? We're doing what?" Since it was Saturday, Justine was home and had just finished her lunch. She left the kitchen and was sitting quietly on the couch in the living room minding her own business when her dad broke the news.

"Justine, it's an opportunity that doesn't come along very often and I think we should take it."

"You have got to be kidding, Dad!" Justine jumped up from the couch and started pacing the floor. "I'm just now finishing my sophomore year of high school. I only have two years of high school left and you expect me to move now from Indianapolis, Indiana to Oxford, England?"

"Please calm down and listen. I thought this would be a wonderful opportunity for our family. You loved the trip to England last August and I thought we could go back and this time really see a lot more of the country. I have been offered a teaching position in the John Radcliffe hospital there. It's the teaching hospital for Oxford University. That is something I've always wanted to do, to help students be good doctors. You would be able to complete your high school education there and Luke can go to college in Oxford. I have already asked the hospital here for a sabbatical leave for two years and they have approved it. I really thought you would be excited about this especially since you've been talking about our trip to England ever since we returned. You said you wanted to go back there someday soon."

"Well, I didn't know someday was going to be now and I certainly didn't think that visit would be for two years! All my friends are here, not to mention the activities I'm in. What am I going to do while you all are doing your thing? What does Mom think about this?"

"She's all for it. She has decided that she can pursue other interests now that she won't be working."

"Mom isn't going to work?"

"No. She resigned her position in the law firm. She's been thinking about it for a while now. She's tired of criminal law and would like to pursue other interests. She would also like to spend more time with you and Luke. And maybe start to write the book she's always talked about writing."

"Oh wow, Dad, I can't believe you and Mom made this decision without Luke and me! Wait until Luke hears about this!"

"Hears about what?" Luke asked as he entered the living room munching on an apple.

"Mom and Dad are moving us to Oxford, England! This coming summer!"

"What?" Luke blurted out as he almost choked on the apple. "And you're just telling us this now?"

"Your mom and I had to make sure all the arrangements were agreed upon before we broke the news to you two. It wouldn't have done us any good to tell you and then have the whole thing fall through. So, I'm telling you now."

"But Dad, what are you suggesting I do for the next two years? I'm 18 years old and graduating from high school. I have plans," Luke informed his dad.

"Well, I want you to know that I talked to Dr. Robinson. Remember, he is the CEO of the hospital in Oxford. He has not only suggested some very good colleges you could attend, but his name means something over there and he can see to it that you are accepted at the one of your choosing."

"Dad, I don't want to go to college! I have been telling you that for the past year but you won't listen. You have this alternate reality in your mind which doesn't include what I want. And no, I don't remember Dr. Robinson. That was the part of the trip where you and Justine stayed at the hospital and Mom and I supposedly stayed in a hotel in Oxford."

"Very true. I had forgotten that you didn't meet him. Parts of that vacation have been such a blur but I do remember being at the hospital, performing surgery, and having to speak to the attendees of the medical conference in London from a conference room in the hospital. That's where I met Dr. Robinson. Well, anyway, I'm listening now. What do you want to do now that you're finishing high school?"

"I want to go to culinary school. I want to be a chef!"

"A chef?" his father yelled! "You want to be a chef? You don't want to go to college? I thought you wanted to be a doctor. At least that's what you've been telling us since you were ten!"

"I know, Dad, but I've changed my mind! I don't want to spend the rest of my life going to school. I'm not like you. You've dedicated your life to being a heart surgeon and you're good at it. You've saved countless lives including the surgery in England. And I admire you for that. But that's not me!"

"I've been trying to work upstairs and can't get anything done for all the yelling! What's going on down here, Drew?" Mrs. Ross inquired as she came down the stairs, rounded the corner to the living room, and looked right at her husband.

3

"Mom, how could you do this to us?" Justine and Luke blurted out at the same time.

"Do what exactly?"

"Dad just told us that we're moving to England this summer. Is that true?" Justine posed to her mom.

Mrs. Ross turned her head toward her husband with a very surprised look on her face. "You told them?" She tried to compose herself enough so she could answer Justine's question. "Yes, it's true. Last summer, Dr. Robinson offered your dad the chance to return to England to work in his hospital. The offer was made at the conclusion of the conference where your dad spoke last August. We tossed the idea around for several months before making any decision. Dad called Dr. Robinson many times to finalize the offer and make the arrangements for the move."

"What? You've been discussing this since last summer?" Justine demanded.

"Justine, do not raise your voice to me, young lady. We did not take this decision lightly and explored all the possibilities. It was not an easy decision and we have thought long and hard about this. But in the end, we both decided that this is a great opportunity for your father and we didn't want to turn it down. So, it's settled. All the arrangements have been made and we leave at the beginning of August."

"But what about our own plans? You certainly didn't consider us in this equation!" Luke yelled as he left the room and bolted out the front door.

"I can't believe this is happening!" Justine said as she started to cry. Then she turned, left the room, and ran up the stairs to her room.

"Well, that certainly went well," Dr. Ross stated sarcastically.

"Drew, I thought we were going to tell them together. Why didn't you wait for me? I was just upstairs. You

4

could have yelled for me to come down. Maybe I could have explained it to them in a way that might have been less of a shock."

"I'm sorry, Stephanie. It just sort of came out of my mouth."

"Well, this is going to be a fun summer! Both of our children are mad at us now and I'm not sure how long that will last!" Then she turned and left the room in a huff.

Dr. Ross found himself standing all alone. Then he sighed and said to himself, "Yep, this is going to be a fun summer all right."

No one in the family talked to each other during the following week. They all went their own way during the day either going to work or school and when home, spent it in different parts of the house. When they did cross paths with someone, they would walk right past and not even acknowledge the presence of that individual. As a matter of fact, each one tried to find something to do outside the house for as long as possible so he/she didn't have to go home. Justine would go to the library or to a friend's house, Luke would go play basketball with his friends, Mrs. Ross would work on a case in the office since she hadn't officially completed her time there, and Dr. Ross would stay at the hospital. Maybe even sleep there.

At the end of a week of not speaking to his family, Dr. Ross couldn't stand it anymore and called a family meeting in the dining room. He figured if it was in the dining room the family would have to sit at the table and face each other. This had to end.

Justine came into the dining room, grabbed a chair and started to pull it into a corner when her dad also grabbed it and put it back where it was.

"We are all sitting at this table, young lady. Do not move that chair."

Next, Luke and Mrs. Ross arrived both looking at Dr. Ross for instructions.

"Please sit down at the table."

Mrs. Ross and Luke both went to opposite ends of the table. That left Justine in the middle. Dr. Ross proceeded to pace behind them as he spoke.

"I realize the events of last week may have left the people in this family a little upset."

"A little?" Justine blurted out.

"No one gets to talk but me until I am finished. Does everyone understand that?"

Each one nodded.

"Ok then. I will finish what I have to say. As I stated before, I realize the discussion held last week regarding the move was done without your mom present, and I apologize for that. We both made the decision and we both should have been there to tell you. Next, telling Justine as I did and not including Luke was wrong and I also apologize for that mistake. I have been doing a lot of thinking this past week about the move and how it will uproot you both from your own lives, Justine from finishing high school here and Luke the chance to move on in the career of his choice. Your mom and I have already made arrangements regarding our lives for the next two years. I think it only fair that we let you two do the same."

At this point, Justine and Luke have a puzzled look on their faces and Mrs. Ross one of concern because she didn't know what her husband was going to say next.

"This is what I would like to propose. Again, no one can say anything until I'm done, please." He looked at his wife and mouthed the word 'please' to her. "Justine, you have expressed to me that you would like to finish high school here and you may do that if you wish."

"What?"

6

"Please, Stephanie, I need to finish. I have contacted Jennifer's parents and they stated they would be happy to have you live with them for the next two years. I know she is your best friend and I trust her parents completely. Luke, you would be moving to a campus, I'm assuming, and would be living away from home anyway, so this wouldn't be any different except that your mother and I would be living in England. You both could come to England for your vacations and during the summer. I don't want any answers right now, I just want you both to think about it and let your Mom and me know your decision. We are a family and I want us to be that again. Families look out for one another and I had forgotten that. I got lost in my excitement about this move and neglected to include the family on the decision. I'm very sorry. It won't happen again. Still, no talking, please. Just leave the dining room and think about what I said."

The three got up from the table, looked at each other and left the room. For the second time, Dr. Ross was left in a room by himself. But this time, he felt good about what he had proposed and knew he had now given Justine and Luke the opportunity to make their own decision regarding their future. Not knowing what that decision would be left him apprehensive as he stood there alone.

CHAPTER 2

THE DREAMS AND
THE DECISION

Justine was still torn about the move. She wanted to finish high school and graduate with her friends. She was making straight A's here but wasn't sure what would happen to her grade point average if she went to a school in England. She loved singing in the choir and being on the volleyball team. She was good at both. Would she be able to continue doing those activities at a new school? So many questions still needed to be answered before she felt comfortable leaving her home. She had lived on the north side of Indianapolis her whole life and now during a critical part of her high school education her parents had decided to uproot the whole family! What if she told them she wasn't going to go and she stayed with Jennifer's family? Jennifer is her best friend but would they still be best friends if they were together 24/7? And if she did stay, when would she be able to see her family? They have always done everything together!

Then there were the dreams she had been having since they returned from England. The same boy always appeared in them but never in the same place. Sometimes she would see him in a castle and they would walk through a beautiful garden together holding hands. Other times, he would visit her in a city where she enjoyed showing him the sites. But no matter the location of the dream, the only thing she knew for certain was that his name was James and she would only have the dreams when she had forgotten to remove her necklace before going to bed, which happened more often than not. So, this James had to be connected to England somehow, but how? That was the only reason she wasn't totally against returning to England. Maybe she could finally get the answers she needed to explain her dreams. But there were other incidents surrounding that trip that she couldn't explain. She knew she had accompanied her dad to the hospital for the surgery but why weren't Luke and their mom part of that memory? Where were the two of them during that week? They remember being at a hotel in Oxford but which one? There were still so many unanswered questions about that trip. She fell asleep still mulling over all the possibilities.

When she awoke in the morning, she remembered having another dream about James. She had never shared her dreams with anyone in the family. But something compelled her to seek out her father right then and share the dreams with him. She felt that if she did, that might help her with her decision to go or stay. She found her dad sitting at the kitchen table drinking a cup of coffee and reading the paper. Good, she caught him before he left for the hospital.

"Hey, Dad, how's your morning going?"

"Fine, why do you ask?"

"Can I talk to you about something? But I don't want Mom and Luke to know, at least not yet. Let's keep this between us for the time being."

"Sure. What's this all about?"

"Well, I need to talk to you about some dreams I've been having ever since we returned from England.

9

But I only have them when I forget to take the necklace off before going to bed."

"Why haven't you mentioned this to me before?"

"I wasn't sure how you would react and I wanted to keep James to myself."

"James?"

So, Justine preceded to tell her dad all about the dreams and about James. She explained how sometimes she saw him in the past and other times he visited her in the present. She told him she felt he was someone she knew but couldn't place where she might have met him. She stated she felt a strong connection to him in these dreams and she often didn't want to wake up because she would have to leave him. She reminded her dad that the necklace had been a gift from someone in England and must have been associated with the person in black she often saw in London and then again at the airport when they were leaving England. She knew James must somehow be connected to England. She also told her dad that James was the only reason she was ready to move with the family because she was hoping she might find him over there.

"Wow, Justine, I had no idea. I know there were some unanswered questions surrounding our trip, some missing moments and lapses in memory. I still don't understand how all of us were affected by it and none of us could remember certain parts of the vacation. We each had bits and pieces we could pull from to try to make sense of the three weeks we were there. So, believe me, I am as curious as you are to discover what happened in England. And now that you have shared these dreams of yours, I'm even more curious. Especially since you only have the dreams while you're wearing the necklace. Very curious indeed. I don't know who James is but we can certainly investigate together to get the answers we're both seeking."

Justine leaned over and gave her dad a hug. "I was so worried about telling you. I thought you would just brush me off or something. But you didn't! I've made my decision and I think I'm ready for this next adventure in our lives even though I won't be graduating with my class."

"I can't tell you how happy I am to hear you say that! I have been stewing over this decision and my proposal ever since I told you and Luke, wondering what your choice would be. I know this was the right choice for your mom and me and was hoping both of you would make that choice, too. At least I know you're on board. Now we just have to convince Luke that this will all work out."

"I think he'll come around. But Dad, please listen to what he is saying about his future plans. He and I have been talking for the past year about this. He didn't know how to break it to you that he didn't want to be a doctor. He knew you would be disappointed in him. The only thing that appeals to him right now is being a chef. He loves to cook! As a matter of fact, he comes home from school and takes over the kitchen. He's made many of the dinners we've had lately."

"I remember hearing it mentioned that he often made dinner, but I didn't put two and two together until just now. Okay, I will make sure I talk to him about this and we can investigate culinary schools in England if that's what he wants."

"Thank you, Dad. I know that will mean a lot to him. He really admires you. You may not realize it but you're our hero!" And Justine hugged her dad again.

"Hero huh! I'll try to live up to the title! Now I have to go to work. I'll talk to him when I get home today. And I'll try to be more complimentary when he makes dinner."

"Have a good day at work, Dad! Love you."

"Love you back."

After work, Dr. Ross returned home ready to talk to Luke and found him in his bedroom, sitting on the bed, with books open all around him.

"Your door was open so I thought I would let myself in."

"Come in, Dad. Glad you found me because I want to talk to you about England."

"Well, it just so happens that's what I came to talk to you about. I know I really haven't been a good listener for the past year. Sometimes I hear but don't pay attention. But I would like to listen now."

"Have a seat, Dad." Dr. Ross looked around, grabbed a chair from the desk and sat down next to the bed.

"What are all these books?"

"Oh, these! Some are cookbooks, and some about culinary schools located in the states and in Oxford, England."

"Oxford?" Dr. Ross asked surprised.

"Yes, I'm still trying to make up my mind and I thought if I did some research it might help."

"It's always a good idea to research something before you commit to it," his father admitted.

"I love to cook and maybe someday own or manage a restaurant. There are culinary schools in Oxford that offer the same opportunities as schools in the states. It might be fun to learn about foods in England and be able to hop over to France sometime. Culinary schools offer degrees at various levels, anywhere from 1-3 years with internships involved."

"Luke, I'm getting the sense that you might have decided to move with us to England."

"Can't break up the family, now can we Dad?"

"No, we can't. I know your mom will be very relieved to hear that the family is moving to England as am I!"

"We're moving to England!" Luke exclaimed. Then he jumped up off the bed, lost his balance and almost fell into his father's lap. Once he regained his composure, he hugged his dad and said, "Thank you, Dad, for letting this decision be my own."

"You are very welcome, son."

CHAPTER 3

LAZY DAYS OF SUMMER?

Once the school year was over, and Luke had gone through graduation, the family began to focus on the move. Luke could now concentrate on finding a culinary school in Oxford after his conversation with his father regarding his career choice. Dr. Ross accepted the fact that Luke wanted to be a chef and even assisted him in locating a suitable school in Oxford to attend. The whole family was ready to move and start their new life in England.

Since the trip was only two months away, they started to gather anything they thought they might need in England. They made piles of items to pack and things to ship. Dr. and Mrs. Ross had decided not to sell the house since they knew the time in England was only to be for two years. Instead, they were going to rent it out to a young couple Dr. Ross knew at work who had just moved to Indianapolis. Also, the neighbors agreed to keep an eye on the place while they were gone and be there to help the new renters if needed. So, the family also had to pack up and store items they wanted to keep but not be part of the rental property. They agreed the furniture could stay and they would replace anything if needed when they returned.

Dr. Robinson had sent pictures of the house where they would be living so they knew how much room they would have, closets, attic space, etc. in which to store items they brought with them. They all loved the pictures. The house was a white, two-story English Tudor trimmed in brown. The English are famous for their gardens, and this house was certainly evidence of that fact. It looked to have gardens in the back with brick pathways winding through the flowers and bushes. It even had a gazebo in the backyard. Whenever Justine looked at the pictures of the garden, it was like déjà vu since it reminded her of the garden in her dreams. Justine had already picked out a room she thought would be great for her bedroom, especially since it looked out on the garden.

The summer was spent cleaning, packing, and storing items from the house. Also, Justine and Luke were able to spend time with their friends before they left. And, of course, they extended an invitation to all of them to come visit anytime although they figured none of their friends would actually take them up on their offer. Justine made a special point to ask Jennifer and her family to come to England since they had so graciously offered to house her for the next two years if she had decided to stay. Jennifer was very excited and told Justine she would see to it that her family made the trip.

The Ross family would often get together to review their travel plans and make decisions about what to see while they were there. Dr. Ross made sure each person in the family had input. They poured over maps of England to see how close they would be to historical sites and towns they could visit. The more they delved into the idea of living in England, the more excited Justine became. After all, this was going to be an opportunity that few of her friends would ever be able to experience and she viewed it as an adventure. More importantly, she hoped it would help make some sense of her dreams and she definitely wanted to find James. In her heart, she knew he was real and she was prepared to search for him if it took the whole two years she was in England. She had a plan all laid out in her mind and needed to run it by her parents. She heard her mother in the kitchen and decided now was as good a time as any.

"Mom, I definitely want to go back to Stonehenge while we're there. As a matter of fact, since I won't be starting school right away, I thought I could go during the first week after we arrive." Justine was rather eager to begin her search.

"Hold on, young lady. Don't start making plans without consulting your parents," her mother stated. "We will be there for two years so you'll have plenty of time to explore England. The first thing we need to do is get the house in order so we aren't living out of suitcases! And, we need to enroll you in high school, or whatever they have over there that's comparable. I still need to look into that."

"Don't hurry on my behalf. I'm perfectly happy to delay that as long as possible! I could stay out for a semester and begin in the middle of the school year." Justine suggested although she knew that would never happen.

"If you don't go until second semester, then you won't have finished high school in either place, here or there. You have two more full years to go. You need to finish high school and that's that!" Then her mom left the room.

"But, Mom!" Justine yelled hoping to get her mom to return to the conversation. She knew her mom wouldn't go for the idea, but she had to try. And even though she hated to admit it, her mom was right. She needed to go all four semesters if she was to finish high school by the time they would move back home.

She spent as much time as she could with Jennifer and her other friends for the rest of the summer. They went to movies, played volleyball, went swimming in the family's backyard pool, learned to play tennis, and even did some horseback riding.

Luke did a lot of cooking trying to improve his skills before culinary school. He used his family and friends as guinea pigs. Many of his dishes were really good, but he also had his flops. He went to the movies with friends and also loved to go swimming. One of his friends asked him to go horseback riding, but he told them there was no way he was going to get on a horse. For some reason, he had a fear of falling off! Even though he couldn't remember the experience he had in Wiltshire, England a year ago when his horse took off with him, it must have had an effect on him subconsciously.

As July ended and August began, Justine and Luke said their final farewells to their friends and promised to keep in touch while they were gone. They said goodbye to the home they had lived in since they were born, to Indiana, and to the United States. It was time to start their new lives in England.

CHAPTER 4

ENGLAND

The family set out for the airport very early in the morning since their flight left at 6:00 am. They had a long day ahead of them. The trip would take nine hours and fifty-five minutes with one stop at Dulles International. But since there is a five-hour time difference, they would actually arrive in London, England at 8:55 pm.

Once in England, their plane taxied to the gate. They deplaned and went to pick up their luggage. They didn't have very much since most of their belongings had been shipped. Then they located Dr. Robinson who was waiting for them outside the baggage claim area.

"So happy you and your family arrived safely, Dr. Ross. And on time no less!"

"Dr. Robinson, it is so good to see you again. Let me introduce you to the two family members you didn't meet last year. This is my wife, Stephanie, and my son, Luke."

"So nice to finally meet you both and to be able to put a face with a name. I'm sure your family must be exhausted from your trip. Let me help you with your luggage. The car is just outside these doors."

The Ross family followed Dr. Robinson outside to the car parked along the curb. Before Justine entered the car, she scanned the back seat for any unexpected items and after she sat down, felt around on the seat just to be sure nothing was there. Maybe there was another present sitting on the seat like last year when she found the necklace.

"Is there a problem, Justine?" her mom asked as she waited for her daughter to get into the car.

"No, no problem."

Justine, Luke, and Mrs. Ross squeezed into the back seat and Dr. Ross sat up front. The luggage they brought just barely fit into the trunk since the trunk was rather small. They left Heathrow and drove out of London on their way to Oxford. It wasn't dark yet and they could still see some of the countryside. Luke and Justine loved pointing out the similarities and differences they observed between England and the United States. They noticed the countryside start to disappear as the area became denser with houses and people. They realized they had to be close to Oxford.

"Oh, by the way," Dr. Robinson began, "your accommodations for the next two years have changed."

"Changed?" Justine asked surprised. She had already, in her head, laid claim to her bedroom. "Aren't we still staying in the house you sent us?"

"No. But I think you'll like this arrangement even better. You see, one of the doctors at the teaching hospital has taken a sabbatical leave as you did Dr. Ross, and has moved to the United States. New York, I believe, for the next two years. When he found out about your family moving here, he approached me and asked that you stay in his house while you're here. He wants to be able to return to his home in two years. I was delighted to accept for you and that is where I am taking you now."

"That is fantastic! Thank you for looking out for us, Dr. Robinson." Dr. Ross stated.

"You are very welcome. This house is north of the hospital in an area called Old Marston. You will only be about a mile and a half from the hospital so it will take you no time at all to travel. It is in a very nice neighborhood on Southcroft. You won't be far from anything in Oxford or Headington, where the hospital is located. If you remember, Headington is the area to the east of Oxford, and Marston where your house is located is on the Northeast side. Ah, here we are now."

As Justine turned to look, her eyes grew large as she caught her first glimpse of the house that would be theirs for the next two years. This house was much bigger than the one the family was to stay in originally. It looked to have a two- story main house, a garage, and an apartment over the garage. She couldn't wait to find out what this house had to offer and as soon as the car pulled into the driveway, she pushed Luke out the door, exited the car, and started for the front door.

"Will you two please wait for Dr. Robinson," their mother yelled after them. "I'm sure Dr. Robinson will give us a tour of the house. Please come back over here and help unload the luggage."

"Mrs. Ross, I took the liberty of having the boxes you shipped transported from the original house to this residence for you. Everything should be inside. Now if you will follow me, I shall unlock the front door for you."

"I can't believe we get to live here for the next two years!" Justine rushed up to the door so she could be the first one in the house.

Dr. Robinson barely had time to open the door before Justine burst inside. Her eyes grew wide as she scanned the inside of the house. This was a mansion! It sprawled out in both directions with no end in sight!

"Please take your luggage upstairs and just leave it in the hallway," Dr. Robinson requested. "Then I will give you a tour of the household. You can arrange your sleeping quarters later."

"If there is a room overlooking a garden, I want that one," Justine declared.

"As a matter of fact, there is one such room. But you'll have to locate it after the tour. It's getting late and I'm sure your family is tired. I know I am."

They took the luggage up to the top of the staircase and left it there. They would distribute the bags later. Then they all joined Dr. Robinson in the front hall so they could see the rest of the house. During the tour, Justine just couldn't stop smiling as she took in all the house had to offer. Her house in Indiana was not small, but this one dwarfed it. And it even had an indoor pool!

"Luke, can you believe this house? And we get to live here for the next two years!" Justine spun in a circle with her arms outstretched.

"I'm glad I decided to make this trip. I almost stayed in the states on my own. But I'm happy I didn't," Luke replied.

"Me, too." And she gave her brother a big hug.

"I think you and I need to do some exploring. What do you say, sis? Let's find out more about Oxford, England."

"You're on!"

"Not so fast, you two. We need to unpack and find a grocery so we have some food to eat," their dad said.

"Oh, Dr. Ross, I forgot to tell you. I requested the refrigerator be filled with some of the essentials so you don't have to rush out to get food. Especially since it is late. And one more thing, the house staff will arrive tomorrow morning. They will see to your needs while you live here. Just ask them about the amenities located in the area. Also, one is a chef and will be preparing your meals for you."

"Oh, wow! Can this get any better?" Justine sighed.

"Drew, I won't have to cook and clean while we're here! This is going to be heavenly!"

"I had no idea we were going to be treated so well, Dr. Robinson," Dr. Ross stated. This is way beyond our expectations. Thank you! But just wondering though, who is paying for the house staff?"

"You are very welcome. As to the staff, there is a benefactor at the hospital who wants to pay for them and any other expenses you may incur while here. When one of the best, if not *the* best, heart surgeons in the world comes to teach and practice in my hospital, I want to take care of that person! I will take my leave of you now and I'll be going home. But I'll check on you tomorrow. Please take the rest of the week to settle in and become accustomed to the time change. You can start teaching next week."

"Thank you, again, Dr. Robinson. I'm looking forward to working with you for the next two years and getting acquainted with England."

"Yes, thank you, Dr. Robinson. I know my husband is anxious to meet his first class of med students." Mrs. Ross gave Dr. Robinson a hug. "And I am looking forward to touring this country. It has so much history to explore."

"I will probably talk to you tomorrow, Dr. Ross. Here are the keys to this house. I hope you find it to your liking." Dr. Robinson handed the keys to Dr. Ross and walked toward his car. Dr. Ross followed him out.

"Oh, Dr. Robinson, before you leave, I have a question to ask you. Remember last year when I did the surgery, I had offered to pay the bill for the patient who apparently was destitute. I never saw the bill because you notified me about a month later of a doctor who came to the hospital and paid that bill for me. I want to personally thank him since I am here but I left the name at home. Do you happen to remember who that was?"

"Oh, yes, of course. That was a big surprise, something I will never forget. His name was Dr. Lange. He wrote a check for the full amount without any questions. But I don't think you're going to find him. He appears to be a ghost. Oh, not in the sense that he is dead, but he seems to have disappeared and no one knows where he is. His records show that he lived in Oxford about three years ago but sold his flat and hasn't been seen since. Very strange."

"That *is* very strange. I'm sorry I won't be able to let him know how grateful I am that he took on that responsibility because I know heart surgeries aren't cheap."

"No, they aren't. Sorry I can't be of more help."

"That's okay. I regret I won't be able to meet him. That was one of the goals I wanted to accomplish while here. I guess I can check that one off my list. Thank you, Dr. Robinson, for everything. I'll see you next week."

"Enjoy your week." Then Dr. Robinson got in his car and left.

CHAPTER 5

SETTLING IN

"This is so much better than I could have imagined! Beat you upstairs!" Justine looked at her brother and then took off for the stairway. "I'm going to claim my room."

"Oh no you don't!" Luke took off towards the stairway, too. He went to grab her, but she was too fast. She ran up the stairs and glanced into every bedroom. There were six of them, more than they needed. She found one that had a little sitting area and was located on the backside of the house. It had floor to ceiling windows and French doors that opened up to what looked to be a balcony.

Before she could investigate, she yelled, "This one is mine!" She had noticed another bedroom that looked to be the master suite, so she knew her parents wouldn't want this particular one.

Luke finally caught up with her and looked into the room. "This one is too feminine for me. You can have it! I found one down the hall that will fit me just fine. And, it's not right next door to you so I can have some peace and quiet for a change."

"Peace and quiet? Who's the one that's always up to the "wee" hours of the morning listening to loud music or talking on the phone? It certainly isn't me! I'm glad you have chosen a room down the hall. That will be perfect!"

"Well, I'm glad you approve, little sis!"

"Okay, you two," their mom yelled as she neared the top of the stairs. "That's enough arguing for one night." Mrs. Ross walked to the door and looked in, "I'm glad you've chosen your rooms because I think we could all use a good night's sleep. We have a big day tomorrow, a lot to do."

"Awe, Mom. A lot to do?" Justine whined.

"Yes, a lot to do. And everyone is going to help. No one is getting out of it."

"I was hoping to be able to do a little sightseeing tomorrow." Justine shared.

"Nope. Not tomorrow. We certainly don't need to hurry. We aren't here on vacation. As I have said before but I guess bears repeating, you have two whole years to do your 'exploring'. You can unpack your own suitcase for now and go to bed, please."

"Will do, Mom! Good night, sis. I'll try not to keep you awake tonight."

"That is so kind of you, Luke."

"Dad and I will be in a room on the other side of the hall if you need us."

"We're not little anymore, Mom. I think we'll be fine," Justine assured her mother.

Mrs. Ross and Luke left to go to their own rooms. Justine followed them to the door, closed it, and then stood with her back to the door. She surveyed her surroundings and a huge smile crept over her face. This room will suit her just fine. What initially caught her eye was the beautiful four poster bed covered by a flowered quilt on the opposite wall. As she stood there looking around the room, her eyes stopped on the French doors opposite her. She crossed the room, unlocked the doors and opened them. There in front of her was a small balcony with a wrought iron table and two chairs. It was hard to see the view since it was dark but she was sure there was a garden down there because the smell of roses drifted through the air. She would look again in the morning. She closed the doors, locked them, and got ready for bed. She didn't feel like unpacking her suitcase and left it on the floor until morning. As she scanned the room, she noticed she had her own bathroom which was a pleasant surprise. Right now, all she wanted to do was climb in bed. So, she plopped down on it, pulled the covers up around her neck and immediately fell fast asleep.

The morning sun streaming through her windows woke her up. It took her a minute to remember where she was. When she did, a huge smile crossed her face. Then she remembered the dream she had about James during the night. They were at the hospital where her dad was going to work. Maybe that was where she might find him, she thought to herself. But in other dreams, she had been with him in a castle. So how could he be both places? She didn't know, but now that she was in England, she was going to find out.

She jumped out of bed and was ready to start the day. But first, she decided to take a shower and wash off the grime from the trip. She removed the necklace, laid it carefully on the dresser, and then jumped in the shower. After she was dressed, she decided it would be best to leave the necklace on the dresser where it would be safe. The family would be doing a lot of unpacking and she didn't want it to get caught on something and break. Then she bounded down the stairs excited to start her first day in England. Before she even hit the last stair, she could smell breakfast and headed toward the kitchen.

"Good grief! Someone made a lot of noise coming down the stairs this morning."

"Good morning, Mom! I got a good night's sleep and am ready to start my day in a new country, in a new city, in a new house."

"Well, someone's attitude sure is different this morning."

"Yep, you can have a whole new outlook on life after a good night's sleep."

"Did you happen to dream about James last night?"

"Who? Who told you...? Dad! He was supposed to keep our conversation to himself; he promised!"

"I had to at least tell your mother," Dad declared as he entered the kitchen. "She is part of the family and I think she needs to know about your dreams. But I haven't told anyone else."

"Told anyone else what exactly?" Luke asked as he strolled into the kitchen.

"Nothing!" Justine affirmed. "Just nothing."

"Okay, already. I'll find out eventually," Luke informed her. "So just calm down for now."

"Ok, you two. We seem to be starting the day where we left off last night! Could we just sit down and have a nice breakfast in this beautiful house, please?" Mrs. Ross pointed toward the table that she had already set. Then she grabbed the platter of food and placed it on the table. "Let's just relax for now, enjoy our breakfast and then we can start unpacking."

The family sat down to breakfast and the conversations centered around the trip, Dr. Robinson, and the house. Justine and Luke were excited about the move and it showed. They couldn't stop talking about the places they were going to see. They would be there for the next two years and were very happy about it.

There was a knock on the door.

"Who would be visiting us? No one knows us here," Mom said.

She soon returned to the table with a smile on her face.

"Dr. Robinson wasn't kidding when he said the house staff would arrive this morning. That was them at the door. I informed them that they weren't needed today as we would be unpacking and they could start tomorrow. I think they were happy to have the day off."

"Before we get started unpacking our boxes, I need to unpack my suitcase. I was so tired I didn't get to it last night." Justine jumped up from the table and as she did her chair fell over. "Sorry, about that!" And she picked up the chair and proceeded to leave the kitchen.

"Okay, Justine, but you be back down here in a half hour," her mom specified.

"Yes, Mom." Then Justine left the kitchen and headed back upstairs to supposedly unpack her suitcase. But what she really wanted to do was see what was outside her doors. As soon as she entered her room, she went to unlock the doors and noticed that they were already unlocked.

"That's strange. I know I locked those last night. Maybe Mom or Dad unlocked them this morning."

She opened the doors and there spread out in front of her was a beautiful English garden, flowers and pathways everywhere. It looked to be very large and she could see a gazebo in the distance. This garden reminded her of the one she often saw in her dreams. She was eager to explore the garden but she knew her mom had other plans for her day. She would have to discover its hidden treasures another time. She went back inside and walked over to the dresser to see how much space she had for her clothes. She found the drawers to be empty and had no problem unloading her suitcase. When she was done, there was still plenty of room for the clothes downstairs still in the boxes. Then she noticed her necklace wasn't on the dresser where she had left it. She panicked! She got down on her hands and knees and looked on the floor under the dresser. But it wasn't there! She started to look around the room and noticed something shiny on the table near the bed. She jumped up and there it was. How did it get there? She was positive she had left it on the dresser like she always did. She shivered and felt a presence in her room.

"Hello. Is someone there? Show yourself cause you're freaking me out."

When no one answered, she thought it might be her imagination. However, the feelings she had on their vacation in London a year ago regarding the figure in a black robe came flooding back and she started to shake.

'This can't be happening again,' she thought to herself. 'Besides, I could see a figure then.' "What's different?" she yelled.

Then it dawned on her. She needed to be wearing the necklace! The necklace was the connection to everything, the person in the black robe and James! The necklace has been in her possession ever since she found it on the seat of the limo a year ago. No one knew where it had come from. It was so pretty she decided to keep it and wear it the whole time they were in England. Eventually, she realized the necklace and the figure in black were connected. Maybe that same figure was with her now? She grabbed the necklace off the table and put it on. As soon as she did, a figure dressed in black began to materialize in front of her and she screamed!

"Justine, are you okay up there?" Her father yelled up the stairs. The figure in front of her put her finger to her lips signaling that Justine should not alert anyone to her presence.

"Sorry, Dad. I'm okay. I thought I saw a mouse."

"Good answer, Justine."

"How do you know my name? Who are you? Did I see you in London a year ago? Were you at Stonehenge? If you don't answer soon, I'll scream again!"

"My name is Gretchen. And I will answer all of your questions. Please tell your parents you will be a little longer and I will explain."

"I'll be right back, don't go anywhere."

"Oh, I will not."

Justine left the room and went to the top of the stairs and yelled down to her parents. "Mom and Dad, I'm almost done and will be down soon."

"You're just taking your time up there so you don't have to help," Luke yelled back.

"Okay, Justine. But please hurry. We could use your help down here," her mom replied.

"Will do!" Then she turned on her heels and ran back to her room.

Gretchen was still there but had taken the hood off of her head. Now Justine could see the person talking to her clearly. She was older, had dark hair and dark eyes. It was almost as if you see right through her, but Justine knew she was real.

"I remember you. I kept seeing you all over London when we were on vacation. You scared me! And then you started talking to me, which was even worse! I seem to remember something happened at Stonehenge. One minute I was standing there talking to you and the next minute I remember being back at Stonehenge two weeks later trying to piece together the events that had happened during those two weeks.

"I am sorry, Justine, for having scared you and cannot explain everything to you at this time. I was seeking something for our town and was alerted to your presence as I felt the necklace call to me. So here I am and very glad to have found you. Why have you returned?"

"My father is going to teach at the hospital where he performed a surgery a year ago. You may have heard of it, John Radcliffe Hospital. Anyway, the hospital director, CEO, Dr. Robinson, requested that he return and teach as well as perform surgeries for the next two years. So, we're back."

"I am glad to see you and hope you will enjoy your time in England. I do need to leave but will return soon."

"You're leaving? But you haven't answered any of my questions. I have so many. My family is still very confused by what happened a year ago and need some answers. And I was hoping you might be able to explain the dreams I've been having. There is a young man who appears in them and the only thing I can tell you is his name is James."

Gretchen looked startled and a small smile appeared on her face. "I will return and we can talk again. Please remember to wear the necklace for that is how I can communicate with you, but only you. No one else will be able to see or hear me when I am around."

"You can't leave."

"I will see you soon." And Gretchen vanished.

Justine stood there in disbelief. Gretchen had just disappeared before her eyes! Was she seeing things? Did that really happen? She walked out on the balcony and stared off into the distance. England sure is an interesting place! Then reality popped back in when she heard her mom yelling from downstairs.

"Coming, Mom." Justine was more determined than ever to discover who Gretchen was and what happened at Stonehenge but for now she needed to join the family to help unpack.

CHAPTER 6

SHE HAS RETURNED

"She has returned, your highness."

"Who?" Prince James asked.

"Justine, your Highness. I have seen her. She is residing in a home in Oxford for the next two years."

"Justine? My Justine?"

"Aye, I was on a mission to find something for Dr. Lange and felt the presence of the necklace. That is when I found her. The necklace is still in her possession."

"I never thought this would come to pass! That she would return to England! And still have the necklace! I must see her. She has been in my thoughts constantly for the past year and I was hoping against hope that she would return. When can I see her?"

"Your highness, I have only just found her. She was not wearing the necklace when I arrived but she could still feel my presence. She must have remembered London because she grabbed the necklace and placed it around her neck. That's when she saw me. She screamed at first when I came into view. She just stood there staring as if she was trying to get her thoughts together and then so many questions came out of her mouth that I didn't have time to speak. What I do know is that she does recall seeing me in London and again at Stonehenge but has no memory of going through the portal. Your highness will be pleased to know that she sees you in her dreams."

"Me? She dreams of me? This is more than I could have hoped! The idea that all memory is lost after one has traveled back through the portal must be wrong. The necklace must allow a person to retain some parts of the visit. But this has never been tested before since Justine is the only one who has left our kingdom with it in her possession. I think it important I share this with my father when I ask his permission to travel through the portal to visit Justine. You must accompany me of course. We must prepare to travel as soon as possible."

"Please, wait, your highness. You need to think on this and know what you are to say before you approach your father. Please remember that it is forbidden to allow anyone to leave the kingdom with the necklace. So, remembering this, it is important you consider how you are going to inform the King and Queen of this information and of your intended departure. But you must be prepared for you may not be granted permission to leave. We have not learned all there is to know about the portal, but, as you stated, it will be necessary for me to accompany you or it seems you will meet the same fate as Dr. Ross and his family and not have any recollection of Wiltshire nor who you are seeking."

"You are right, Gretchen, as always. I will first think of what I will say and then find my father so preparations may be made as soon as possible." Then he murmured to himself, "She remembers me."

"May I come with you, your highness? It may be necessary for me to explain the circumstances surrounding my discovery."

"Aye, Gretchen, you should. If you are present, my father may be more inclined to grant my request. And, I will make sure he understands that you would be accompanying me on my journey."

A very elated prince left to locate his father. As he walked, he was practicing what to say to convince his father that he needed to leave. Gretchen followed him and often commented with approval or disapproval on the argument James was preparing to use on his father. Prince James found his father in the throne room talking to Arius, the sorcerer for the kingdom and always at the King's beck and call.

"Father, I am sorry to interrupt, but I have some exciting news to share with you."

"Ah, Prince James. And I see Gretchen has accompanied you. Excuse me one moment. Arius, we will continue our conversation after James departs this chamber. Please remain until I have concluded my conversation with my son."

"Yes, your Majesty." Arius bowed and moved to the side of the room.

"What is so important that you needed to interrupt..."

"Father, Gretchen has located her! She has returned to England!"

"Who has returned my son?"

"Justine."

"The young lady who was here last year? Her father being Dr. Ross who saved my life?"

"The very same, Father. Gretchen has seen her and she is still in possession of the necklace."

"Gretchen, is this true?"

"Yes, your majesty."

"How did we allow her to leave with the necklace?" the King bellowed. "No one is to take anything from this kingdom through the portal! How did this happen? Gretchen, how did you not sense it when you escorted the Rosses through the portal?"

"I am truly sorry, your majesty, I must have missed that in the confusion as the whole family passed through the portal."

"Father, please don't blame Gretchen for this. I am to blame. I ordered Gretchen to allow Justine to keep the necklace. It was my hope that she would return someday and I would be able to find her again."

"James, you went against everything we have done to try to ensure the portal and this kingdom remain a secret to the outside world. You have placed this kingdom in danger! What am I to do with you?"

"Father, please! May I speak so that I may defend my actions and tell you what Gretchen has discovered regarding the necklace?"

"Before you say anything, I would like to hear from Gretchen. Gretchen, I need you to tell me of your last visit. I understand you left to locate some needed medical items for Dr. Lange."

"Yes, your majesty. That was my charge when I left."

So, Gretchen proceeded to explain the circumstances of her visit to Oxford and how she came to find Justine and the necklace. She also informed him of her visit to Justine's room and the encounter she had with Justine. She relayed the details of the conversation they had and the revelation that Justine had dreams of Wiltshire when she wore the necklace to bed at night. But Justine did not seem to have these recollections when she was awake even though she was wearing the necklace. When Gretchen finished there was an overwhelming silence in the room. King William just sat on his throne and stared out into the room.

Finally, King William looked over in the direction of Arius.

"Arius, I have always relied on your counsel and trust you to guide me when making decisions. I seek that now. I am very disappointed in my son and his decision to choose love over the safety of our kingdom. I will deal with him later. But right now, I need to hear your thoughts on this information Gretchen has shared with us. Is it possible the necklace has been the cause of these dreams? And could this happen in the future?"

"Aye, it is possible. We have never had anyone retain a necklace after having traveled here nor go through the portal more than once, as she and her father did, other than Dr. Lange. This is something we have not experienced before. I also wonder if the connection she had with James may have had something to do with the dreams. I find it very curious that Justine traveled across an ocean, to the middle of another country and still experienced these dreams."

"I, too, sir, wonder how this could have happened when she was so far away," Gretchen added. "I have found when using the necklace to communicate with someone that if that person travels too far from London, Stonehenge, or me, the necklace loses its power. It must be that Justine is truly in love with your son. Their bond must be very strong."

"Father, if I may speak."

"You may."

"I am truly sorry for telling Gretchen to ignore the rules and allowing Justine to retain the necklace after leaving. I know that was wrong of me and it will not happen again. But at the time, I would have done anything to have Justine not forget me. I was also hoping the necklace would lead her back to me and from what Gretchen has shared, she has returned with a memory of me even if it is only in her dreams, but that is something. At least I am a memory."

"Thank you, my son, for your apology but I fear your love for Justine clouded your judgement this time. You must promise me that this will not happen again, ever! It must not!"

Prince James knelt before his father and stated, "Aye, Father, I understand. It will never happen again. This I promise."

"Please rise, my son, I accept your apology and will hold you to that promise! The task at hand now is to remove the necklace from Justine and return it to Wiltshire."

"Father, if I may, I would like to offer a suggestion as to how that may occur. It would serve two purposes, first to retrieve the necklace and two for me to find out how deep her memory of me is. If I find that she does not recognize me or remember our time together, then I will do as you have asked and come back to Wiltshire and marry a young lady in the kingdom. But I must know if I mean anything to her."

"And if she does indeed remember, what then? She will not want to return to Wiltshire and live out her days here with you. James, you know how I feel about you choosing someone from our own time period to wed. Not someone from the future!"

"You have made that very clear, Father. But as hard as you have tried during the past year to find me a match, you must have realized by now that my heart is elsewhere for no one here is Justine. I must know. It is eating me up inside knowing she is so close. I cannot live another day and not know if she feels as I do."

"Gretchen, do you know of this? Has my son informed you of a plan to carry this out?"

"Aye, King William, and that is why he came to this room with me in tow, to tell you of his plan to visit her."

"Leave Wiltshire? That is out of the question. You may not go through the portal! I forbid it!" King William ordered.

"I do not understand, Father. The Ross family has returned to England. And now you are denying me the chance to see the one person I love? If you are worried about me, Gretchen has agreed to accompany me on this journey. I will be safe."

"Your majesty, I have only agreed because I did not want Prince James to attempt to go on his own."

"I need some time to think. I will talk to Arius. James, you are dismissed and Gretchen, you will stay."

"But, Father!"

"Not another word from you, James. I will discuss this with Gretchen and Arius as to what can be done. But you, my son, will remain in Wiltshire until you hear anything different."

"Does that mean you will consider my request to go through the portal?"

"I do not know the answer to that question right now. What I do know is you are to remain here for now."

"Yes, Father. I will remain here..., for now."

Prince James left the throne room very dejected as he didn't know what the outcome would be. He wanted to plan his reunion with Justine. But there would be the issue of memory for she would not remember the time they spent together in Oxford at the hospital. Gretchen had erased the fact that the King and James were there. It was as if Dr. Ross had operated on someone else. She would also not remember Wiltshire because once someone goes through the portal, all memory of Wiltshire is lost. At least that was the common theory until now. He knew what would happen to him, as Gretchen had reminded him, if he attempted this journey on his own. And could he even go through the portal without Gretchen's help? Also, he wasn't sure how he would be received when he did find her. Would he need to get her to love him all over again? But he did have one thing in his favor he hadn't counted on: he was in her dreams. So, she must remember something. That was what he needed to find out. Either she needed to come back to Wiltshire or he had to meet her in Oxford. He was hoping he could revisit the future. He had really enjoyed his time there and had learned a lot. But for now, he had to wait to see what his father would decide.

CHAPTER 7

THE GIFT

After Prince James left the throne room, King William motioned to Gretchen and Arius to approach the throne so he could consult with his best seeker and his sorcerer as to how to resolve this.

"Arius, what do you have to say about all of this. You are my sorcerer. Is there any way you can do some magic and have the necklace return without someone having to go get it?"

"No, your majesty, it is my understanding my magic does not go beyond the portal. I do not know if my magic would even work on the other side. It is something that has never been tried."

"Gretchen, you actually saw Justine, not someone who looked like her? And the necklace was still in her possession? And the family? Did you see Dr. Ross in particular?"

"Yes, your majesty, I did see Justine. She looked to be in good health, still very beautiful and most inquisitive. She asked a lot of questions which I did not have time to address. But no, I was not around anyone else. I did catch a glimpse of the family through the windows of the house. I saw Dr. Ross, Mrs. Ross and Luke unpacking boxes."

"That is good news, good news indeed. Now that he has returned to England, I would like to send a gift to

Dr. Ross to thank him for saving my life. After my return from Oxford, Dr. Lange told me the surgery Dr. Ross performed would have been truly expensive. I asked James about it and he said Dr. Ross had paid for it. I did not think that to be fair and wanted to cover my own debt. I gave Dr. Lange some gold and sent him through the portal accompanied by a seeker. He was able to go to the hospital and pay off the debt owed by Dr. Ross. Now I would like to give a gift to Dr. Ross."

"May I suggest something, your majesty?"

"Please, I would welcome anything you have to offer."

"You have been talking about not being able to properly thank Dr. Ross for the past year now. I was wondering if I might take the gift to him. I could deliver it to him when I go to get the necklace."

"That thought had not crossed my mind until now. To not only retrieve the necklace but to thank Dr. Ross at the same time seems like an excellent idea. I accept your suggestion, Gretchen. Now I must think of a proper gift to give someone who saved my life."

"What are you thinking of sending, your highness?" Arius asked.

"I would like to send some of the jewels we have stored in my bedroom."

"I do not think Dr. Ross will be able to use jewels in his time period," Gretchen suggested. "They use paper money to pay all expenses."

"Well, we must find a way to deliver the jewels to him and he can do what needs to be done to change them into this paper money. I would like you, Arius, to accompany Gretchen on this journey."

"Me? Is it really necessary that I travel to the future? I just relayed to you that a sorcerer has never left the kingdom that I know of. I do not even know if my magic will work in the future. What if I am needed here? It would take me awhile to return. And as I stated before, this is something that has never been done so I would rather not put it to the test."

"I do not anticipate anything that may come up in the immediate future where we would need your services. It is important to me that I do this and therefore you will help Gretchen with this task. Now, I need to locate the jewels I will send with you so I must retire to my bedchamber. I will summon you both when I am ready to send you through the portal."

"Yes, your Majesty. I will be ready," Arius replied reluctantly.

"I will be ready as well, your Majesty," Gretchen stated.

They both bowed to the King, turned and walked out of the Throne Room.

"I understand why he asked you to complete this task, but why me?" Arius didn't want to travel into the future for he wasn't sure what would happen.

"I think he just wants to make sure the gift gets there and if there are two of us, he will not have to worry."

"I have an idea. You and James could deliver the gift. He wants to travel to Oxford to see Justine and this would be a great opportunity for him to do just that."

"And of course, you would be staying in Wiltshire."

"Aye, I would! I will have a conversation with the King and inform him of my thoughts. I think he will agree with me. We cannot leave this kingdom unprotected especially since King Henry has sent soldiers to prowl the border."

Since the day Luke rode over the hill, King Henry has had his soldiers patrolling the border. Arius felt that his leaving the kingdom would be unwise under the current circumstances. Arius was positive that reminding King William of this would help ensure he remained in Wiltshire. Arius and Gretchen returned to the Throne Room to try to convince the King that Arius needed to remain in Wiltshire.

"You are right, Arius. I was not thinking clearly. Having you leave is out of the question. I understand your concerns and I also share the same ones. I do agree that lately, King Henry has been more aggressive regarding the number of soldiers checking the border. I would hate for something to happen and you not be here. King Henry has also been trying to send spies into our kingdom. You are the only one who knows when they are coming and can send alerts to the guard. And so far, he has not been successful. You should remain in Wiltshire. I have great faith in Gretchen and think she will be up to the task of delivering the gift safely."

"King William, may I offer another suggestion?" Gretchen asked.

"By all means, speak."

"Prince James seems determined to see Justine. I am afraid he may try to leave on his own and we are all aware of what happens to someone once they go through the portal unless accompanied by a seeker."

"Go on."

"I was thinking it might be in the best interest of all if Prince James would accompany me on this journey."

"I just told him he was not to leave this kingdom. Do you think he will disobey his father, the King?"

"I do not think he would do it on purpose, your majesty, but he is listening to his heart and not his head right now."

"I agree with Gretchen, your majesty. I think the Prince needs to know if he is in her heart or just a memory. If he does this, he will be able to move on with his life, as you have requested, and he assured you he would do just that a little while ago. He seems very eager to leave the kingdom. So that he doesn't do anything foolish and attempt to leave on his own, I think it would be best for him to visit with Gretchen so that she may guide him and keep him safe."

"Arius, you have always been a trusted advisor in many matters, and this time is no different. I do think you are correct in your prediction and it would be best if he left the kingdom with Gretchen so she could watch over him." Then to Gretchen, "You will be his chaperone on this journey. He does need to forget about her and find a nice young lady from our own time. And you both think this will be the way for him to do just that?"

"I do, your majesty," Arius assured the King.

"And I do, too," Gretchen affirmed.

"Then, we have come to a decision. Prince James will deliver the jewels and, Gretchen, you will accompany him on this journey. Gretchen, you must keep him safe."

"I will be with him always. I will not leave his side."

"I need to inform the Prince of this change. I will get the gift and you can be on your way."

"Yes, your majesty."

CHAPTER 8

A NEW HOME

Now that all the boxes were finally unpacked and their things put away, a very tired family sat down to eat supper. They had ordered a pizza from a nearby restaurant since Mrs. Ross did not want to make anything after working all day. When the family had finished eating, Dr. Ross and Luke excused themselves from the table, both going in separate directions and Mrs. Ross and Justine were left sitting at the table together.

"We had pizza tonight and who knows what the chef will create for us tomorrow night! I wonder if I need to sit down with the chef to decide on the meals for the week or does the chef do that alone. I guess I'll find out tomorrow."

"This is going to be so neat having people here to do all the housework. I won't have to do the dishes anymore! Yay!" Justine cheered.

"Don't get too excited, Justine. You may not be doing housework but you will be going to school here and I'm sure you will be doing homework."

"Gee, thanks, Mom, for succeeding to bring me right back to reality! I don't even want to think about school. Speaking of school, where have you and Dad decided I am going?"

"I guess we never really talked about that with you, did we? So sorry. Dr. Robinson suggested that you attend the Headington School which is south of where we are currently. It is located in the same area as the hospital."

"Headington? Wow, I think that's a good choice! Before we came, I did my own research and checked out the high schools in the area. Did you know that there are different names for the levels of schools over here than at home? But I think I have figured it out. I think they call it Sixth Form for ages 16-18. So that would definitely be me. But I hope you're not considering having me board there."

"Of course not. You'll be living here at home and commuting to school."

"Great! I was a little worried about that. Hey, some very famous women went there. Did you know that Emma Watson went to Headington?"

"Emma who?" her mom asked.

"Emma Watson. She played Hermione Granger in the Harry Potter movies! I think it would be pretty cool to claim that I attended the same school she did. Can we visit the campus before we make the final decision?"

"Yes, of course we can. We could go any day this week if you would like. Dad doesn't have to start at the hospital until next Monday. How about Wednesday? We could also plan to ride the Hop on Hop off bus to get a tour of Oxford sometime this week. I like to ride the bus on the whole route the first time in order to get a feel for the lay of the land, so to speak."

"I like that plan, Mom. I'm really looking forward to touring Oxford. I read up about it and a lot of history has happened here. Did you know that C.S. Lewis lived here?"

"Yes, I did. I have his home, The Kilns, on my list of places to see while we're here. Next summer, I might even sign up for one of the seminars."

"Hey, I just noticed that Luke hasn't walked in here and interrupted our conversation even once. I wonder where is he?"

"I think he's already gone to his room. He's probably on the computer. Tomorrow morning, Dad and he are going to visit the culinary school he wants to attend. They will need to fill out the paperwork so he can enroll. Afterwards, they are going to tour the hospital since Luke hasn't seen it and Dad needs to refresh his memory of the place. It's been a year since you and your dad were there. It still seems very strange to me that you and your dad recall a place for which Luke and I have no recollection. Maybe, now that we are back in England, we will finally get the answers to what actually happened a year ago."

"I am hoping that, too, Mom, more than you know. But after working so hard today, I think you and I need a break. You know what I would like to do tomorrow? I would like to go swimming in the indoor pool."

"That does sound relaxing. I think I will join you. But right now, I'm very tired. It's been a long day and I'm having trouble adjusting to the time change. So, I'm going to excuse myself and go to bed. See you in the morning. Love you."

"Love you, too, Mom. See you in the morning."

Justine walked up the stairs hoping there would be no surprises once she got to her room. She was too tired to deal with anything. She quickly opened the door, turned on the light and peered into the room. Seeing nothing, she got into her jammies, brushed her teeth and climbed into bed. She hadn't removed the necklace, though, so she would be prepared if anything happened during the night. And she hoped James would visit her in her dreams.

CHAPTER 9

THE TRIP IS ON

King William thought it best, even though he had already made the decision, to consult with his wife before he broke the news to Prince James about the trip. He thought he would approach the topic while they got ready for bed that night. He felt the Queen was always more receptive to ideas then, being that she was tired from the events of the day and did not have the strength to argue.

"My love, this day has been most tiring for me. I wish our children would not quarrel over small things that do not matter. And then there were matters that needed attending in the castle which I saw to on my own. I did not think it necessary to trouble you with such trivial things. I know you had your own matters to deal with today. It must have been something important for I saw Arius and Gretchen leaving the Throne Room this afternoon and then Arius disappeared." The Queen then climbed into bed, fluffed up her pillow and waited for her husband to join her. She was fishing for information regarding the meeting with Arius and Gretchen.

The king walked over to the bed and then stopped.

"I would like to talk to you about that meeting with Arius and Gretchen today as well as the interruption by our son, Prince James."

"Interruption. Why, whatever for?"

"Gretchen has seen Justine."

"Justine! Where?"

"The Ross family has returned to England. They are in Oxford. I was not aware of this, but Justine is still in possession of the necklace. Gretchen felt its presence while she was seeking items for Dr. Lange. Gretchen went to a house where she sensed it would be and located the necklace. She picked it up to examine it and while she was holding it, Justine walked into the room. Gretchen quickly put it down on a table near the bed. Justine must have felt her presence for she put on the necklace and screamed when she saw Gretchen."

"She still has the necklace!" the Queen exclaimed. "How is that possible? Is Justine here, in Wiltshire? Did Gretchen bring her here?"

"Yes, and no, Justine is not here. She remains in her own time. Gretchen did talk to Justine for a short time. Then she told Justine it was necessary for her to leave, but that she would return. However, Justine continues to be in possession of the necklace. When Gretchen arrived back in Wiltshire, she told the Prince what had happened. I have also learned that Justine sees James in her dreams. That is why James came to see me and interrupted my conversation with Arius. Gretchen came with him so that she could explain the encounter."

"She dreams of him? What did James say? What was his reaction?"

"I am getting to that part, please be patient. James informed me that he must go see her, in her own time."

"I hope you told him no."

"I did...then."

"Explain, please."

"I am trying to my dear." King William now realized that no time would have been a good time to explain this to the Queen, especially when their son was involved. "You know I have wanted to give Dr. Ross a gift to thank him for all he did, but have not been able to since his departure. This news is giving me the opportunity to do that now. I talked to Arius and Gretchen about delivering the gift together..."

"Do you think it wise for Arius to leave?" the Queen implored.

"No, I do not. Arius explained why he thought he should not leave and I agreed. Then Gretchen expressed her fear regarding James and his desire to see Justine again. We both know our son has a mind of his own and if he wants to leave Wiltshire to see Justine, he may just try to do it."

"When James gets a thought in his head, it is hard to reason with him. That is true," the Queen agreed. "Well, I have a thought. Since Gretchen is traveling through the portal to deliver the gift, I think we must allow James to accompany her. That way we know he will be protected on this journey into the future and he will be able to visit Justine."

The King looked at her surprised since she had just offered the very remedy that he was going to propose.

"That is a very good idea, my dear. Why had I not thought of that? We can send James with Gretchen and resolve two issues at the same time."

"You are welcome. I wonder how he will be received by her. We thought she would have no memory of him. Yet, she dreams of him, curious. This trip may be a good thing. He will realize she does not care for him the way he cares for her. Then he can stop thinking of her and move on. He can return home and marry someone in our own kingdom as you have requested. I feel her return may be a blessing. Now that that is settled, please climb into bed so we can get some sleep."

King William still worried about Justine's dreams and the fact that she may not have completely lost the memory of her time with them. Perhaps, the reason would be something James and Gretchen would discover during this journey and return with some answers.

The next morning, King William wanted to tell James his decision regarding the trip. He searched for him but to no avail. His search finally led him to the Great Hall where he found the rest of the family eating breakfast.

"Oh, Father, have you heard the good news? Justine is back! Not here but in England in her own time! Isn't that wonderful?" Madison was older now, almost fourteen, and more inquisitive about life and the world around her. "May we go see her?"

"Who informed you of this? And no, you will not be leaving Wiltshire."

"James did, this morning while he was eating breakfast." John responded quietly. When James announced that Justine was back, John's heart skipped a beat. He had feelings for her that he had never divulged to anyone. She belonged to James. And besides, when she left, he thought he would never see her again. Now the thought of her back in their lives left him weak in the knees. What would he do if she ever came back to Wiltshire? John had turned twenty during the past year and his father was pressuring him to find a spouse. His father had introduced him to a young lady from the kingdom to their north who his father thought would be a good match. John knew their union would strengthen the alliance between the two kingdoms and help to ensure that peace was maintained in the country of England, despite King Henry to their south. Finally, Justine had become but a mere memory. But now James was talking about going to find Justine and his feelings for her came flooding back.

"And why can't we go? James said he is going," Madison stated.

"He what? I must talk to him. Do you know where he might be?"

"I do, Father," Bethany chimed in, "he said he wanted to walk through the garden. He said Justine was there. But I don't think he is telling the truth because Justine is still in her own time, right Father?" Bethany was now eleven and had grown at least an inch in the last year. She was almost as tall as Madison.

"Thank you, Bethany. You are right. Justine is not here."

"I hope she comes to visit. I really miss her." Bethany added.

"Me, too. Are you sure we can't go through the portal with James?" Madison inquired in a hopeful way.

Then John heard himself blurt out, "I'll go with him! I mean, I can go with James, Father to ensure his safety."

"Thank you, John, but James cannot go through the portal without a seeker and that will be Gretchen. She will go with him and will be able to see to his safety. Now I must find James."

The King left and went to the garden at the back of the palace. He remembered that was where James had said good bye to Justine the morning before her family left. He found James walking among the flowers along the path to the gazebo. James walked up the steps to the gazebo, put his hands on the railing and just stood there staring.

"James. James, my son, I need to talk to you! James, can you hear me?" King William said as he approached the gazebo.

James turned around and noticed his father standing there.

"Oh, Father. I must have been deep in thought and did not hear you approach. I am sorry."

"James, I would like to talk to you about Justine."

"If you are going to tell me I cannot go see her, then you might as well not say any more."

"You were ready to defy my order? I told you not to leave Wiltshire and yet at breakfast I learned from Bethany that you were leaving. Explain why she said that!"

"She relayed this information to you incorrectly. I told her I was hoping to leave, not that I *was* leaving. I wanted to talk to you further today in hopes I could convince you to let me go."

The King relaxed a little when he heard this and said, "I was going to tell you that you may go through the portal and Gretchen will accompany you."

"What!!? I am confused. Yesterday you said I was not to leave Wiltshire."

"I did say that. But I also said I needed to talk to Arius and Gretchen about a matter concerning Dr. Ross and I told you to remain here for now. After talking to Arius and your mother, we have decided you and Gretchen will be the ones to deliver a gift to Dr. Ross."

"A gift? Mother said it was fine with her?"

"Aye, as a matter of fact, the suggestion came from your mother. As for the gift, I have wanted to thank Dr. Ross for saving my life but did not know how to do that. Now that the Ross family has returned, it will be possible to show my gratitude for giving me my life back."

"When may I go?" James responded excitedly.

"That is still to be determined, but I think within the next day or so. I have already gotten the gift ready and have placed it in a decorative chest to be delivered. I need to talk to Gretchen about this decision and have her make arrangements for your departure."

"I still have the clothes Arius created for me a year ago when you had your surgery. I will locate those and see if they still fit. I know I have grown a little since the last time I wore them."

"It is good that you still have those clothes. I will instruct Arius to make any changes to the clothes for you if needed. Now I need to find Gretchen and inform her I have changed my mind regarding your departure."

"Thank you, Father. This really means a lot to me."

After his father left, he turned around and, in his excitement, he hit the rail on the gazebo with the edge of his fist. He was eager to travel and was overjoyed his Father had given him permission to go.

CHAPTER 10

LUKE ENROLLS

"This pool is just what I needed this afternoon. I'm glad you thought of it, Justine."

"Me, too, Mom. I love just floating around on the water. It's so relaxing. I also can't believe the walls open up like they do. There are so many sliding glass doors. When they're all open, it makes it feel like you're outside. When closed, you can use it in the winter. Maybe we ought to do this to our pool at home? But, then again, trying to heat it in the winter months would be very expensive! When do you think Dad and Luke will be getting back? I hope Luke likes the school he's enrolling in today."

"I do, too. Your dad says it is well known throughout Europe and later on in his education, Luke would be able to decide where he would like to intern. There would be several countries over here from which to choose."

"Wow, I didn't realize that. That would be a real advantage for him when he goes back home to the states."

"Assuming he wants to go back."

"You don't think he'll want to go back home after these two years are up?"

"Justine, we can't assume anything when it comes to your brother."

"That's very true."

"Hey, there! We wondered where you two were," Luke said as he approached finding Justine and his mom floating in the pool.

"Go get your suit on and come float with us. You can tell us all about the school."

"Okay. Be back before you can say culinary school!"

"Culinary School. You're not back yet!"

"Very funny, sis! See you both soon."

"So, this is where you two have been spending your day. Must have been a rough one." Dad said as he walked into the pool area and sat on one of the lounge chairs.

"Yes, it's definitely been rough. How was your day? Did everything go as planned?" Mom asked.

"I think I'll wait until Luke gets back and he can fill you in since it all centers around him."

"You can't even give us a hint?" Justine pleaded.

"It went well; that's all I'll say," her dad replied.

Luke returned, dropped his towel on one of the lounge chairs and proceeded to run toward the pool.

"Bombs away!" and he jumped into the pool making a huge splash.

"Thanks for getting us all wet!" Justine yelled as she wiped the water off her face. "We can always count on you to stir things up around here!" Justine was rather perturbed at her brother since he had just destroyed the quiet day her mother and she had had up to that point.

"You're welcome!" Luke grabbed a float, climbed on, and for the rest of the afternoon proceeded to tell them all about the school, where it's located, how many students go there, how long it will take to graduate, possible internships, how prestigious it is, and the cost, which he saved for last.

"You sound so excited about this. I'm very happy for you, Luke. Now, aren't you glad you came to England with us?" his mother asked.

"Yes. It was the right thing to do. And tomorrow, it's your turn, little sis. You get to visit the school where you will complete your high school education! Are you nervous?"

"Me, nervous? Yes, yes I am. I've never been to a school that's all girls before."

"That's a good thing. It will keep your mind off boys so you can concentrate on your studies," Mom added.

"Oh, Mom, I don't think boys are going to be a problem for Justine. Her mind is only on James, the boy of her dreams!"

"Now you've done it!" And Justine hopped off her float and turned Luke's float over. He came up from under the water and splashed her. Then a splashing and dunking competition began.

"Okay, you two. Now you're getting *me* all wet! Well, if you can't beat them, join them I always say!" And their mom fell off her float and joined in the splashing. They even splashed their dad who was minding his own business.

"I know when it's time to leave!" he said as he got up from the lounge chair and started to leave the pool deck.

"Dr. Ross, should I serve dinner now?" It was Jennifer, the chef for the house. She wasn't very old, in her early twenties. She had dark hair and big dark eyes and close to Justine's height. She was very polite and a very good cook. She had graduated from the culinary school Luke was to attend and this was her first job after graduating.

"Yes, go ahead. I don't think they'll be in the water much longer."

"Thank you, sir." And she retired to the kitchen.

The three very water-logged swimmers finally decided they had had enough and got out of the pool.

"I haven't had that much fun in a long time!" Justine said. "I'm glad we came."

"Me, too," Luke responded.

"Me, too," their mom added. "Now, let's get out of these wet bathing suits and go inside and change for dinner."

They dried off and went upstairs to change. When they came back downstairs, Jennifer had finished preparing the dinner and everything was already out on the table.

"This looks great!" Justine said as she took her seat at the table.

They all sat down and passed the food family style around the table.

"Please give my compliments to the chef. This is delicious!" Mom said as she took her first bite.

"You know she went to the same school I'm attending," Luke informed his mom.

"No, I didn't know that. Well, maybe she'll be able to give you some pointers while you're going to school."

"Maybe she can. I hope we can discuss a lot of things, related to school that is!"

"Does my big brother have a crush on our chef?"

"No, I will be grateful for any help she can offer."

"Sure, you will!"

"Let's not finish this wonderful dinner with a spat between you two," their mother asked. "I think we need to thank Jennifer for this fabulous meal and move someplace more comfortable."

After dinner, they moved to the living room since no one was ready to retire for the night. They sat and talked for several more hours. Luke was still talking about the day he had had when, finally, Justine stood up and yawned.

"Well, brother, I know you're excited about culinary school, but I think I've heard enough for one day. I for one am going to bed. It's my turn to tour tomorrow and I want to have a good night's sleep."

"That's a good idea," her mom chimed in. "I think we should all go to bed. So, for now we will say good night to you two and Dad and I will see you in the morning."

"Good night, Mom and Dad. Thank you again for bringing us to England and for helping me enroll in culinary school. I know it's not what Dad wished for me but it's what I really want to do and I thank you."

"You're welcome, Luke. You need to follow your dreams, not mine. Now we can look forward to many great meals from our own family chef! Good night you two," their dad replied.

"Good night," Luke and Justine responded in tandem. They all walked upstairs and went to bed.

CHAPTER 11

JUSTINE VISITS HEADINGTON

Justine opened her eyes and looked over at her clock. It was 7:00 am, too early for her to make her appearance downstairs so she just lay in bed staring at the ceiling. She knew today she was to visit the high school she would be attending and she was not eager to get the day started. Maybe she should just wait until her mom came to the room to wake her up. But she decided against that idea since she needed to take a shower. It was important she look her best when she went to Headington. There would be a lot of girls crisscrossing the campus and she wanted to be looked at in a positive way, accepted even before she started school.

After she felt she had made herself presentable, curled her hair and put on her makeup, she went downstairs for breakfast.

"There she is. I thought I was going to have to wake you up. But then I heard the shower and knew you were up. Here, sit down and have some breakfast. We have a big morning ahead of us," her mom informed her.

"Yes, I am a little apprehensive about today. I don't know how I'll be accepted, an American student at a prestigious English high school. Maybe they won't like me, the girls I mean."

"You have nothing to worry about. You are a great student, a wonderful, kind person, and any one of them would be lucky to have you as a friend," her mom assured her.

"That's easy for you to say: you're my mom!"

"They are going to love you at that school and if they don't, they don't know what they're missing," her dad added.

"Well, I know what they'd be missing. Another ditsy blonde!" Luke decided to add some levity to the conversation. "Just kidding. You'll do great, sis! Don't even think about the girls there. But if you meet one that is really pretty, tell them about your good-looking brother and they'll be your best friend!"

"Very funny, Luke. If I tell them about you, they'll run away!"

"That's enough you two. Justine, finish up. We have an appointment at 9:00. Dad is going with us. So, go do whatever you need to do to finish getting ready and let's go."

"I'll run upstairs, brush my teeth, get my purse and be right back down."

Justine went into her bathroom and brushed her teeth. She checked the room to make sure she had put her phone and her iPad in her backpack. She also got some paper and a pen and put them in the backpack, too, in case she needed to make any notes about the school. When she went to grab her purse, she noticed her necklace was still sitting on the dresser. She had forgotten to put it on when she dressed earlier. But, as she stared at it, she decided today wasn't the day to wear it. So, she wrapped it in a hand towel and put it in the top drawer of the dresser for safe keeping. Now she was ready to go.

"I'm ready, Mom and Dad. Hurry up. Let's go," Justine declared as she bounded down the stairs.

"Wow, that's a switch. She's telling us to hurry up." Her dad grabbed the information they had printed about the school, yelled goodbye to Luke, and walked out the door.

"Okay, Let's go. I have the directions right here. It won't take very long to get there. Stephanie, please read the directions to me while I drive."

The three Rosses left their house and began the drive to the Headington School. They located the school and drove up the circular drive to the front door. They were greeted by a student who asked them their purpose for being there and whom they were to meet. Another student was summoned to the front door and escorted them to the main office. There, they were introduced to the director for the Senior School. She ushered them into her office for the initial interview which took about an hour. After the interview, the director took them on a tour of the campus. There were a lot of brick buildings each housing a different area of study. Justine was very interested in the building dedicated to the arts for she could pursue music there. Her parents informed the director that Justine would be living at home and commuting to school daily so the director skipped that part of the tour. Justine learned the school motto was "Fight the Good Fight of Faith" and had been the motto since the school was founded in 1915. She also learned if she was to be in Sixth Form, she would not have to wear a uniform. But she did have to be mindful of how she dressed and would need a black, grey, or navy suit for formal occasions.

The three were very impressed with the school and agreed that Dr. Robinson had made a great suggestion. Dr. Ross asked if there was any paper work they needed to fill out so Justine could enroll. The director gave him a folder that contained the enrollment forms which they could take home and complete. Justine was to return with the forms on Monday, her first day at school.

Justine thanked the director for meeting with them and for the tour. The tour had taken only about an hour and it was now around 11:00. She told the director she was excited to complete her high school experience in England. They shook hands and the director walked them to the front door.

The Rosses left very impressed by what they had seen and drove back to their house.

CHAPTER 12

A SURPRISE AWAITS

"Hey, Luke," Justine yelled as she came through the door. "We're back from the school." Luke came out of his room and started down the stairs. "I didn't want you to be surprised in case you're doing something you shouldn't."

"Me?" Luke replied as he reached the bottom step. "I'm surprised by what you are insinuating, sis. I would never do something I shouldn't do, at least not so anyone would know!"

"Very funny! Anyway, we're back and had a great visit at the school. I really liked it. The curriculum has a lot to offer. I can still pursue music but they don't have volleyball. They do have something called Net Ball. I guess it's kind of like basketball. But I'm not really sure. Anyway, I start on Monday."

"That's great! We both are able to attend schools we like. I wasn't sure what to expect when Mom and Dad first suggested this trip. But it looks like everything is going to work out!"

"And, I don't have to wear a uniform!"

"That may be good for you but now we have to listen to you every morning trying to decide what you're going to wear! The usual every day thing!"

"Speaking of what to wear, I think I'll go change out of these clothes so I can get back to being comfortable.

Be back in a few," Justine called back over her shoulder as she went upstairs.

Justine went into her room. She felt really good about her choice of schools and was looking forward to her first day but was nervous at the same time. She still wasn't sure if she would fit in. Then she remembered she wasn't wearing the necklace and went over to get it from the dresser. She opened the dresser drawer, unfolded the towel, and there it was, safe and sound. She had worried about it while she was gone and was glad it was still there. She placed it around her neck where she knew it would be safe.

"Hello, Justine."

Justine, surprised, spun around and there was Gretchen standing in her room.

"You're back! I can't believe you're back so soon. You were just here! Why have you returned? This is so weird! I can't believe we are actually having a conversation!" Justine was talking a mile a minute.

"Justine, please be calm. I would like to explain some things to you if I could just be allowed to speak."

"Oh, I'm sorry. By all means, please speak."

"I have returned with a gift for your father..."

"My father? I don't understand," Justine interrupted.

"If I may continue, the person I work for was the person your dad operated on a year ago. The operation saved my King's life and he wanted to thank your father with a gift."

"King? You just said King."

"Did I? I am sorry. I did not mean to say that. He is like a King to his family is what I meant to say. But my purpose here is to deliver the gift and I need your help to do so."

"But you did say King. From what country? There aren't too many left that have kings. And you work for him? You have the ability to appear and disappear.

How is that possible? That doesn't happen in the 21st century. Or in any century for that matter. Unless... you're a magician." Justine had to sit down on her bed since she was beginning to feel light headed. "I have had dreams about a king and a castle but they're never very clear and the people are blurred. I only have those dreams when I'm wearing this necklace. Would you be able to explain why I'm having those dreams and who is this King you are talking about?"

"I will try to explain everything to you. I wasn't sure if the necklace would affect your memories and now, I know. I will explain later, but first, I need you to come with me, please." And before Justine could say anything, she and Gretchen disappeared from Justine's room and reappeared in the garden. "There is someone here who is eager to see you. Just start down the path and you will see him."

"Him?" Justine gasped.

She looked at Gretchen and then looked down the path. Gretchen nodded for her to go ahead. Justine walked slowly into the garden. This was a scene that had played over and over in her dreams for the past year. Was this real? Her breathing quickened as she neared the gazebo and then she saw him. Was it James? It looked like the boy she saw in her dreams. But she couldn't be sure. She walked closer and he turned around. There was a look of surprise on both of their faces, James because he couldn't believe she was actually standing in front of him and Justine because she wasn't sure he was real. She approached the gazebo cautiously and then abruptly stopped in front of it. She grabbed the edge of a bench near her to steady herself.

"Is your name James?"

"Aye." James was ready to rush over to her and hold her and never let her go. But he knew he had to be patient and not scare her.

"May I touch you? That didn't sound right. What I mean is, I need to be sure that this isn't a dream, that you're actually here."

"You may." And he stood there with his hand outstretched.

Justine walked up the steps to the landing, reached out her hand and touched his. A tingle surged through her body and a smile appeared on her face.

"You're real," she said quietly looking down at their hands.

"I am," and James' hand folded around hers.

At that moment, Justine looked up and into his eyes. "I have been dreaming about you for the past year," she said as she started to cry. "You were always there, but I could never touch you. My heart kept telling me that you were someone special but I didn't know how or where to find you. I didn't know if you were just imagined or real. And now, here you are. Standing in front of me, as real as I am."

Then James couldn't help himself. He grabbed Justine and just held her until she stopped crying. He felt whole again now that Justine was back in his life. They stood entwined for a while and Justine's crying subsided. Then James stepped back, put her head in his hands and kissed her gently. Justine felt warm all over and knew what her dreams were trying to tell her. She was in love with James. She kissed him back and then they embraced again.

As they stood together, Justine whispered, "I don't know where you came from, why you have been in my dreams, and why you've been gone for a year. But I don't care, you're here now and I'm very happy."

James continued to hold her and kissed her every so often. "I have not been able to get you out of my heart. You have stayed with me for the past year and it has been torture to not be able to hold you and be with you. I was afraid you would not return to England. But here you are and I do not want to lose you ever again."

"Here I am. I fell in love with a dream. At least that's what I thought. I'm still trying to wrap my head around all of this." She paused and then said, "Gretchen brought you here, didn't she?"

"Aye. She was the one who told me of your return and that you were living in Oxford. I knew I had to come find you. So, when my father asked Gretchen to deliver the gift to your father, I thought this to be the perfect time for me to leave home."

"I need to sit down for a moment. I feel kind of dizzy." They walked over to the bench located along the edge of the gazebo and sat down holding hands.

"I have a lot of unanswered questions, but I'm going to ask you just two right now. My first question, do you live in a castle where there is a king?"

"There is no easy way to answer this, but aye, I do."

"That's the second time you've used the word Aye. And my second question, were you with me in Oxford when my dad operated on the King, according to Gretchen?"

"Gretchen told you that your father operated on the King?"

"Yes, I don't think she meant to but she let it slip."

James sighed took a big breath and then answered her question. "Aye, I was with you in Oxford. The King is my father."

"Your father?" Justine asked shocked.

"Aye, and you taught me a lot about your time while we were in Oxford."

"Well, that explains why you have appeared in different places in my dreams." Justine stopped and realized he was talking as if he didn't live in the present. "But what do you mean, my time? Isn't this your time, too?"

67

"No. I am from the past and live in a kingdom called Wiltshire."

"What?" Justine stood up from the bench and started pacing. The only way she knew how to deal with her nerves at this point was to walk. "This is impossible! How can this be true?" She continued walking back and forth. James has to be lying to her. What he is saying isn't possible, or is it? There was something that happened at Stonehenge which no one in her family could recall. Then there was the fact that her dad and she remembered being at the hospital, but her mom and Luke did not. Why? Some of this was finally becoming clearer the more they talked and from the answers James gave her.

"Justine, please stop walking back and forth. I do not think I should tell you anymore right now. I know it is confusing. I think I should wait until Gretchen and I can explain this together. But you must promise me to not say anything to the rest of your family." He stood up, grabbed both her arms and looked her right in the face. "Promise me you will not tell them at least not right now."

"I promise. How can I tell them about something I don't understand myself?" Justine reached for James and hugged him. "James, just hold me. I feel safe in your arms, no matter who you are."

James held her tightly, passionately kissed her, and continued to hug her. Justine finally relaxed and looked up at him.

"How am I going to explain you to my parents?" she asked. "Up till now, you have been someone I have been dreaming about. But you're real, and boy am I glad of that!" Then changing the subject, "So, how long are you staying and where are you staying?"

"I will not be leaving for a while. I still need to deliver the gift to your father. And, I am not aware of any living accommodations at the moment. I will need to seek that information from Gretchen."

Justine sat back down on the bench, grabbed his hand and pulled him next to her.

"I have an idea. You could stay with us! We have plenty of room in this house and there is an apartment over the garage."

"I do not know either of these words, apartment or garage."

Suddenly, Justine saw herself doing this very thing at the hospital, explaining things to James. She gasped, "I remember," she murmured. Then louder she declared, "I remember! I had to explain things to you at the hospital, didn't I? Just like now. This all seems so surreal! That my dreams weren't dreams at all but my mind recalling the events of last summer. That means the castle *is* real, and your father *is* the King, and my family was there! But how?" At this point, Justine jumped up from the bench and started pacing again. "This can't be happening. My logical mind tells me none of this could be real, but my dreams and my heart tell me it did happen!"

James stood up and placed himself in front of her. "This was not supposed to be possible for you to remember all of this. This was not to happen."

"What wasn't to happen?"

"You were not to remember Wiltshire or the trip to the hospital. The portal was to take away your memory so our kingdom would continue to remain a secret."

"Portal? There's a portal? That must be why we were at Stonehenge, isn't it?"

"I think I have said too much. We need to find Gretchen."

"I am here, your highness. I have heard all of what was said. I am certain her memories must be because Justine still has the necklace in her possession. She is the only one who has taken the necklace with her after leaving Wiltshire. Neither Arius nor I were aware this would be a problem upon her departure. We have also not had someone leave Wiltshire in love, your highness. I think the bond between you two may have strengthened the magic of the necklace and helped her remember, but only in her dreams."

"I am so relieved to know that this isn't a dream any longer. And I'm sorry to have dispelled your belief in the magic of the portal, Gretchen, but very glad to have kept the necklace and to have found James again. James, you were the main reason I came to England with my family. I was determined to find you no matter what. I knew in my heart you were real. But instead, you found me which is great because I had no idea where to start looking for you."

"I think it best to now explain last summer to Justine so she knows how and why all of this took place, Gretchen."

"I agree, your highness. Please sit down, Justine, and I will relay the events of last summer to you as they took place."

So, Gretchen explained everything, starting with the first moment Justine found the necklace in the limo at the airport to the last moment when Gretchen said goodbye to Justine's family after going through the portal. The whole time, Justine held on tightly to James' hand. She was afraid if she let go, he might disappear.

When Justine thought Gretchen was done, she threw in, "But I remember seeing you again in the airport before I boarded the plane. That was you, wasn't it?"

Then Gretchen added, "Prince James could not rest until he was sure you were safe and that is why you saw me in my black robe at the airport."

Justine just sat there for awhile not saying anything. She was trying to absorb all the information she had just heard which went against everything she knew to be true. This wasn't something that happened in real life, but yet it did and James and Gretchen were proof of it.

"Justine, are you alright? You look very pale!" James asked concerned.

"How all right would you be if someone had just told you what you told me? I will be fine, just let me sit here for a minute. I do have a question, though. You mentioned everyone goes through a portal. Why don't I remember that? You would think something like a portal would stick in my mind. What is it like to go through it?"

Gretchen spoke up to answer this one, "You do not remember it because when you enter from Stonehenge, I place the visitors under a spell so I can get them through the portal without anyone hearing or seeing them. Then, once on the other side, the spell wears off. It is like walking through a door, a portal to another world. When a visitor enters from Wiltshire, the portal erases all memories and therefore the memory of the portal would be gone."

James moved their clasped hands and held them close to his heart.

"Please take comfort in knowing I am right here and not going anywhere."

Justine looked at him with tears in her eyes, "You are the one thing in all of this that is finally real and here beside me, now. Don't ever leave me again."

Then Justine reached up and cradled his face in her hands. She looked into his eyes and then gently pressed her lips to his and hugged him.

James whispered in her ear, "I will not leave you."

7 1

CHAPTER 13

JAMES MEETS THE FAMILY

By now, it was late in the afternoon and close to dinner time. The three of them had been in the garden all afternoon not realizing how much time had passed.

"Justine! Where are you? I think you're out here in the garden somewhere. It's time to come in and clean up for dinner." It was Mrs. Ross and her voice brought Justine out of her thoughts.

"Oh, my gosh, that's my mother! She's on her way over here."

"Not to worry. I will disappear and no one but you and James will know of my presence. But I am afraid you will need to introduce your mother to James." And Gretchen disappeared just as Mrs. Ross was coming down the path to the Gazebo.

"Justine, what have you been doing out here all afternoon?" Then she saw James. "And who is this young man? Have you two been out here by yourselves all this time?"

"Mom, this is James."

"Nice to meet you, ... Did you say James? As in the James in your dreams?"

"Yes, Mom, the very same."

"It is an honor to meet you, Mrs. Ross," and James bowed.

Stunned, Mrs. Ross replied, "It is nice to meet you as well, James. I am at a loss for words right now." Then Mrs. Ross backed up toward the bench because she needed to sit down.

"Mom, James was told that I was living here and he came as soon as he could. He remembered meeting me last summer and wanted very much to renew that relationship."

"Renew? What relationship? I don't even remember meeting him last summer." And then under her breath she murmured, "But then again there's still a lot about last summer that is up for grabs." She gathered herself together and stood up. "James, you must join us for dinner. We have plenty. There is much we need to talk about and I'm sure Dr. Ross and her brother would like to meet you as well."

"I would be honored to see Luke again and join your family for dinner."

"Luke? How did you know his name was Luke and you said 'again'?"

"Oh, I told him, Mom, about our family and everyone's name and he didn't mean again as in again, just that he will be happy to meet my family," Justine added.

"Oh, yes, I see. Well, you probably did tell him about us. Okay then, I'll go tell our cook there will be one more for dinner and prepare Dr. Ross and Luke for your visit."

"We will be there shortly, Mom."

Mrs. Ross started to leave and then turned around, pointed her finger at Justine. "No dawdling, now!" Then she turned back toward the house and walked briskly down the path.

"We'll be right behind you, Mom." She turned and looked at James. "This is going to be an interesting meal. My whole family knows about you. But you've only been a figment of my imagination until this moment!"

"It will go well, Justine," Gretchen said as she reappeared. "I will help Prince James while he is here. I have been in your time period often and am aware of how things are done."

"Thank you, Gretchen. Knowing you are here is most comforting." Prince James informed her.

"Thank you from me, too, Gretchen. I think we're going to need all the help we can get. Come on, James. Let's go meet the rest of the family." Justine took James's hand and they walked to the house, together.

"I will be with you, your highness. You and Justine will only be able to hear me for I will remain invisible for now."

As they neared the house, Justine wasn't sure how James would be received. She had already seen her mother's reaction which was calmer than she thought it would be. But how was James going to present her father with the gift? What was he going to say? And what was the gift?

She didn't have long to find out. The whole family was waiting for them on the back porch.

"Family, this is James. James, this is my family."

"James, you will need to shake the hands of Dr. Ross and Luke," Gretchen advised him.

James extended his hand toward Dr. Ross. "It is my pleasure to meet you, Dr. Ross." Dr. Ross shook James's hand. Then James turned toward Luke and as they shook hands he stated, "And Luke, I am pleased to meet you as well. I was honored to have met Mrs. Ross in the garden."

"So, you're the famous James!" Luke responded. "I really didn't believe there was such a person, but Justine was convinced you were real. And here you are! James from her past. So maybe you can help us understand how you and Justine met!"

"Luke, please leave our guest alone," Dr. Ross interrupted. "It is nice to meet you, James," Dr. Ross said. "You know, I can't help feeling like we have met before... at the hospital? But then again, maybe you have one of those faces that looks like someone else."

"Dinner is served, Dr. Ross." It was Jennifer, the house chef.

"Thank you, Jennifer. We'll be right there."

The family walked into the dining room where they found steaming plates of food awaiting them on the table.

"James, you may sit next to Justine and the rest of us will fill in the other seats," Dr. Ross directed.

Dr. Ross picked up the platter of meat, placed some on his plate and passed it on to Justine. Justine passed it in turn to James when she was done. As she did, she whispered, "This is a serve yourself meal. Take some meat and put it on your plate. Then pass it on to Luke."

"What do you call this most tasty meat I am eating?" James asked.

"That is steak. Haven't you ever eaten steak before?" Luke inquired.

"Ah. Steak is what you have named this? It is wonderful. Most flavorful. It far surpasses anything we have at home." James stated.

"I'm very glad you like it. I'll give my compliments to the chef." Mrs. Ross added.

"So, James, back to the original question. How *did* you and Justine meet? How were you two able to spend time together without us knowing about it?" Luke asked anxiously. He was determined to get to the bottom of this and would persist until he got some answers.

"Your highness, you must answer these questions very carefully in order for the family to understand your relationship," Gretchen coached.

75

"Ah, aye, how Justine and I met. The man Dr. Ross operated on in the hospital was my father."

"Your father!" Dr. Ross interrupted. "I knew I had seen you there. The hospital wasn't able to share with me the name of the patient. They stated it was to remain confidential. I was also told that a Dr. Lange arranged for the bill to be paid. I wanted to thank him personally once we arrived in England but no one can find him. There are records of him living here up to around three years ago and then he appears to have vanished. Maybe you can help shed some light on this for me."

"Shed some light? I do not know this saying."

Justine immediately interrupted, "What my dad meant was that he thinks you could help him find Dr. Lange."

"Aye, I fear that to be impossible for he has moved far away from here. The reason I am here now is because I have been asked to deliver a gift to you as a thank you for saving the life of my father and... well, just for saving father."

"A gift? That certainly isn't necessary. He was a patient who needed surgery which I performed as his doctor. You do not have to give me a gift for that."

"But you still haven't answered my question, James," Luke interrupted.

"Luke, leave him alone. We met at the hospital," Justine explained. "He was there for his father's operation and then stayed during the week while his father was recuperating. That's when we met."

"I think I'm confused, as I think we all may be," Luke persisted. "If he was there that week, then why didn't I ever meet him?"

"I was actually wondering the same thing," Dr. Ross queried.

"If I may, I will answer that question, Dr. Ross."

"Please do. I'm as anxious as Luke to hear this answer."

"My father is a well-known...um...person and the hospital was asked to keep his presence in the hospital confidential. So, that went for me as well. I met Justine by chance while waiting for the surgery to be over. I explained the circumstances to her and asked her not to tell anyone, even her own family. That is why you may have seen me at the hospital, Dr. Ross and Luke did not meet me then."

"Okay, that explains how you two met, but that doesn't explain why Justine could only remember you in her dreams. She wasn't sure if you were real or not." Luke wasn't sold on this explanation. The whole thing seemed too fishy to him.

"Your highness, I think it best if you state that you disappeared after that first encounter and she never saw you again. That would help explain her not being able to remember you." Gretchen worried that Prince James might not be able to explain his way out of this one.

"Um, I did not want my presence to be known and I remained in the room of my father for the rest of the week. When Dr. Ross arrived to check on my father, I would go into the closet so as not to be noticed. I only met Justine one time while there. But she made such an impression on me that I could not get her out of my mind this whole year. It means a lot to me that I am here and able to see her again."

Justine blushed and replied, "You must have made a big impression on me as well since I have been dreaming about you this past year." Then trying to change the subject, "James said he doesn't have anywhere to stay while he's visiting and I suggested he stay here! What do you think? He could stay in the apartment over the garage. No one is using it."

"He doesn't have anywhere to stay? That seems odd since he knew he was coming to give your father a gift," Mrs. Ross queried.

"Mrs. Ross, we only became aware of the presence of your family two days ago. My father thought it best to deliver the gift as soon as possible. He did not want more time to pass before he could show his gratitude. That did not give us much time to prepare and that is why I am without a place to stay."

"Where are our manners? Of course, you may stay here. I think the apartment over the garage is a great idea, Justine. James, please accept my apologies for the members of my family. I think they are too caught up in who you are and where you came from to remember how we treat guests. Justine, please take him to the apartment after dinner is over so he may get settled."

"Thank you, Dad. I will."

"And, I think it best if we don't ask any more questions of our guest tonight."

Since no one could ask questions, Justine presented some information about her high school and Luke talked about going to culinary school. James was fascinated by the conversations even though he had a hard time following the topics.

CHAPTER 14

THE APARTMENT

After dinner, Justine and James excused themselves and Justine took James to the apartment to show him where he would be staying while he was in Oxford. It was a nice two bedroom with a kitchen and a sitting area.

"I know this has a kitchen but you will be taking your meals with us so you won't have to worry about cooking. Behind that door is a bedroom with a king size bed and a bathroom attached. The other bedroom has a queen size bed. Then this is the sitting area and there is a small table over in the corner for whatever."

"I am glad to know I will not need the kitchen as I do not know anything about cooking." James stated. "And you have had a King and a Queen stay here as well. That must have been very exciting."

"What? Oh, you must be referring to the beds I mentioned." Then she laughed and replied, "That's the name we give to the biggest bed someone can have and a queen is the second largest."

"I still have much to learn. It is very nice of your family to offer this fine place for me to reside while I am here." James looked around and then asked, "What is outside those doors?" James walked over to the French doors that led to a small balcony and opened them.

"This is called a balcony. There is a small table and chairs for you and you can see the garden from here. That's my room over there on the corner." Justine pointed to her room. "I have a balcony, too. I love going out there. It also looks out on the garden. Every time I view the garden, it reminds me of the one that haunts me in my dreams. Now I realize it wasn't just a dream. What happened in that garden? Why do I remember it?"

"That was where you and I said good bye to each other. My father told me that your time in our kingdom had come to an end and you needed to return home. I did not know how I was going to bid you farewell for you and I had been together every day since your arrival. That is why I walked in the garden that day, to be alone for I could not face you knowing this. Then you appeared before me in the gazebo and I held you close as long as I could. I told you that you would soon be going back through the portal. At first, you suggested that you might remain in Wiltshire. But I knew this was not possible as you had another life in another time and needed to return to it. And here we are again, together but separate. For I know I will need to return to Wiltshire soon."

Justine turned toward him and grabbed his hand, "Why can't I go with you? I would love to visit your home and see your family, again."

"I would love nothing more than to have you to journey to my home with me. But our time together would be as before. You would return home with memories in a dream as they are now. The portal makes one forget Wiltshire and the time spent there. It was too hard to lose you the first time. I am not prepared to face that again. But this does not have to be settled right now. We are here, together, and I want to be with you as much as I can. For now, I think it best if you retreat to your house and your own room as I may not be able to control myself around you if you remain much longer."

Blushing, Justine replied, "I think that would be best as well. Tomorrow morning, come over to the main house for breakfast and after that, we can spend the whole day together. We can tour Oxford if you like."

"I would like that very much. I will see you in the morning."

James gave Justine a peck on the cheek and as she turned to leave, he grabbed her arm, turned her back toward him and kissed her again, but this time on the lips. Then he let her go. She paused for a moment looking longingly at him and then swiftly walked to the door and out of the apartment.

He turned around and just stared at the wall. It took all he had to dismiss her. It had been a whole year since they had seen each other and he wanted her to stay with him. But he knew it was too soon to expect their relationship to be where it had been then.

"Your highness, I am so glad you made this trip with me," Gretchen's voice startled him as he had forgotten all about her.

"Gretchen! Have you been here the whole time?"

"I was in the room at first but then thought better of it and waited outside until Justine left. Now, I realize how much Justine means to you. I was not with you both at the hospital last year for I remained in the room with your father. I did not see how your feelings for her had grown while we were there. I can see that you are in love with her. This relationship is going to be very difficult for you both since you have the added problem of being from two different times. I will try to stay at a distance when you two are together. But you must remember that I cannot be very far away at any time because you will lose the memory of who you are and where you come from."

"I understand, Gretchen. And I am well aware of the challenges we are facing. I am not going to think about that right now and enjoy this time together. I am weary and in need of rest. The day has been long. I will sleep in the bedroom with the king bed and you may rest wherever you like."

"Thank you, your highness. I will see you in the morning."

James walked into the bedroom and closed the door. He saw the bathroom Justine had mentioned which was attached to his room. He had used one in the hospital and was glad that he remembered how to operate the toilet, the sink and the shower. When done in the bathroom, he walked over to the bed, plopped down on it, and fell asleep in his clothes.

CHAPTER 15

THE PRESENTATION OF
THE GIFT

Morning came and James woke up soon after the sun came up. As he lay there, his thoughts turned to Justine and he was excited to be able to spend the day with her. He sat on the edge of the bed and examined his surroundings. Much of what he saw he remembered from his days at the hospital. Then he recalled taking a shower and how good it felt. He definitely had to take one before he left for breakfast for that wasn't something they had in the castle. He took off his clothes, went into the bathroom, figured out how to adjust the water temperature, and stepped into the shower. He just stood there and let the water run down his back. He found the soap and shampoo on the shelf in the shower and loved the lather each one created. He lost track of the time and heard a knock on the door.

"Is someone there? Who is it?"

"It is Gretchen, your highness. You have been in the shower for a very long time and I was beginning to worry about you."

"Please forgive me, Gretchen. We do not have these at home and I was enjoying the warmth of the water. Maybe we can return home with one of these! I am finished now and will soon join you."

"I am glad to know there is nothing wrong. Also, we have been summoned for breakfast in the house."

"Thank you, Gretchen."

James quickly finished in the bathroom, got dressed and joined Gretchen in the sitting area.

"What am I to do about my clothes? I can not wear this all week."

"Arius thought you might need another set of clothes and I have brought them with me." Gretchen handed him the clothes she had hidden under her robe.

"You think of everything, Gretchen. What would I do without you?" James walked back into the bedroom, put on the clean clothes and then returned to the sitting area. "Let us be off for breakfast. Should I make a plate for you, Gretchen, and bring it to you here?"

"Please do not be concerned with me. I will eat when I can."

James left the apartment, walked down the stairs to the driveway and entered the house through the dining room doors. He found the family already seated at the table.

"Good morning, Dr. Ross, Mrs. Ross, and Justine. What a fine morning we are having today. Where is Luke?"

"Good morning, James. Please join us for breakfast," Mrs. Ross said. "Luke is still in bed. He has a hard time waking up in the morning. Do you have any plans today?"

"Aye, Justine thought it a good idea to take a tour of Oxford today," James replied as he sat down.

"Yes, Mom, I thought we could do the hop on hop off tour you told me about. And I wanted to visit the hospital where we first met."

"It sounds like you have your day all planned out. I guess you and I will have to do the bus tour another time. I hope you two enjoy it."

"This food looks wonderful. Is this meat bacon? I remember eating it at the hospital. It was rather tasty!" he said as he pointed to the bacon.

"I can't believe you do not know what bacon is!" Mrs. Ross stated astonished. "You need to get out more often, it seems."

"Mrs. Ross, we have meat like this bacon, but not prepared as this is. It is much different where I come from."

Trying to change the subject, Justine mentioned the gift James had brought.

"Justine, thank you for this reminder. Dr. Ross, before I leave with Justine, I need to share with you the gift my father has sent."

"That is really not necessary as I said before," Dr. Ross threw in.

"My father would be very angry with me if I were not to deliver the gift to you. Please excuse me and I will return with the gift." James got up from the table and walked outside.

"Gretchen, are you here?"

"I am, your highness."

"May I please have the gift for Dr. Ross. I will deliver it to him now."

Gretchen reached into an inner pocket in her robe and retrieved the small chest which housed the jewels the King had chosen. James took the chest and asked Gretchen to come into the house so she could advise him on his presentation. He didn't want to say or do the wrong thing. He could not make any mistakes that might jeopardize the whereabouts of Wiltshire.

James walked in the door and up to Dr. Ross. "This small chest belonged to my grandfather and in turn my father. He placed the gift he chose for you inside. Please take this along with deep gratitude from my father. He wished he could present it to you in person but he was not able to travel at this time."

"Very nice, young prince," Gretchen said in approval.

James handed the chest to Dr. Ross and awaited his response.

"This chest is exquisite, James. These markings appear to be very old, but yet this chest looks like it's hardly been used. Well, let's take a look at what is inside."

Dr. Ross opened the box carefully for he didn't know what to expect. Once the lid was open, the jewels inside glowed in the light. He just sat there staring at its contents mouth open but no words coming out.

"Drew, what's in the box?" Mrs. Ross asked. "You have a look of shock on your face."

Dr. Ross handed the chest to her. When she glanced down, she almost dropped it after she saw what was inside.

"Mom, what's wrong? Is it something awful?" Justine was surprised at her parents' reaction to the contents of the chest. "May I see it?"

Her mom closed it and gave it to Justine. Justine handled it gingerly since she wasn't sure what she would find especially after seeing how her parents had reacted. She opened it very slowly and peered inside.

"Wow, James! These are awesome! I bet they're worth a fortune! This is the gift your father wants my dad to have?"

"Aye, my father chose them for Dr. Ross. Is it not enough?"

"Those jewels are more than enough, James," Dr. Ross replied. "Thank you for this thoughtful gift, but I can't accept them. These are probably worth millions and should remain in your father's possession. How did he come by them?"

"They have been in our family for generations. My father chose these to give to you. He will be most offended if you do not accept them."

"I understand your predicament, trying to do what your father desires and knowing that I can't take the gift. Maybe there is a compromise here. I will take two of the jewels and the rest you may return to your father with my thanks. He also must understand I will be questioned regarding the origin of these jewels when I have them appraised. I would rather have fewer of them to explain."

"Dr. Ross, I do not know this word appraised. What does that mean?"

"You don't know what appraised means?"

"Dad, he isn't from here...he lives in the...countryside and probably has never had to get the jewels appraised." Justine tried to smooth things over so her dad wouldn't ask too many questions.

"I see, I think. Well, appraised means I need to talk to someone who knows the value of jewels and can tell me how much money I could exchange them for."

"Ah, I understand. Thank you, Dr. Ross. I agree. I think it might be wise to talk to this person first and then we will decide if you will keep them all."

"Agreed. But for now, I think it will be best if I store them in a safe place. I don't want anything to happen to them."

"James, those are beautiful. You must tell your father how grateful we are for his thoughtful gift." Mrs. Ross didn't want James to think they were offended by the rather generous gift.

"I will pass these thoughts on to my father."

"Well, now that my dad has his present, I think it's time for you and me to go on that tour we talked about," Justine suggested trying to change the subject. "I'll go get ready and meet you in the front hall."

"I will be there."

"What tour? Have I missed something? Guess I shouldn't have slept in," Luke admitted as he walked sleepily into the dining room.

"We will tell you later but for right now, just eat your breakfast," Mrs. Ross suggested.

"I think I have forgotten something in the apartment. I will take my leave of you and will return shortly."

James walked outside through the dining room door and looked around for Gretchen.

"Gretchen, are you here?"

"Yes, your highness."

"Did you hear our conversation about the gift?"

"Aye. The King will be very disappointed to hear Dr. Ross would not accept it. I am glad you were able to talk to him about taking some of the jewels at least. But please, your highness, if you do not understand something, seek me out first and I will help you to find the answer. We do not want them to start asking too many questions."

"Aye, you are right, as always. I am still learning about the future. There is so much to know in this time period and so many things I would like to take home with me. Right now, Justine and I are going on a tour of Oxford and I would like you to accompany us."

"I must, your highness, for we do not know how far this tour will take you."

"That is true. I had forgotten about that. We need to go inside for we are to meet Justine in the house."

James and Gretchen entered the house and waited for Justine in the front hall.

CHAPTER 16

THE BUS TOUR

Justine came down the stairs and met James in the front hall. Together they started their walk to the bus stop where they could board the Tour bus.

"This is going to be so neat. I'm looking forward to seeing the town and some of the historic sites in it. And I'm so glad we get to do this together. I really didn't want to go with my mom. She would have been a chatter box regarding all the history we would see."

"Chatter box?"

"Oh sorry, that means someone who talks too much."

"My mother would be the same. My mother is always educating us on our heritage. Justine, what is this thing you call a bus?"

"Oh, wow. I keep forgetting you don't know about all this stuff. Just keep asking questions and I'll try to answer. Do you remember the van we took back to Stonehenge from the hospital?

"Aye."

"It's like that only bigger. It has more seats. It's called a double decker because it has two layers, or decks, for seats. The bottom layer is closed and the top layer has no covering, or roof. You will see people getting on and off the bus, but I think we will stay on the whole time so we can hear about everything before we decide to get off anywhere."

"Thank you for helping me understand. You helped me a lot at the hospital."

"I do remember some of that. I'm surprised I just remembered about the van we took back to Stonehenge. Is Gretchen with us?"

"I am, Justine. Prince James and I must not be too far apart while he is here."

"Then you will be able to tour Oxford, too. Maybe that will help when you are seeking something in our time."

As the bus approached the stop James grabbed Justine and jumped backwards.

"What's going on?" Justine yelled.

"I was saving you from that large beast that was heading toward us!"

"James," Justine said quietly, "that is the bus."

"That is very large!"

"Yes, it is. Take my hand and we will climb on board."

James put his hand in hers and he followed her onto the bus. He approached it slowly not knowing what to expect, and then walked up the steps with her to the top of the bus. She led him to one of the open seats and they sat down.

"This is most unusual! But I like sitting on the top. You can see much from up here."

"Yes, you can. Okay, I need you to listen to me so I can give you some more instructions on what to do now."

"Aye, I am listening."

Justine picked up some headphones and gave them to James.

"These are called headphones. In order to hear what the guide has to say, you need to put these on your head over your ears."

"But if I put those over my ears, it will make it hard to hear. How will I hear anything?"

"Trust me, James, it will work. Here, let me show you with the ones I will wear."

Justine put her headphones on and showed James how to put them over the ears. James took his, and put them on.

"See, that wasn't so hard."

"What did you say? I told you I would not be able to hear."

"Just wait."

So, James waited and all of a sudden, he heard a loud voice. He looked all around and couldn't see anyone talking. Then he grabbed the headphones, took them off very quickly, and looked around again. Justine realized what James was doing and she pointed to the headphones.

"The sound, voice, is coming from these," and she pointed to the headphones on her head.

"But where is the person who is speaking?"

"It's kind of like Gretchen sometimes; you can hear her but you can't see her. Just listen and the person will tell you all about Oxford. Now, put them back on."

James put his headphones back on and immediately removed them again.

"This person must talk softer. He is very loud!"

"Oh, sorry! Do you see this on the headphone? It will make the voice louder or softer."

"Thank you."

So, James turned the knob and lowered the sound coming from his headphones. Then he settled back into his seat and started listening to the voice of the guide. As they traveled on the bus, Justine would help James by pointing to the places being described. Toward the end of the tour, the guide announced the hospital would be the next stop.

"James, take off your headphones. We'll be getting off here. The hospital is at the next stop."

James removed his headphones and waited for Justine to instruct him what to do next. She took his hand and together they disembarked from the bus. There, in front of them, was the hospital where they had spent a week together over a year ago. Memories of their time together began to flash through James' head for his memories were much more vivid than Justine's.

"Before we go in, I need to know if we did anything we shouldn't have."

"I know you do not remember all of this, but our time here was one I will never forget. This is where we had our first kiss but that is all. I would not dishonor you by doing more."

"Thank you, James. I'm sure that would be something I would remember, I think. Anyway, can you show me where we kissed?"

"There is a cemetery behind the hospital with a small church there. We must walk there first. But before we go, Gretchen are you here with us?"

"Aye, your highness, I am here."

"I knew you must not be far away as I have not lost my memory of home. But I needed to check."

"Please believe me, I would not allow you to go very far away from me."

"That is good. Now, let us go find the church."

The three walked around to the back of the hospital and across a street. James looked around and then saw a familiar sight, the sign for the Headington Cemetery.

"This is it, the place where people are buried after they die. You called it a cemetery. We have some in my time, but many royals are buried in the church. Come."

James took her hand and led her to the chapel located on the grounds of the cemetery.

As they neared the door to the chapel, Justine stopped. "I remember this," she gasped. Then she looked at James intently, "I remember this! We went inside and sat on one of the pews and that's where you kissed me! Oh, wow! This is so exciting! We really did spend time together last summer! I remember!! The surgery, the cafeteria, the walks around the hospital... we wore scrubs because we didn't have any other clothes to wear, and this chapel."

They walked into the chapel together, down the aisle to the front pew and sat down. She sat there in silence for a moment trying to recall this moment in her mind. Then, as before, James turned to her, cradled her face in his hands and kissed her gently. Immediately, Justine put her hands around his neck and held him close.

"This was the part of that walk I loved the best," she whispered in his ear.

"Me, too."

She straightened up, turned toward the front of the chapel, and sighed.

"What now?" she whispered. She scooted closer to him, grabbed his hand placed it in her lap and repeated. "What now? You live in the 16th century and I live here, in the 21st century. I don't want to let you go home. I can't lose you again and have you haunt me in my dreams. That was torture!" She paused for a minute. "I already suggested this but, I can go back to Wiltshire with you! I really would love to see your family again, especially your sisters. And we don't have to say good bye to each other. At least not right away. What do you think of that idea?"

James sat and continued to look forward. "I must talk to Gretchen outside. I will return."

James got up and walked out the door leaving Justine sitting by herself on the pew. Did she just ruin everything? Was their relationship over now? This was not an easy remedy to their situation, but she was willing to try. Now, she just had to wait to see what James was going to say after talking to Gretchen.

It seemed like she had been waiting for hours when James finally returned. He walked in with Gretchen and sat down beside her. At first, he didn't say anything. Then, he finally spoke.

"Justine, after talking to Gretchen, I would like to invite you to return to Wiltshire with me."

Justine couldn't contain her excitement. She jumped up off the pew, spun around and yelled, "Yes, I get to return to Wiltshire!"

James immediately grabbed her arm, pulled her back down to the pew, and covered her mouth with his hand. "What are you doing?" he whispered. "We are trying to keep everything a secret and you just yelled so everyone could hear you!"

"There's no one here. And besides, Wiltshire is still a county in England. I want you to know how excited I am that you asked me to return with you. This will be such a fantastic trip, especially since I remember so much about the first one now."

"Justine, you must not tell anyone, not even your parents, that you are going with me."

"What do I tell them, then? How about this? I could tell them that you have invited me to your farm in Wiltshire for the weekend. Remember? I told them you're from the country, or rather a farm when I was trying to explain why you didn't know certain words they used. They would be okay with that, I think."

"Justine," Gretchen interjected, "you will not remember, but the magic of the portal allows visitors to return to the moment in time they left. That would mean your parents would not even know you had gone. But that can only happen once."

"Is that what happened the last time we were here? There were two weeks that none of us could recall what had happened. Dad and I remembered being at the hospital but Mom and Luke remembered nothing."

"Dr. Ross was needed to attend to the King and I was sent to bring you through the portal, which I did. You had not been there very long when the King became gravely ill. Dr. Ross made the decision to transport the King to your time where he had what he needed to do the surgery. Prince James went with us. That was the one time you both could go through the portal and return to the moment you left. But that could not happen the second time, which we have learned since Dr. Lange's arrival. So you were returned a week later. For your family, that would be the two weeks they could not remember as the portal erases all memory of Wiltshire."

"At least, that is what we thought until you left with the necklace and had memories of us in your dreams," Prince James added. "You must know that will happen again if you visit Wiltshire with me. Even though I would like you to go through the portal with me, I cannot bear the thought of you leaving me again."

"I don't know what else to do. The only way we can be together is if I return to Wiltshire. I have a question which just popped into my head. How long can you remain in the future? Will something happen to you if you stay too long?"

"I will answer that for the Prince. He can only remain as long as I am with him. I have been told that I may not visit the future for a long time period. I am not certain of that but will look for the answer when I return. As for the Prince, he too can lose his memory of Wiltshire if he goes through the portal without a seeker. You must know, that would mean that he would have no memory of you."

"What? I would forget Justine? That will not work!" James yelled. "How is this to work if neither of us can remember the other?"

"I am sorry, your highness, but that is for the safety of our kingdom. I cannot remain much longer in the future. I am a seeker and I must be available when I am needed." Then Gretchen paused as if listening to someone, "Yes, your majesty. I understand."

"Were you just talking to my father, Gretchen?"

"Aye, Prince James, I am able to talk to the King through Arius even when I am in the future. The King has told me that we must return very soon. The King has declared that once you deliver the gift to Dr. Ross we must go back through the portal. You are needed in Wiltshire."

"That settles it! I will return with you. We don't need to make any decisions about the future right now. We will cross that bridge when we get to it."

"What bridge are we to cross?" James asked.

"Never mind. I meant that we can decide later what will happen. We don't need to decide anything right now. For now, we need to make plans to leave for Stonehenge."

"Aye, we will need to leave soon, your highness, as you have already bestowed the gift on Dr. Ross as your father asked."

"Let's get back on the bus so we can return to my house."

Justine took Prince James by the hand, led him out of the chapel and walked to the front of the hospital. There, the three of them were able to catch the bus that would return them to Justine's new home.

CHAPTER 17

PREPARATIONS

So many questions went through Justine's mind as they rode the bus back to the house. Had she made the right decision? Would her parents allow her to leave? And if they did, how long would she be able to stay in Wiltshire? Would she miss her family? She couldn't bear the thought of being so far away from them, and this wasn't just distance but time as well! She didn't know the answers and she didn't have much time to work all this out since Gretchen stated she and James were to leave very soon.

"You are very quiet, Justine. What is troubling you?" James asked.

She turned and looked at him and saw the worried expression on his face. Then she took his hand in hers and kissed it.

"Please don't worry about me. I was just thinking about my family and Wiltshire, not knowing how this is all going to work out. There's a lot to consider regarding both and not a lot of time to come up with a game plan."

"A game plan? I need to learn all of these expressions so I do not to have to ask so many questions all the time."

"That's okay. I love it when you ask questions about things I say. It makes me love you even more."

"Then I will not worry about asking them!"

"Here's our stop," Justine announced.

They got off the bus and walked to the house which was about a block away. When they reached the front door, Justine grabbed James' arm and pulled him in front of her.

"I don't know how my parents will react to all of this, but I want you to know I really want this to happen despite any obstacles we may face along the way. Let's not hit them with this right away. Maybe tell them at dinner when everyone is relaxed and having a good meal."

"I will follow your lead on this for I do not know your parents very well and cannot pretend to know how to approach them. Let us go in and greet your family. Gretchen, please stay close by as I will need your counsel."

"I will always be by your side, Prince James, and will be glad to help in any way I can."

"Thank you, Gretchen. You are our most trusted seeker whose advice I value at all times."

"Okay, here we go!" Justine stated.

Justine opened the door and as the three entered the front hall they were greeted by Mrs. Ross.

"There you are! I was starting to get worried. I texted you about an hour ago and hadn't heard back. You usually answer your text messages right away."

"Oh, I'm sorry, Mom. We were so busy touring I didn't even look at my phone!"

"That must have been some tour! Well, anyway, we are getting ready to have dinner. Please go wash your hands and meet us in the dining room."

"Okay, will do. See you soon."

Justine pushed James up the stairs and stopped once they were in front of her room.

"Please let me do all the talking. I will mention that you are needed at home and you asked me if I would like to go with you since our visit here was so short. I will tell them you live near Stonehenge and we will take a bus to your family farm."

"You're going back to Stonehenge? I want to go!"

"Luke, what are you doing up here?"

"Well, I was cleaning up for dinner and my room is right there so I could hear every word." Luke shared as he approached them. "You're not going back to Stonehenge without me! We never really got to tour it the first time we were there. And besides, maybe I can figure out the mystery behind the two weeks that seemed to magically disappear from our memory!"

"You can't come with us!"

"Why not? I can at least travel with you to Stonehenge and then you can go on your merry way. That's okay with you, right James?"

"I..."

"Great! It's settled! When do we leave? Never mind. That won't matter cause I can leave anytime. Now, we'd better go downstairs for dinner before Mom gets mad. Wait till she hears about this!" Then Luke turned and briskly walked away and down the stairs.

Justine stood there speechless. She had worked it all out in her head exactly as it was going to happen and even anticipated her parents' response. But she certainly didn't see this coming.

"What just happened? I didn't plan for that to happen! Oh, no! He's probably going to tell Mom and Dad! Hurry, we need to head him off before he says anything." Justine said as she took off running down the stairs with James and Gretchen close behind. She slowed down just before she got to the dining room.

"Well, we're here for dinner. Let's all sit down and eat," Justine suggested as she started toward a chair.

"What's this I hear about you going to Stonehenge and visiting James' farm? Luke started babbling about it the moment he came downstairs."

"Mom, we were going to tell you about it at dinner and ask your permission but Luke overheard us talking in the hallway and spilled the beans!"

"Justine, you're starting school next week on Monday to be exact and you don't have time to go galavanting around the countryside right now. And neither does Luke for that matter." Mrs. Ross declared.

"Okay, let's all calm down. We can discuss this rationally over dinner," Dr. Ross said. "Please, everyone sit down. Jennifer went to a lot of trouble to prepare this meal and I think we need to eat it before it gets cold. Justine, would you please pass the serving dishes to our guest so we may start eating."

After the food had been passed, James spoke up, "I am truly sorry to have caused this disagreement within your household. That was not my intent. I am to return home soon and when Justine became aware of this, she asked if she could come with me. We had planned to ask your permission during this meal."

"Thank you, James. I understand things got a little out of hand because of my son. I want you to know we think you are a wonderful young man and I know Justine thinks the world of you. I have not talked to my husband regarding this visit, but I cannot give my permission for such a trip right now. We have just arrived in England, both Luke and Justine start school on Monday and Drew starts his job at the hospital. There are too many things happening all at the same time."

"I have to agree with my wife, James. This isn't a good time for Justine to leave. Maybe during one of her school breaks would be better."

"I understand, sir."

"Well, I don't," Justine chimed in. "What better time to visit his family than before I even start school? I can go to school when I get back. I wouldn't be gone very long and no time will have passed!"

"What she means is, she could begin a week later, if necessary," James interjected.

"Yes, that's what I meant."

"I have an idea on how to solve this," Luke added. "Since tomorrow is Thursday, why don't we all go! We can tour Stonehenge, again, since we really didn't see very much of it a year ago, and Mom and Dad can see the farm and meet James' family. That way they'll know where you are and won't be so worried. We really don't have anything to do until Monday."

"You're all coming? You can't! That won't work!" Justine was becoming frustrated that her plan had fallen apart. "James, please say something."

"I think my family would be honored if you came to visit them. My father has not seen Dr. Ross since the surgery."

"What? What about the ..." Justine began.

"This would work very well, I think. Your family would be with you and not back here in Oxford. Would that not work well, Justine?"

"I agree, your highness. The family would be together for as long as Justine remains and she will not miss them. It would be a surprise for your family, especially the King." Gretchen decided to add her opinion on the matter.

"That it would be."

"What did you say, James?" Dr. Ross inquired.

"I was thinking out loud, sir, regarding my father, who will be very happy to see the doctor who saved his life."

"Wow, I can't believe we are going to Stonehenge for the weekend! We should leave after breakfast tomorrow morning so we can get an early start. Way to go, sis! You made all this possible!"

"I certainly did," Justine said under her breath. "Well," turning to James, "at least we get to be together. And are we still going to your house?"

"Aye, that we are!"

"Since we have a car, we will be able to drive there this time and not have to call an Uber," Dr. Ross suggested.

"No, you can't!" Justine yelled.

"Justine, what's wrong? Why can't we drive there? We'll be going to Stonehenge and then to James' farm. How are we to get there if we don't drive?"

"Bus, yes, we can take the bus. James told me it goes by both places, right James? That way you can relax and not worry about driving. You'll be able to take in the sights along the way. You can't do that if you're driving. And you need to relax, Dad. You look a little stressed."

"Stressed, how do I look stressed? But, you're probably right. I am worried about beginning my job next week. It might be relaxing just to sit on the bus and watch the English countryside go by. Okay, we will take the bus."

"Yes! I mean, good choice Dad. We will take the bus. As a matter of fact, I think it stops at the end of our street," Justine stated relieved. She knew if they took the car that it would be sitting as if abandoned at Stonehenge and she didn't want that. Then she had a thought: if they are returned to the day they left when coming back through the portal, does that mean that time moves differently in Wiltshire than it does in the future? Does that only happen when someone is visiting Wiltshire from the future? James had aged the same as she did. How is this all possible? She knew she was only able to understand this according to her own reality. This was something she needed to explore once they were in Wiltshire.

No one could talk of anything else during the remainder of the meal. Once the decision was made to travel to Stonehenge, they needed to discuss the agenda for the weekend. James just sat and ate his meal for he already knew what was to happen once they all arrived at Stonehenge.

As soon as dinner was finished and plans were made, the family retired to their own bedrooms to pack for the weekend, except Justine and James.

"Could this have gone any worse? I can't believe my whole family will be traveling with us tomorrow. They have no idea what is to happen to them, again. How will we tell them?"

"Please do not be troubled about the trip. We will leave this to Gretchen."

Then Gretchen spoke up. "Justine, do you remember the first time you went through the portal? We talked at Stonehenge that day about leading your family through the portal. There is a spell I can cast on them so that they aren't aware of anything until they come out on the other side."

"Oh, yes, I remember that now. I followed them through the portal and you were behind me. I was the only one who knew what was happening because of the necklace."

"So, that is what I will do this time as well. It will go very well for your family. I will make sure of it."

"I guess I will see you two in the morning then. I need to pack some things for the weekend."

"Please do not bring too many items as you will arouse suspicion on the part of your parents," Gretchen advised.

"I won't, at least I'll try not to. But I must know, will the rule regarding the portal apply to us no matter how long we stay?"

"There are many commands decreed by the King surrounding the portal. Which one are you thinking of?" Gretchen asked.

"You have said that when a person steps back through the portal to return to the future that that person will be returned to the exact day of departure. That would mean, if I am correct, that my family and I could stay for any length of time and it wouldn't matter since we could all return as if we never left. Right?"

"That is true. But in the past, we have never had anyone visit us for very long except Dr. Lange. So, we do not know how long that stay may be."

"Well, Gretchen, I guess we will be the guinea pigs, then."

"Guinea Pigs? I do not understand," James asked puzzled.

Laughing, Justine replied, "I'm sorry, James, another expression to explain. It means we will be the first ones to test this rule especially since I'm not planning to return any time soon!"

"I do not know what a guinea pig is, but it is a funny way to say you will be the first. And I am very glad to know that you want to stay in my kingdom for a long time." Then James reached over, pulled Justine close to him and kissed her. "Till tomorrow."

CHAPTER 18

THE PORTAL

Justine was so excited she couldn't sleep. She had packed what she thought was light and was ready to go, only it was still nighttime with hours to go before they were to leave. She opened the doors to the balcony and decided to sit there for a while. The night air was so warm and fragrant with the scents of the garden billowing toward her in the breeze. She closed her eyes and remembered the first time she had entered the garden at the palace to find James. It made her all warm and tingly inside and she grabbed her knees and pulled them close as she sat. When she opened her eyes, she saw James standing on the balcony outside the garage apartment staring at her. She immediately jumped up out of the chair and made it crash to the floor. She turned around and pulled the chair upright and then just stood there. She looked over at James and saw him laughing and she started laughing, too.

James yelled, "You could not sleep either?"

"No," she yelled back. Then she heard a knock on the door.

"Justine, everything okay in there? I just heard a loud crash."

Justine rushed to the door and opened it, "Sorry, mom. I couldn't sleep so I was sitting on the balcony.

When I got up, my chair fell over. I'm fine. Nothing to worry about."

"That's good to know, you scared me! Well, try to get some sleep, okay? I'll see you in the morning."

"Okay, Mom."

Justine hugged her mom and closed the door. She ran back to the balcony but James wasn't there anymore. She stood there for a moment then went back inside and got in bed. She left the balcony doors open so she could breathe in the night air while she slept.

When she opened her eyes, the morning sun was shining in her window. She lay there just stretching and relaxing. Then she remembered what was to happen that day and jumped out of bed. She ran out on the balcony and yelled, "Good morning day. Good morning sun. Good morning garden!"

"Good morning to you as well!"

She looked over the edge of the railing. It was James! He was already up and walking to the house for breakfast.

"Oh wow! So sorry you had to hear that."

"I am not."

She stared at him for a second and then said, "I'll be down in a minute."

She ran back inside, closed the doors, and quickly got dressed.

Everyone was already in the dining room eating breakfast when she finally came downstairs.

"Well, there you are! I guess you were able to fall asleep after all," her mom commented.

"Yes, I did. And now I feel refreshed and ready to begin our adventure!"

"I would hardly call this an adventure, missy. We're just going away for the weekend."

"Yes, Dad, but I like to look on every trip as an adventure."

"Well, I'm ready to go," Luke announced. "I'm excited to start our time in England with an adventure, as Justine says. What time does the bus come?"

"I think it stops around 10:00," Justine answered.

"Well, it's 9:00 right now, so I think we should finish up here, gather our bags, and meet in the front hall in half an hour."

"Okay, Mom. Will do." Luke got up from the table to leave and paused. "Did anyone tell Jennifer we'll be gone? She won't need to show up to cook if no one's here."

"I'll make sure she knows," Mom replied.

"May I be of some service, Mrs. Ross? I have no belongings to gather and can help if needed."

"Thank you, James. That is very thoughtful. I think since we are just going away for a weekend, we should be able to handle our own bags. But I may need your help when we leave for the bus."

"I am happy to help."

"Come on then. You can come with me to get my things," Justine said as she grabbed his hand and led him upstairs. Once in her room, she turned toward James and asked, "When we arrive, what will happen? How do I greet your parents, the King and Queen? Do I curtsy, bow? What should I say to them? Will they know what I know and that I know about them and remember my first visit there?"

James gently put his hand up to her mouth to silence her. "Justine, please do not be so worried. My family loves you. Madison and Bethany think of you as their sister and wanted to come with me on this journey. And as for my mother and father, I am aware they desire me to seek out someone from our own time, but I cannot. My heart was yours from the moment we met and I cannot change what is. So let us return to Wiltshire now that we have found each other once more, and not worry about what the future may hold for us." Then James pulled her to him, wrapped his arms around her and held her close.

"I love it when you hug me. I feel so safe, as if nothing can harm me when you're around. I promise I'll try to relax and just go with the flow. I mean, just not worry about what is to come and only be in the now. For now, we are together and that's all that matters."

They heard Dr. and Mrs. Ross yelling from downstairs that it was time to leave.

"Oh my gosh, I forgot the time. We'd better go downstairs before my parents get upset. Will you please grab that bag over there and I'll get this one?" Before the two of them left her room, Justine quickly put her hand up to her neck to make sure she was wearing the necklace and it was there. She was so used to wearing it all the time now that she didn't notice it when it was around her neck anymore. She sighed with relief. Then she picked up the suitcase and she and James descended down the stairs.

"Glad to see you two could make it since this trip was your idea," Luke said. "Now, let's go so we don't miss that bus."

The family, along with James and Gretchen, walked out the front door, made sure it was locked, and then proceeded to walk to the bus stop. It was a good thing they left when they did since the bus arrived not 10 minutes later. The driver got off the bus to welcome his passengers.

"Is that luggage accompanying you on this trip?"

"Why, yes, it is." Mrs. Ross answered.

"You are aware that this is a tour bus and will be returning to Oxford when the tour is over. Are you staying somewhere in the area?"

"Yes, this young man's father will be meeting us there and we are planning to visit them for the weekend.

Isn't that correct, James? Your father will be meeting us there?"

"Aye, someone will meet us and take us to my home."

The driver loaded the luggage in the compartment on the side of the bus and they all boarded the bus. The bus departed for Stonehenge with four very excited family members.

The English countryside was so beautiful with lush emerald green pastures extending toward the horizon in both directions. It was covered with old English charm, crooked rooftops, creeping vines and chunky cottage doors. Many of the sights gave the feeling that one had stepped back centuries in time. The roads were bordered by drystone walls. The cottages were nestled at the bottom of small valleys with sheep grazing on the hillsides.

As they drew closer to Stonehenge, the landscape changed. The hills seemed to contain a white substance exposed at the surface and the grasslands were covered with wildflowers. This area didn't contain as many farms as there were around Oxford.

"James, do you know what that white stuff on the hills is?" Justine inquired.

"I was told by Dr. Lange that you call it chalk. He called this area the Downland. You can see it all around the area here. I am told that the cliffs along the sea are called white cliffs because of it."

"Chalk? That's interesting. Some day I need to look that up to find out why it's here."

"I can tell you," Luke chimed in, "and who's Dr. Lange by the way? To answer your question, Justine, we learned about it in high school. Remember when we were trying to decide what we wanted to see last summer and I told you we had learned all about Stonehenge in class and that was one of the reasons

I wanted to go there. Anyway, the Downs are called that because there is a word in Old English, I think it was something like dun, that means hill. We learned that the chalk was deposited about sixty million years ago and is made up of microscopic skeletons of plankton."

"Thank you, Luke. I guess you did learn something in high school," Justine replied.

"Luke, you used the word microscopic. What does that mean? And what are plankton?" James asked.

"Oh, well, microscopic means something you can't see with your eyes and you need to look through a microscope to see them. And plankton, they're minute organisms that live in the oceans. Whales eat them. Where did you say you live? I can't believe you're not familiar with these words."

Justine interrupted, "He's been on the farm and doesn't go near the sea."

"But, didn't he go to school?" Luke asked confused.

Just then the bus driver announced they had arrived at Stonehenge and those departing the bus for the tour would need to gather their belongings and be ready to get off at the stop. Justine breathed a sigh of relief since she knew Luke wanted answers and she couldn't give them to him.

The family got off the bus and each one grabbed their own luggage or backpack.

"Enjoy your weekend," the bus driver offered.

"Thank you, we will. Now, James, where should we put our luggage while we walk around to see Stonehenge?" Mrs. Ross was scouring the area to find somewhere to put the bags but could not see a likely spot.

"Mrs. Ross, I know of one not far from here. Please follow me." Then he whispered, "Gretchen, are you with us?"

"I am your highness. I am beside you."

"That is good. Please tell me what I am to do."

"You will need to stop for a moment so that I may cover them with a spell. They will follow your commands and you can lead them to the portal. I will need to use the invisible spell once I am sure we are not noticed and it will be safe."

"Does that include me," Justine blurted out.

"Does what include you?" Luke pipped in.

"Oh, nothing, nothing at all. I was just talking to myself."

Then Gretchen cast the spell over the family which made them zombie like.

"They will answer to your voice only. Start leading them to the portal."

So, James told the small group of followers to carry their bags and walk behind him. As they got closer to the portal, the travelers became invisible so as not to draw attention.

"I still see the family. Why have you not made them invisible?"

"I have, your highness, to all who are here, but not to you."

"Is it safe to travel through the portal?"

"Aye, it is. You must lead them and I will be the last person to go through."

Then Gretchen said the words to open the portal and James led the family through it into the kingdom of Wiltshire.

CHAPTER 19

A REUNION OF SORTS

James sat down next to Justine as they waited for the rest of the family to awake from the spell. Gretchen was visible now as she didn't have to remain out of sight from the family anymore. One by one the glazed look in their eyes disappeared and was replaced by one of confusion.

"James, where are we? I don't remember anything after we picked up our bags. How did we get here and who is that?" Mrs. Ross asked pointing to Gretchen.

"Family, meet Gretchen. She is a seeker and she brought James through that portal over there to visit me in Oxford. I know this will be hard to believe, but we have been transported back to 16th century England."

"That is impossible!" Dr. Ross insisted. "There is no such thing as time travel. I admit things have been a little strange ever since James arrived. A lot of unanswered questions, but nothing to make me think that James is from another time period."

"Is this what happened last summer?" Luke declared. "All the holes we've been trying to fill for the last year, the memory lapses? And Justine and the dreams she's been having weren't dreams at all but memories she was reliving. And why could she remember and we...the necklace! That has to be the connection we were missing!"

"Aye, the necklace was not to remain in her possession. That is why we ask our visitors to not take anything with them from our kingdom when they leave," Gretchen explained. "We were not aware the necklace remained in her possession until I noticed she saw me at the airport last summer. I did not try to retrieve it from her as I knew the distance you were to travel was great and a seeker would not be near her. The necklace allows its wearer to see and hear a seeker who has been sent to bring that person to our kingdom for a specific reason. Once a visitor goes back through the portal when leaving the kingdom, all memory of Wiltshire disappears. But what we did not know was that the connection she had with James would increase the magic of the necklace and cause Justine to remember her time in Wiltshire. That was unexpected, but good information to know in the future."

"So, what you're saying is, we have gone through a portal, apparently again, and have been transported back to 16th century England in the company of a young man..."

"He is a Prince, Daddy."

"Oh, that's even better! In the company of a Prince and a seeker who came to the future to find Justine and this is the family home we are visiting?"

"Yes, Dad. That is what happened. I'm sorry I couldn't say anything once I realized James was real and not a dream. There have been many times when I almost let the cat out of the bag, so to speak."

"I need to summon Arius so that he may know we are here and can inform the King and Queen of our arrival. He will come get us." Gretchen seemed to go into a trance at that moment and James told the family that Arius is able to connect to Gretchen through their minds. "Aye, we will be vigilant and ready when you arrive." Then Gretchen announced to the family, "Arius is on his way but we must stay out of sight. Arius has informed me that King Henry has patrols of soldiers moving in our kingdom and they must not see us."

"I will not ask right now, but I hope you will let us know what is going on after we have arrived wherever we are going."

"Aye, Dr. Ross, we will explain later," James assured him. "We must hide in the brush until he arrives."

"Who is Arius?" Luke asked.

"Please remain silent right now," Gretchen implored.

The small band of travelers did as they were told and hid in the bushes while they waited for Arius. Then someone appeared out of nowhere in the small clearing in front of them. It startled them, but no one made a sound. Arius motioned to them to come out of hiding and join him. They grabbed their belongings and joined him in the clearing. He silently indicated they needed to place their bags in front of him. Then he took Justine's hand and motioned to everyone to grab a hand and form a circle. Once they were all connected, Arius whisked them to the castle. Next thing they saw was the main hall of the castle.

"Wow! I want to be able to travel like that more often!" Luke announced as he regained his footing.

Justine looked around and the hall was just as she had envisioned it in her dreams. She was still trying to convince herself that this was all real and she was actually in 16th century England. It didn't take long for her to accept that fact for there, standing in front of her, were the King and Queen.

"I have delivered the Ross family, your Majesty," Arius stated as he bowed toward the King and Queen.

"Ross family, I would like to introduce, again, my father and mother, King William and Queen Marianne of Wiltshire."

Justine curtsied with Mrs. Ross following her lead, and Dr. Ross and Luke bowed.

"It is good to see you again, Dr. Ross. I know you do not remember being here last summer but we would like to welcome you again to our fair kingdom. However, I am aware there is one member of your family who does recall the last trip to Wiltshire due to a gift she took with her when she left our kingdom. That was unfortunate, but cannot be helped now."

"You were the patient in the hospital, weren't you? I remember your face. I never forget someone who has been in surgery. I seem to remember the surgery was an emergency and I needed to replace a valve."

"That is correct, Dr. Ross, but I am surprised to hear you say you remember me. This is something we need to investigate, but not right now. I want you to know I owe my life to you. I am still King and able to be with my family because of you. We were very happy Gretchen found you when she did and brought you here."

"I am grateful as well, Dr. Ross, for I still have my husband with me. I do not know what would have become of us if he had died."

"I'm glad I was able to help."

Just then two young ladies entered the hall and when they saw Justine, broke into a run. Once they reached her, they hugged her so hard that Justine cried out in pain.

"Justine, we are so happy to see you," Bethany shrieked. "We thought when you left, we would never see you again. But here you are!"

"Yes, here I am. And you two have grown since I last saw you."

"And you are just as pretty as I remember," Madison affirmed.

"Madison and Bethany, that is enough. That is not how young ladies act. I do understand your excitement, however. I am glad to see her as well."

Then Queen Marianne broke protocol and walked over to Justine and hugged her but more gently than her daughters. "We have a lot to talk about, young lady. But you must get settled first." She stepped over to a table, picked up a bell and rang it. A man entered the hall. "Cedric, please show the Ross family where they will be staying during their visit." Then addressing the family, "Cedric will show you to your chambers so you can clean up. Dinner will be served in a little while so you have time."

"Mother, where is John?" James asked.

"He is out on patrol and will return soon. This is something your father and you must discuss at a later time, my son."

Meanwhile, the princesses had each grabbed one of Justine's hands and were leading her into the Great Hall. They were asking her so many questions she didn't know where to begin with her answers.

"My girls, please let Justine alone. She will be here for awhile and you do not need to ask her so many questions right away. I know she will be happy to talk to you both but later."

"Aye, mother. But we have so much to ask her."

"I know you do, but it will have to wait. Justine, please follow Cedric. He will show you to your chambers. It may even be the one you were in last summer."

"Thank you, your majesty. I am looking forward to being with your family again and to see more of your kingdom."

The family followed Cedric to their bedrooms so they could unpack and settle in before dinner.

"How is it with you, my son? There is so much to discuss. You must meet with me in the throne room after you clean up from your travels."

"Aye, father. I will be there soon."

The King kissed his wife, "I will not be long. I need to discover our son's intentions toward Justine and will apprise him of the situation with King Henry."

James wasn't sure what his father was going to ask him but he had a good idea. He knew his father would want to know how he felt about Justine. This relationship was not what his father and mother wanted. But James had his own mind and knew whatever he proclaimed right now needed to be very clear because he wanted his parents' blessing. Later, he would seek that from the Ross's but didn't need to cross that bridge yet. What mattered now was his father, the King.

He walked up to the door of the Throne Room, took a deep breath and proceeded to knock.

"You may enter," he heard his father say.

"Father, I am here as requested."

"Please, come sit with me. There are several things we must discuss. First and foremost, I need you to explain to me why Justine and her family have returned with you."

So, James began with the meeting in the garden where Justine admitted to having dreams about him. He also learned that her dreams took place at the hospital and in Wiltshire. He and Gretchen were very surprised by this revelation and the fact that the tie between Justine and him was stronger than anyone realized. No one had ever remembered a visit to Wiltshire until Justine. Then he filled his father in on the rest of his visit. He told his father that initially, Justine was to be the only one traveling with him and how it was decided the whole family would be going on the trip to Wiltshire.

"I must admit I am pleased to see Dr. Ross again. I may even ask him to check me while he is here. But what I am more interested in at the moment is you and Justine. Have your feelings changed for her? When you saw her again, it is obvious from what you have said that she remembered you."

"Father, the moment I saw her I knew she had my heart. It took everything I had not to rush to her and hold her in my arms. She stood there, said my name as if I were a dream, and she asked if I was real. She wanted to touch me to make sure. As soon as she touched me, I reached out for her and pulled her close to me. She started crying and telling me she kept reaching for me in her dreams but could never touch me. We were in the garden for a long time talking and sharing our feelings for each other. If nothing else, this visit made me love her even more than I did."

"I thought this trip would help you get over her, not bring you together. You love someone who does not belong here, does not understand our ways, our customs. She is from the future where so much has changed."

"We have talked about this, father, and she wants to stay here with me. I thought it would be good for her family to accompany us to help with that change. And then there is the portal. If she stays and only goes through it one time, she will come out on the other side on the day she left. That will mean she won't be missing the life she has now if she ever decides to return."

"I need to consult with Arius on all of this. We have never had anyone stay for a long time except Dr. Lange. He travels back and forth now to add to his medicines and it doesn't matter how long he's been gone between his travels. But for someone to stay a long time and possibly not return? I am not sure if the portal has that kind of memory.

"It is my intent to marry her, father. And I want your blessing."

"I was not prepared for this and must have some time to think on this further. I will need to consult with your mother and Arius as well before I can tell you anything."

"I understand, Father, and I will eagerly await your decision."

"On another matter, I must tell you what has taken place since you departed. King Henry has stepped up his patrols and some of them have even crossed over into Wiltshire. We must be vigilant at all times. John is out in the kingdom now following our borders to make sure there are no intruders."

"Do we know what has caused this action on his part?"

"We think he is still convinced after last summer, that there is something happening in this kingdom that we are keeping from him and his obsession has only gotten worse. He was not satisfied with the story his spies told him when they returned home last summer. I have decided I need to travel to his kingdom for a visit to gain more information. I will be leaving within the week and I want you and John to be with me."

"But I have only just returned."

"You are my son. It is important we show King Henry we act as one so he thinks twice about any plans he may have to attack our kingdom. I have also arranged to visit neighboring kingdoms to ensure our alliance with them is secure."

"If it is your command, I will be at the ready when you decide it is time to leave."

"Thank you, my son." King William grabbed the back of James' neck, pulled James toward him and they touched their foreheads together. "Now go and ready yourself for dinner. We have guests to entertain."

"Aye, Father."

CHAPTER 20

A DINNER SURPRISE

James left the Throne Room in search of his mother for he knew he needed to plead his case to her before his father did. He found her in the garden walking among the roses.

"Mother, I am glad I have found you. I have something to ask of you. Do you have a ring in your possession that I may give to Justine? My feelings for her have only grown over these past couple of days in Oxford and I want to ask her to marry me."

"Marry you? My son, I feel you are too hasty? You have not known her very long and more importantly; she does not even live in our own time. She has only come for a visit and nothing more. I heard her parents say as much. How does your father feel about this? I am sure he does not approve."

"We talked of this just now. I told him of my intentions and I wanted his blessing. He, however, did not say anything one way or the other. He informed me that he needed to talk to you and Arius and could not let me know anything right now."

"Arius? Why must he speak to Arius?"

"There may be some information of which we are not aware surrounding the portal that may affect Justine in the days to come. She has told me she intends to remain in Wiltshire and not return with her family when they leave."

"Does she know what she is giving up when she says she wants to remain? I am afraid she says that now and may later regret her decision. She knows nothing of our customs and she is not of royal blood. She could one day very well be queen. Do you think she is prepared for that?"

"We agree that to be together, one of us must sacrifice the life we now have. But, if I leave Wiltshire to live in her time, I will need a seeker with me so that I do not forget who I am or her. It will be easier for her to remain here with me. But we may still visit her family in the future and return. That is why Father needs to talk to Arius, to see if this is possible. Father has also told me that John and I are to accompany him on a visit to King Henry's kingdom. We are to leave within the week. Father wants to determine if the King poses a threat to Wiltshire so that we may be ready. It was after Father and I talked that I thought of asking you for the ring. I want to ask her before we depart for Dorset. I do not want to wait until we return."

"My son, I can not pretend to know your heart. I do know that you are head strong and very passionate about life. I also know you would defend those you love until your last breath. Therefore, I know your love to be true as you have said. It has been a year since you saw her last but that did not matter. You have loved her since last summer and nothing your father or I have said or done since then has changed your mind, including the possibility of an arranged marriage. You are our beloved son and as your parents, we want you to be happy and marry for love. I do not want to lose you and I fear that would happen if we did not give you our blessing. Because of that, and this is what you desire, then I will not stand in your way. I do have a ring in my bedchamber which I think would befit this occasion. I have not worn it but have kept it these many years because it belonged to your grandmother. I will tell you the story behind the ring when I bring it to you at dinner."

"Thank you, Mother. I will be forever grateful. Please tell Father that you have given me, us, your blessing and I hope he will find it in his heart to bless us as well."

James left the garden confident in his decision and eager to ask Justine for her hand in marriage. He didn't know when the right time would present itself so he decided he would always carry the ring on his person. It didn't matter the look of the ring, only that he had one to put on her finger.

As he entered the palace from the garden, he encountered John who had just returned from patrolling the kingdom. John gasped when he saw him.

"James! What are you doing here? I thought you were still in the future!"

"John, my brother, I only just arrived but a few hours ago. And, since you have obviously just returned you have not heard the news. Justine and her family are here with me. They have returned to Wiltshire."

"Justine is here!" Then John tried to contain his obvious excitement. "It is good to have you back and to be able to see the Ross family again."

James looked at his brother suspiciously, "You seem to be rather excited that Justine has returned."

"That is because I know how much she means to you and therefore I was expressing my excitement that she is here for you."

"That is good to hear," James stated with a sigh of relief. "For a moment there, I got the feeling you were more than just glad she has returned."

"No, brother. It was only for your sake that I showed my excitement."

"Good, for I am going to ask her to marry me and I think she wants to marry me as well."

Surprised but not trying to show it, John replied, "I am happy for you, brother. You are good together. Now I must go clean up for dinner. Please excuse me."

John walked away with a look of disgust on his face. How was he going to forget about her now while she was right there under their roof?

Dinner was announced to the household and everyone began to arrive from different areas of the palace. Justine arrived with Madison and Bethany in tow still asking questions about her activities for the past year. John had time to clean up and had just come down the stairs.

"John," Bethany yelled, "Justine is back! Isn't that great!"

John looked up and there she was standing in front of him. He couldn't bring himself to say anything. He just stared.

"Hi, John. It's good to see you again. John?"

"What, oh, sorry. We are so glad you are back among us."

The Queen motioned to James to approach.

She leaned over and whispered, "Here is the ring. It is the one my father gave to my mother when they were married. They had a long and happy life together. I hope it will be the same for you and Justine." Then she placed it in his hand.

"Thank you, Mother." He opened his hand and there he saw a beautiful sapphire stone set in a gold ring. "Are you sure you want me to have this? It is more than I could have hoped."

His mother closed his fingers around it and cupped his hand in hers. "If she is the one, then the ring shall be hers."

James walked over to Justine, "May I escort you into dinner, Miss?"

"You may." James took her by the arm and escorted her to a seat by him.

"James, she was to sit between Bethany and me," Madison announced to her brother.

"I think you have had her all afternoon and now it is my turn to sit with her."

"Then, we will sit next to Luke," Bethany declared.

"I would love to have you two young ladies sit beside me."

"May we ask you some questions?" Madison inquired.

"Ask away."

"I know two young ladies who are forgetting their manners and may talk to Luke if asked a question or are informing him of something."

"Aye, Mother, we will remember."

The King and Queen sat at the ends of the table with Madison and Bethany sitting on either side of Luke and Dr. Ross on one side, and John sitting next to James and then Justine and her mother all on the other side. The servers proceeded to place plates filled with food in front of each person. Then filled the goblets on the table with wine.

Justine reached for her goblet and took a drink. "Oh yum! Mom, this is wine not water. May I drink it? It tastes really good."

"It is the custom to drink wine with our meals, Justine. We must be careful of the water. It can make one very sick," the Queen cautioned. "It is very important to drink water that has been boiled."

"Yes, you may drink it, but only one glass, please," Mrs. Ross noted.

"Thank you, Mom."

Then the King stood up which in turn made everyone else at the table stand.

"I have something I need to say. James, John and I will be leaving in the morning to travel to King Henry's kingdom. When talking to James earlier today, I told him that we would leave within the week. But I have since learned that tensions are increasing in Dorset and feel we must not wait any longer. This trip is important for the relationship between our two kingdoms. Around twenty knights are making preparations to leave as we speak. I am sorry to inform you of this, but it can't be helped. This was planned before we knew the Ross family would be arriving today. We will not be gone long." Then King William sat back down followed by the family members.

As soon as everyone was seated, James, still standing, spoke up, "Father, you expressed to me we would have a week before this trip. I have only just returned and the Ross family hasn't had time to settle in. Since I have now learned we will be leaving tomorrow and no one knows what tomorrow will bring, I would like to say something," James stated. Then he turned toward Justine, pulled the ring out and said, "Justine, you are the love of my life. I cannot imagine living my life without you and I want us to be together always." He got down on his knee and looked up at Justine, his heart ready to burst, "Will you marry me and make me the happiest person on the earth?"

Justine gasped and sat silent for what seemed an eternity to James and then looked at him excitedly and said, "Yes, yes, I will marry you!"

John's heart dropped for he knew he had no chance with Justine now. She was definitely in love with James.

There was an overwhelming silence in the room as Justine and James hugged and he placed the ring on her finger.

Dr. Ross looked at his wife and mouthed the words, "Did you know about this?"

She mouthed back, "No, I had no clue."

The King immediately stood up, and those at the table stood as well, "James, I must speak with you. Please follow me immediately," the King ordered.

"And I must speak with you, young lady," Dr. Ross proclaimed.

James and Justine looked at each other, hugged, and then followed their fathers out of the room.

"James, you just let me know of your intention to marry Justine in the Throne Room this very afternoon. You asked me for my blessing and I did not give it. Yet you chose to ask her anyway. I will have an explanation."

"Father, please know I had not intended to ask her at dinner tonight. I approached Mother after our meeting and asked if she possessed a ring I might be able to give to Justine when I proposed. She offered one that belonged to her mother and gave me her blessing. I knew this was to be discussed at some time by the two of you and was going to wait until you rendered that decision. But you announced at dinner that we are to leave tomorrow morning, which when we last talked, you said it would be within the week. I panicked! So, on impulse, I asked Justine to marry me."

"Your impulse went against my wishes. It is futile now to offer you my blessing on this marriage. I will now act as though you have it when we go back into the dining room for it will be expected of me. However, I did not tell you this, but there was also the proposal I wanted to make to King Henry hoping to join our kingdoms through marriage if our meeting went as planned."

"Marriage? Of me to one of his daughters?"

"I had hoped it would be one of my sons. The more likely person would be John as he is the eldest and heir to this kingdom. But your impulsiveness has made that decision for me. Now, the arranged marriage will have to take place, if agreed upon, with one of the daughters of King Henry and John. How could you be so foolish as to think only of yourself in this matter? You are my son, the King's son, and must put your kingdom above family. This may yet work as John cannot, much like you, find a suitable maiden within Wiltshire. But all of this will be dependent on the outcome of the meeting with King Henry."

"But, Father, what about the portal and the items we have brought here from the future. If one of the daughters is here, she will certainly see all of this and report it back to her father."

"I have discussed this with Arius and he assures me he will be able to control what she says to her father or to anyone outside the castle walls. We not only need to ensure our secret is safe but to also reestablish the positive relationship between our two kingdoms."

"Please forgive me, Father, for thinking only of myself. I know I should have waited as you asked, but my love for Justine overcame my better judgement. It will not happen again."

"We will discuss this further at a later time, but we need to return to dinner and the family."

Meanwhile, in another room. Dr. Ross was addressing his daughter on this very topic.

"Justine, you are only seventeen and have yet to finish high school! I will not allow you to get married. You have not even discussed this with your mother and me. You and James have been together for what, not even a week, and you have now declared your intent to accept his proposal. How could you do such a thing?"

"Because I am in love with him. Isn't that reason enough? And we haven't been together for just a week. James has been with me for a year now. Yes, it was only in my dreams, but my feelings for him have only grown stronger during this past year. And when I saw him standing there before me in the garden, I almost jumped out of my skin. At first, I thought he was a ghost until I touched him and realized he was real. Then he held me and for the first time in a year I felt safe, home. He is my home, dad. People can fall in love in high school and later marry that person. Why can't I?"

Then Dr. Ross walked over to Justine and hugged her. "Please know that your mom and I love you very much and want you to succeed in life and be happy with your choices. This one, however, is difficult to accept knowing that you are from two different worlds. Where will you live? Will we ever get to see you again if you choose to remain here? What happens if you travel back and forth through the portal? Have you really thought this through?"

"All I know is I want to be with him wherever that may be. We will figure this out, I promise. And you know I would never be anywhere where I couldn't see my family again."

"We will definitely discuss this further, young lady, with your mother present, but right now I think we need to return to dinner. They're probably worried about us."

With his arm around her shoulders, Dr. Ross and Justine returned to the dinner table. King William and James were entering the dining room at the same time. The two fathers stopped when they saw each other. Dr. Ross made it a point to walk over to King William and greet him. The King spoke first.

"I want you to know that James has our blessing and we welcome Justine into this family."

"And we as well welcome James into ours."

Madison and Bethany couldn't contain their excitement any longer and jumped out of their chairs to hug Justine. Luke walked over to his sister and also gave her a hug.

"Congratulations, sis. This really caught me off guard, but I'm very happy for you. I can see how much you love him and hope you will be happy together."

As the two approached the table, Mrs. Ross excused herself from the table and walked toward them. She looked at them both and stated quietly, "We need to talk about this and not just you and dad, but the family. I want you to know I do not approve of you getting married so young but for now, I will put on my happy face and act as though everything is fine."

"Stephanie, I told her the same thing and said she and I needed to talk to you about this. But for now, I have given my blessing."

She started to cry. Justine reached for her and hugged her.

"We'll be okay, Mom. I really do love him and need you to be happy for me."

"I am crying for happy and sad at the same time. I want you to know how much you mean to me, us. Your happiness is all I have ever wanted. But how will this work? That is something we need to discuss. Plus, I cannot live the rest of my life without ever seeing you again."

"That will not happen, Mom. This is something James and I know needs to be addressed and will do that before any final plans are made."

"That is very good to hear. Now, let me see that ring." The three walked back to the table and waited for the King to seat himself. Then everyone proceeded to sit down.

"Queen Marianne, I know you were not expecting James to propose tonight and am sure there is a story behind this ring that has not been shared. This is a very beautiful sapphire. It must have some history behind it. I would love to hear the story of this ring."

"Thank you, Stephanie, for inquiring as to the history of that ring. As you stated, I was not expecting James to ask Justine for her hand in marriage this evening. It was my intent to have the story of the ring written down so he could pass it on to Justine. But circumstances have changed. The written story of the ring will be passed on but at a later time. For now, I will relay the story as I know it.

"My father was once a revered King in the north of England. He became King at the age of twelve and certainly wasn't ready to assume his kingly duties. He had a guardian, or steward, who was to advise my father regarding the affairs of the kingdom until he came of age, which was sixteen. During that time, there were people in the north who did not think a young boy should be telling them what to do and they revolted. However, the armies of my father were successful in quelling the rebellion and restored peace to the land. With the peace came offerings from the lords in the land and one of those was the sapphire in that ring. When it was presented, my father was heard to say that a sapphire like that deserved to be on the hand of his queen when he married. He had it set in gold so it would be ready when that day came. My father fell in love with the daughter of a king from the south and they were married. Their love was one that lasted for many years. They died within days of each other for neither one wanted to stay on this earth without the other. Because I was the oldest, the ring was passed on to me, and now I pass it on to my son as his love for Justine reminds me of the love I witnessed in my parents."

The room was silent after Queen Marianne finished. Everyone seemed overwhelmed by her story and no one knew what to say. Finally, Mrs. Ross spoke up, "Queen Marianne, that was a beautiful story about your parents. You must have loved them very much. Their legacy lives on in you and now in James and Justine. I am so very grateful you have shared this with us so Justine knows how much that ring means to you and your family. She has been the recipient of a great gift and we are honored."

"Aye, Mother. I was not aware of any of this until now. I am so very sorry I did not ask about the ring when you presented it to me. I am ashamed of my behavior today toward you and my father as I was only thinking of myself. I am not one who has much patience in many things but will promise to do better."

"Thank you, James, for your apology. It is accepted," Queen Marianne acknowledged. "Now, let us feast on this meal before it is cold and celebrate this upcoming marriage."

Finally, the meal was over and everyone was stuffed after having sat at the table for so long. So much had been said at dinner that there was silence in the room as everyone began to excuse themselves from the table. In the silence, Justine's mind started replaying everything that had happened that evening when suddenly, reality set in. Had she just agreed to marry James? She was so caught up in the moment that she didn't have time to think about her answer. What did the future hold for them?

'I hope this was the right thing to do,' she thought to herself. 'I am only seventeen and have agreed to marry someone. But I do love him, very much. It seems like we have known each other forever! But it has only been a year and that year has been in my dreams! How much do we really know about each other? We will need to make sure everything is settled before my parents leave for home. This is not going to be easy.'

Then James stirred her from her thoughts by taking hold of her hand. "Let's take a walk in the garden now that we have finished our meal."

"I would love that."

"Please excuse us, Father. Justine and I would like to take our leave to the garden."

"You may do so, James. I think we have all finished eating and may retire elsewhere. Dr. Ross, I would like to talk to you privately if I may. Please walk with me."

"Gladly, King William." Then to his wife, "Stephanie, you might want to talk to the Queen about this upcoming marriage. Now would be a good time since the King and I are meeting, I'm assuming, about this very topic."

"I'll see if she is available right now."

"Good. I'll let you know what is discussed in our meeting and you can do the same. Compare notes so to speak. And we need to talk to each other. This isn't just any young man asking to marry our daughter. This is a prince in a kingdom from the past and the only way to get here is through a portal. No one would believe this if I told them. But, of course, we can't tell anyone because we won't remember any of this when we leave through the portal!!"

"Please, calm down, Drew. We are not leaving here until we have some concrete facts about all of this. So, let's start now. You meet with the King and I will meet with the Queen!"

Dr. Ross left with the King, Mrs. Ross left with the Queen and Justine and James left together for the garden. That left John, Luke, Madison, and Bethany standing around the table by themselves. They all just stood there not knowing what to say.

"I am so excited that Justine will be our big sister!" Bethany finally blurted out. "It is wonderful to see James so happy. have not seen him this happy since Justine left."

"I wonder when the wedding will be? Of course, we will need new dresses to wear!" Madison added.

Then the two of them locked arms and left the room talking about their own plans for the upcoming wedding.

"It appears my two sisters will have this whole thing planned soon," John assured Luke.

"Not if Justine has anything to say about it. I know my sister, and she will definitely want to have her say in the matter." Then Luke addressed John with a look of concern on his face. "What do you think about all of this?" Then talking to himself, "Truthfully, I can't believe James proposed to my sister so soon after they were just reunited. This trip through the portal for my whole family wasn't supposed to happen. I overheard the two of them talking about traveling to Stonehenge and I didn't want to be left out, so I made Mom and Dad aware of their plan. That's when we all decided to make the trip. But it was only supposed to be a trip to Stonehenge for the weekend and to visit James' parents who we thought lived on a farm near there. Then this trip through the portal happened and, suddenly, here we are! In Wiltshire, in a castle with a King and Queen in the 16th century no less! And now, my seventeen-year-old sister is engaged to be married to a Prince! Who doesn't even live in our time period! How does this happen?"

"Believe me, I am just as confused as you are, Luke. My brother has talked of nothing else this past year than when he would be able to see Justine again. My father has introduced him to many young ladies from our kingdom who would be a suitable match, but he would have nothing to do with them. Then recently, Gretchen informed us your family had returned to England, and she had seen Justine. My father wanted to take advantage of this fact and made it known he wanted Dr. Ross to receive a gift from him for saving his life. Gretchen would be the one to deliver it. James learned of this and convinced our father that he should accompany Gretchen on her journey. They left, and James returned with your family and now this! What was he thinking?"

"That's just it! I don't think he was thinking. He just acted on impulse. I think he heard your father talking about leaving tomorrow and didn't want any more time to pass before he asked her to marry him. I think he was afraid of what might happen on this trip. At least that was what it appeared to me."

"Your observation may be correct. That did not cross my mind. I have also been made aware that Father was considering an arranged marriage between one of the daughters of King Henry and either James or me. My brother may have just succeeded in spoiling the plan my father had, leaving me, the only eligible son. I do not think James was aware of this. But I saw the daughters from a distance about a year ago and would not choose either of them for my wife."

They looked at each other, smiled, and then laughed.

"Let us go find some ale to quench our thirst and talk some more," John suggested.

"That sounds like the best thing I've heard all night!"

They left in the direction of the kitchen where they knew they would be able to find someone to help them.

They had just entered the main hall when they met James and Justine on their way in from the garden.

"Where are you two off to in such a hurry?" James asked.

"We're looking for some ale to drink. Want to join us?" Luke inquired. "We can drink a toast to your upcoming wedding!"

"Aye, I think a toast is in order," James proclaimed.

"If you will excuse me, I think it is time for me to leave and let you three have some time together," Justine suggested.

"Good night, Justine. I will see you in the morning before I am to leave." James gave her a kiss and she walked up the stairs. John turned and watched her leave.

CHAPTER 21

THE NEXT MORNING

The King was up bright and early for he knew he had a long day ahead of him. His attendants helped him dress and then he proceeded to the Great Hall for breakfast.

"Where are my sons? They should be here for breakfast. Cedric, please see to my sons and tell them to come down for breakfast. They are late!"

"Aye, your majesty, I will see to it."

"I have arrived for breakfast before our sons? I am very surprised by that," Queen Marianne said as she entered the Great Hall.

Justine walked into the hall with a big yawn. "Oh, I'm sorry, your majesties. I didn't mean to be yawning in your presence. That was very rude."

"Please do not apologize. It is morning, is it not? Have you seen James this morning? He and John are to be eating right now. They know we have a long ride ahead of us."

"No, your majesty. I have not seen him. When I went to bed last night, John, James and Luke were going to find some ale and toast to our upcoming wedding."

"Ah, a toast, was it?"

John then entered the Great Hall. "Father, I am so very sorry I am late for breakfast. I must have slept too long this morning. Where is James?"

"He, like you, has not yet arrived."

"Father, did you need to send Cedric to my room to wake me and is it necessary to leave this early? I am not really feeling my best this morning," James moaned as he entered the Great Hall.

"Brother, you do not look so good," John declared rather loudly.

"John, could you please not use such a loud voice. It makes my head hurt."

"Maybe you should not have had so much ale to drink last night, brother."

Rather perturbed, the King roared, "My sons chose the night before a very important trip to drink to excess and begin this morning feeling ill. I want you to know that I do not care how you feel this morning. That problem belongs to you, not me. You must get ready to leave this palace and be outside, mounted on your horse in short order. Is that clear?"

"Aye, Father, very clear. We will be there," John assured him. James and John both grabbed some food from the table and departed the Great Hall to prepare for the trip.

The Queen approached her husband and calmly asked, "My husband, do you think it wise to take both of our sons on this trip?"

"What? Are you questioning me right now?"

"I am only reminding you that initially, you were only taking John since James had not yet returned. To take both of our sons would leave our kingdom without an heir if anything were to happen. I do not trust King Henry, and I know you do not as well. His constant patrols for the past year have been most concerning."

"I am very aware of King Henry and his intentions. This trip is to try to quell those suspicions and finally put them to rest. I do not intend to remain in his kingdom very long and will be vigilant the whole time we are there. However, I do agree with you though regarding our sons. Therefore, James will remain for the reason you have addressed and John will accompany me."

"And what have you decided regarding the daughters of King Henry? Do you still think it wise to arrange a marriage of one of them to John?"

"I have not made a decision yet. John approached me last night and has asked that I not require him to marry one of them. He would like to be able to choose his own bride. He did not think it wise to bring in an outsider. I do have to agree with him on that."

"Will Arius be accompanying you on this trip? I do hope so."

"Aye, he will be with us, but visible only to John and me at times. For I do not think it wise to make King Henry aware of his presence."

They were interrupted by several voices entering the Great Hall talking all at once. The Ross family had appeared for breakfast at the same time as did Madison and Bethany. John and James returned and approached the King and Queen.

"Father, James and I have donned our armor and are ready for the trip. We are prepared to leave when asked," John informed the King.

"My sons, there has been a change. John will accompany me and James, you will now remain in Wiltshire."

"Remain? Why, father? You might need me on this trip. I am just as good a fighter as John and will not let anything happen to you."

"As good as me? I think not!" John retorted.

"Aye, James, you have become a very good swordsman, but that is not the reason you are to remain. I think it best to have one of my sons remain in Wiltshire. James, this was planned while you were gone and therefore I think it best to keep the plans as they were and have John with me."

"Aye, father, as requested, I will remain here in your stead. You will be taking Arius with you will you not?"

"Aye, Arius will be with us. I do not venture out of the castle walls without him."

"That is good to know. Gretchen will remain here I hope."

"Aye, she will be here as she will be able to communicate with Arius and keep you abreast of our whereabouts. Now I think it is time for us to take our leave. Come, John. We must be on our way."

King William and John left the Great Hall. Arius met them at the palace door. The three walked outside into the courtyard followed by the members of both families. There they were met by twenty soldiers standing next to their horses. The King mounted his horse first followed by John and Arius and then the soldiers mounted their horses. The horses became restless as they sensed they were about to travel somewhere. The King's horse began to prance but he was able to steady it.

After a nod to the Queen he ordered, "Let us depart." King William and the small band of knights started off on the road to the castle gate. Madison and Bethany both yelled goodbye as their father rode away and the Queen waved with a slight movement of her hand.

As the group of riders disappeared from sight, Queen Marianne motioned for the families to reenter the palace. Once inside, she offered some instructions to those who were left.

"It is very important that we continue to carry on as though the King were here. James and I will make decisions together regarding issues that may arise. King William will be gone for at least a week and maybe two but I do not anticipate any major problems coming to our attention during that time. For now, Dr. and Mrs. Ross, you will need to remain in Wiltshire. You may not return to your own time just yet. We do not want to call attention to anyone or anything while the King is gone. James, you need to keep your intentions toward Justine a secret for now. It would not be good for the people of Wiltshire to be spreading this amongst themselves. At least, not now. Also, I want the Ross family to don clothes suited to our time and I will request it of Cedric to ensure that will happen. Madison and Bethany, you will need to attend to your lessons as you do each day. The rest, we will figure out as we go. Now, please, if you have not eaten, return to the Great Hall and enjoy your breakfast."

James started to walk away but instead turned and approached his mother.

"Why didn't I go with Father instead of John? If anyone were to remain in Wiltshire, it should have been John, not me. He is first born and heir to the throne. When father needed surgery, I was chosen to accompany him and John remained in Wiltshire. Why is this time different?

"There were many reasons why you went through the portal with your father a year ago. The main reason, as you stated, was because John is first born and we did not know what the outcome of the surgery would be. Your father was very sick and he might not have survived the trip."

"You said there were reasons. What might another one be then?"

"You are inquisitive and have never met a stranger you could not talk to. We knew that trait would be beneficial as you traveled with Dr. Ross and Justine into the future."

"If those were good reasons then, why not now?"

"This time, your father wanted John to be part of the conversations with King Henry especially if there were any decisions to be made regarding the relationship between our two kingdoms. And we hoped this would be good for you as well since you will be at the head of this kingdom in the King's absence."

"I will not disappoint Father or you while he is gone. I will do my best in his stead and make him proud of me."

"I know you will, my son. He is already very proud of the man you have become even though he is not always forthcoming with his praise."

Then James gave his mother a nod along with a slight bow and left to join the families at breakfast. But before he did, he removed the armor he was wearing and asked Cedric to take it to his room.

When he entered the Great Hall, Justine beckoned to him to sit by her. After he sat down, she leaned into him, put her head on his shoulder and whispered, "I'm glad you stayed here with us and me."

"I am glad I remained as well," he whispered back.

CHAPTER 22

THE TRIP TO DORSET

King Henry ruled the small neighboring kingdom of Dorset which was Southwest of Wiltshire and bordered on the south by the English Channel. The county town where King Henry's castle was situated was called Dorchester, which was inland about eight miles from the coast. The journey would take King William around four days to traverse the countryside to reach his destination.

"Do they know we are coming?" Prince John asked his father as they rode.

"I sent a messenger last week to inform the King of our visit and we received word back that King Henry is awaiting our arrival. How we will be received is not clear to me. That will be made known when we arrive. But I feel it will not be pleasant. I have been communicating with him through a messenger for the past year for I have not had the opportunity to travel until now nor have I had the desire to meet with him. But I fear if I keep neglecting this issue between our kingdoms, it will continue to worsen."

"King Henry's soldiers have been venturing ever so close to our borders and have even been seen crossing over the top of the hill between our two kingdoms," John reported to his father. "I hope we can ascertain the reason for this continued behavior and resolve any differences we may have. This all began last year while you were gone when Luke's horse took off with him and he crossed over into Dorset. Not soon after, King Henry made the trip to Wiltshire thinking he would find something amiss. But we were very careful, Father, not to give him any cause to question it as anything but a mistake."

"I was and still am very proud of the way you and your mother took charge of that situation. You could not have known that King Henry would leave spies behind in the castle after he departed. King Henry has a very suspicious nature and it seems to be getting the better of him." Then to Arius, still visible at that point, "Arius, please approach so I may talk to you." Arius nudged his horse to speed up so he could catch up with the King. "Arius, I am worried about King Henry and our safety throughout our visit. As we get closer to Dorchester, I would like you to go ahead of us, invisible of course, and assess the situation there. Then return to us before our arrival and inform us of what you have observed."

"No one will know of my presence there, your majesty. I will learn as much as I can. I will do as you have asked, but please know that I will not be able to protect your majesty while I am gone and want you to be most vigilant. Our ability to communicate will be hampered by the distance between us, and therefore you must continue to shorten that distance."

"I am aware of the problem this may cause, but I feel it is important to know of King Henry's intentions and I am willing to take the risk."

"King Henry would not dare attack us on the road, would he, father? It would be unwise and could begin a war between our two kingdoms. Please be assured, Arius, I will keep my father safe until you have returned."

The commander of the guard, Sir George, suddenly rode up alongside the King. "Your majesty, I have observed someone watching us from the top of those hills. It looks to be a soldier from Dorset. I have not seen anyone else, but there may be more."

"Thank you, Sir George. You have a keen eye. We will need to continue to watch for any movement in the hills. That is why we will not be traveling on the roads where they could easily ambush us. At night, we will set up an empty camp in a clearing near a wooded area, in case they intend to attack at night, and we will be waiting in the trees."

"That is an excellent strategy, Father. I am concerned that if Dorset soldiers have been watching us since we left, they may know that Arius is with us for he has remained visible up till now. The spies in the hills may have already seen him. We will need to make it look as though Arius is still here. Otherwise, they may suspect something."

"That thought had not crossed my mind. Very good, John! Arius, what do you suggest?"

"I could conjure up a replica of me riding on the horse. It will not be able to react to its surroundings, but will look like I am still here. I would suggest someone lead the horse I have been riding since my double will not be able to direct it."

"Then that is what we will do. Thank you, Arius."

Arius got off the horse and led it to the spot where he had previously been riding. Sir George placed his horse right next to it in order to hide the real Aruis. Then Arius handed him a lead rope. Arius appeared to remount his horse taking the reins in his hands and the real Arius vanished.

"Let us continue to Dorchester."

The King kicked his horse and took off in a canter followed by John, the fake Arius, and the soldiers.

Sir George asked the soldiers in the group to be on the look out for anything unusual. He asked the last two soldiers to hang back somewhat and be vigilant regarding their surroundings.

Throughout the day, King Henry's spies continued to keep their distance in the hills as they followed King William. As night fell, King William's soldiers set up camp to look as though they were there but remained at a distance watching for any sign of movement within the camp. Throughout the night, the soldiers took turns keeping watch while the King slept.

The next morning, the soldiers quietly entered the tents from the back and came out the front yawning and looking as though they had just awakened. It gave the appearance they had been in the camp the entire night. They made something to eat, broke camp, mounted their horses and proceeded on their way. They would continue this pattern for the remainder of the trip so as to ward off any dangers they might face along the way.

The countryside in Dorset was very picturesque. The group encountered rolling grasslands covered in wildflowers and sheep grazing in between fences made of stones and bushes. The hillsides offered great views of the surrounding area. From that vantage point, Sir George and the other soldiers could easily keep track of the whereabouts of King Henry's spies. It also enabled them to locate any woodland areas adjacent to a clearing where they could set up camp for the night. The trees were necessary if they were to stay hidden during the night.

They knew there would be one river to cross and that would be the River Stour. The river was approximately 61 miles long and ran from Wiltshire through Dorset. There was one bridge that had been built across the river but they dared not consider using it as it would be a good place for an ambush. They would need to find somewhere to ford the river. King William knew this would be the best time to cross since the water level often ran low in the summer. As they crossed the lowland around the river, they noticed it was teaming with wildlife and they were able to hunt. They now had enough deer and rabbits to eat for several days.

It was near dark when they arrived at the river's edge. King William ordered his soldiers to make camp and they would cross in the morning. They found a small group of trees nearby and set up camp there. Once the tents were up, the soldiers began preparing the meat for the evening meal and King William and John met with Sir George regarding the plans for the coming days.

"We have not heard anything from Arius yet and do not know what to expect..."

"I am here, your majesty!"

"Arius!" the King yelled in surprise. "You are here! It is good to see you. I was beginning to worry that something had happened to you. I hope you have some information for us."

"I do. It is my recommendation you turn back and not finish this journey to Dorchester. King Henry is conspiring with his captain of the guard, Sir Gregory, to capture you and John once you have entered his palace. He will then torture you until you confess everything. He is convinced our kingdom has access to something he should have. He has no idea what that is but he is willing to find out no matter what the cost. I did hear the captain try to reason with him to give you the chance to present the purpose for this visit. He felt there would be no need for bloodshed and that this could be resolved peacefully."

"I will give him a reason for bloodshed if he even tries to take King William and John prisoner," Sir George stated emphatically.

King William put his hand up to calm Sir George and then asked, "And what did King Henry reply to that? I am assuming he would have nothing to do with the suggestion made by Sir Gregory."

"No, your majesty, he would not. I studied him while I was there, and he was not himself, almost as if he were possessed. There was no reasoning with him. He could not be deterred from this path he is on. His mind could only see that which he has conjured up and nothing else. I think his guards could be persuaded to stand against him if given the chance. Otherwise, this will lead to an unnecessary confrontation."

"What are we to do, Father? If we leave, I think he will only gather his soldiers and come to Wiltshire. Maybe, since we now have the advantage Arius has given us, we could catch them off guard and attack them instead."

"Your Majesty, if I may speak," Sir George requested.

"Certainly, I am interested to hear what you have to say."

"I do agree with Prince John that if we attack them, we might have the advantage. But our soldiers are few and not enough to go against that army. I do not see us even getting through the front gate. And if we do send for reinforcements, the spies will surely see them approaching and report back to King Henry."

"That might be a good thing," King William paused as he reflected on what was just proposed. "Arius, do you think King Henry would be able to stay behind his walls when he knows my army is assembling in his kingdom? Do you think, in his frame of mind, he would believe his army could defeat us on the battlefield?"

"I do, your majesty. I feel he could not bear to have our soldiers in his kingdom. In his mind, it would mean only one thing: our kingdoms would be at war. This strategy just might get him out from behind the walls of the castle and give us the advantage we need to defeat him."

"I concur, your Majesty," Sir George added. "I suggest we immediately send a messenger to Wiltshire and return with our army. The messenger would need to leave under the cover of darkness so as to not be seen. He will be far enough away by morning so the spies in the hills will not know he is gone. I suggest we camp here for several nights so it looks as though we still intend to continue to Dorchester but have paused so we can rest the horses and the men along the river. That should be time enough for the messenger to reach Wiltshire if he rides through the night as we are only halfway to Dorchester."

"Arius, I would like you to return to Dorchester for two reasons. One, I want you to continue to monitor King Henry and his activity and two, I want you to take John with you and look for an opportunity to have an audience with Sir Gregory."

"For what purpose, your Majesty," Arius inquired.

"Aye, Father, for what purpose? And wouldn't I better serve you if I remained here?" John insisted.

"My reason is this. If you are able to convince his Captain that the King is not in his right mind and is obsessing over nothing, then we might be able to prevent this battle from ever happening."

"But why me, Father?"

"I think you will have more influence on Captain Gregory than Arius and together you must explain the situation to him. I am certain he accompanied the King to Wiltshire a year ago and may agree that King Henry is in pursuit of a ghost. This conflict will only amount to many on both sides meeting an unnecessary death."

"Your majesty, how can a Captain prevent what is to take place if the King orders it? I do not understand the recourse he may have. I am the Captain of the

Guard under your command and would never, under any circumstances, question your orders." Sir George stated emphatically.

"That is most gratifying to hear you say that, Sir George. But under these conditions, the Captain of the Guard may declare the King to be an unfit ruler and temporarily take control of Dorchester."

"But what about his daughters? Are they not to be next in line to the throne?" Prince John asked.

"Yes, they are but only if one of the daughters marries and then there would be a King and Queen to rule over the kingdom. According to the laws of Dorset, there must be a King. We are fortunate this has presented itself at this moment. I would never have dreamed this could very well benefit our kingdom and cause a very serious situation to end in peace. If the Captain agrees to this plan, then, as a solution to the matter of a king, I will propose that you, John, marry one of the daughters and become the new King of Dorchester."

"The King of Dorchester? We already talked about this back in Wiltshire. I stated there would be problems bringing in someone from the outside to marry me. I am next in line for the throne in Wiltshire, to succeed you, Father. You have been teaching me the ways of the kingdom for many years. It should be me on the throne after you!" Prince John exclaimed. "Are you suggesting that James will now be the heir to the throne? He is not ready for that! And he is to take Justine as his bride. She is certainly not ready to be Queen!"

"I agree with your father, Prince John. This will ensure peace between our two kingdoms with you as King in Dorset. The portal will remain a safely guarded secret as you and your queen will reside in Dorchester." Arius affirmed. "This solution which has presented itself at this time is much better than your marrying one of King Henry's daughters and bringing her to Wiltshire."

"I agree. To have you as King of Dorset, someone I have raised and guided all your life, would be as if our two kingdoms were but one. Let us explore this further for it is not decided as yet. Only supposition on our part. First things first. You and Arius must convince the Captain of King Henry's mental state and then we will decide the next steps in this plan."

"Aye, Father. Arius and I will proceed with the first step and report what we learn to you."

Prince John stood next to Arius and the two disappeared.

CHAPTER 23

THE MESSENGER ARRIVES

"What is it, Cedric?" the Queen asked as she looked up from her needlepoint.

"Queen Marianne, there is a messenger from the King. He said it is important that he see you right away."

"From the King?" The Queen immediately placed the needlepoint on the table next to her and stood up. "This must surely be of great importance. Send him in, Cedric, and then inform James that he is to come here at once."

"Aye, your majesty." Cedric bowed, turned, and left the sitting room.

The Queen grew impatient and began pacing the floor. 'There must be something wrong,' she thought to herself. 'I certainly hope they have not run into any trouble from King Henry.'

Cedric finally appeared along with the messenger. "Here is the messenger, your majesty, as requested."

"Thank you, Cedric. Has James been summoned?"

"Aye, he is on his way."

"Thank you, Cedric. You are dismissed."

As Cedric was leaving the room, James entered and crossed over to stand next to his mother.

"Thank you, my son, for arriving so promptly. This messenger was sent by the King and I am anxious to discover why he is here. I thought it important that you be here as well." Then to the messenger, "Please tell us why the King has sent you."

"Your majesty, I have been sent to amass an army to accompany me to Dorset. The King was camped along the River Stour when I left. This will explain."

The soldier handed her a folded message stamped with the King's seal. The Queen anxiously broke the seal and opened the document. As she read the message, her expression changed from one of worry and concern to one of surprise then anger.

"How could King Henry even think he could capture my husband and my son without a fight?"

"What?! King Henry has captured my father and John!" Then to the soldier, "That is why you are here to gather an army? How did you escape?"

"You must read this from the King. He has not been captured for he was warned of this by Arius who he had sent to spy on King Henry. We must send as many soldiers as we can spare for we must also maintain a small force here to protect Wiltshire."

"By my father's own words, he is planning to draw King Henry out of his castle and meet his army on the battlefield. He writes of a plan that he hopes will lead to peace rather than a fight, but he does not say what that is." Then James questioned the soldier, "Has my father told you of this plan? Do you know if the life of the King is in danger, or my brother? How soon was he expecting this army to join him?" James' voice became more angry with each question.

"Prince James, I was not privy to any of the plans that were discussed. I was told only to ride as fast as I could to deliver this message to the Queen. King William told me to return as soon as possible which would be a period of two days from the time of my arrival unless we ride with haste and push the horses to their limit. He stopped traveling before he crossed the River Stour. That is when Arius reappeared after he had been in Dorchester."

"Then we must immediately gather an army, as requested, to leave for Dorset as soon as they can," the Queen ordered.

"I will go with them."

"The King did not mention you in the message and I would like you to remain here with me. I cannot face the possibility of losing all three of you in a battle."

"Nothing will happen to me, mother. I also should be at the head of the army. I have been trained well and am one of the best soldiers in Wiltshire. I need to be there! I will keep my father safe and as long as I am in the battle, he will not be captured or killed! You have my word."

"I know you are a great soldier, James, and I know you want to be there for your father. It is also important King Henry and his army be defeated. Knowing this, I will allow you to leave. But you must promise me that you will return along with your father and brother."

"I will stay with him, your majesty. I would give my life for your family," the soldier affirmed as he pulled his sword and saluted her.

"Thank you for your loyalty. I am sorry, I have not asked your name before now."

"It is Sir Gawain, your majesty. I am a knight in the service of the King."

"Thank you, Sir Gawain. It is good to know you will fight alongside my son. Now, please gather as many soldiers as you can and quickly begin the journey to Dorset."

Sir Gawain bowed to the Queen as he backed up to leave the room so he could do the Queen's bidding.

"James, you must be very careful. I do not trust King Henry and do not know what your father has planned. But I am sure he knows what he is doing. I would like for Dr. Lange and Gretchen to accompany you. You may be in need of their services. Dr. Ross will remain and can attend to anyone who may need his help."

"I will be careful, mother. Father is very good at creating battle plans and I have every confidence that he has already done so as he awaits our arrival. I must go say my goodbyes to Justine, put on my armor and join the soldiers." Then James kissed his mother on the check. "Do not worry, mother. We will be back soon."

James left the sitting room to put on his armor and find Justine. He was afraid if he saw her first, he might not have the strength to leave. But if he was dressed for the journey, it would be easier to bid her goodbye. As least that was what he thought. He found her seated in the garden reading a book. She didn't hear him approach and his voice startled her.

"It was not my intent to scare you. Please forgive me."

"That's okay. Umm, why are you dressed like that? You were dressed like that the day your father left and you stayed behind. It is a good look for you! But you look like you're dressed for battle or something."

"I am."

At that moment, Justine quickly stood up and faced him, "What? No one has told me that there's a problem here. As a matter of fact, it's pretty quiet!"

James took a deep breath then said, "I have come to tell you that I am leaving with some soldiers at the request of my father. There may be a battle and that is why I am dressed as I am. We will meet my father in no more than two days' time and I will learn of the plans then."

"You are leaving? You may be in a battle? But you don't know that yet? How can that be? Who is this battle with and why are you going to fight? Will you be okay? Oh my gosh, you could be killed! Could you be killed, James?"

He knew if he reached out to hold her at this point, he wouldn't be able to leave. So, he stepped backwards one step, took another deep breath and continued, "King Henry is threatening to capture John and my father and by sending an army, my father is hoping King Henry will rethink that and there will be peace between our two kingdoms."

She started to reach out to him but he put his hand up to stop her. "Please, do not come any closer. This is hard for me to tell you I am leaving. I want to hold on to you and never let go. But I cannot do that. I need to leave. It is my duty as Prince to be with my father. I hope you understand and will not come near me right now."

Justine put her arms down and looked as though she was going to start crying. Then she shook her head, got hold of herself, and looked him in the eyes. "I understand, I don't like it, but I understand. If I hugged you right now, I know I wouldn't be able to let go. May I at least kiss you on the cheek?"

"Aye." They leaned toward each other, not touching, and she gently kissed his cheek after which they both backed up so as not to give in to temptation. Then James nodded, turned and walked briskly out of the garden.

Justine stood there staring. What just happened? James might be going into battle and he was wearing armor. Would this happen again? Was this what she had to look forward to if she married him? Would his life always be in danger? He is a prince after all and could one day be King. She really hadn't faced the reality of the situation in which she now found herself. All she knew was that she was in love with James and that meant she would have to take the good with the bad, no matter what century he lived in. But right now, James was leaving and she knew she had to be there when he left. She took off running and ran through the garden, past the kitchen, into the main hall and out the front door. There in front of her was a large group of soldiers on horseback. To their left was James. She watched as he mounted his horse and rode to the front of the army. He turned to make sure all the soldiers were mounted and ready and then he saw her. She nodded and waved. He turned away momentarily and just sat there. He realized he may never see her again. He wasn't sure how this battle was going to go and just couldn't leave her like this. Then he suddenly turned his horse back toward the castle and took off at a gallop. When he arrived at the spot where Justine was standing, he stopped the horse, jumped off, ran toward her, grabbed her and passionately kissed her.

"Now we have said goodbye as I should have before. I love you, Justine. No matter what happens, always remember that." Then he mounted his horse, rode back to the front of the army and they all rode out through the castle gates.

Justine suddenly felt alone. She had just said good bye to the love of her life not knowing if he would return. As she looked around her, she realized the villagers were staring at her and whispering to each other. Guess the secret was out about James and her and that couldn't be undone. He just kissed her in front of the whole town. She politely smiled, backed up, turned and walked into the palace. She closed the front door and placed her forehead on the door and began to sob. Then she felt arms reach around her and enfold her in them.

"It will be okay, honey. James will come back and everything will be as it was," her mom said as she tried to comfort her daughter.

"As it was? You don't understand! I love him, there is no question about that, but he could become King someday and that would make me his queen. And will there be other battles to fight where I will have to watch him ride off into the sunset wondering if he'll return. And I live in the 21st century! Am I willing to give that all up to live with him here? There is no 'as it was' for this is no ordinary love story. All of this became clearer and more real when he told me he was to ride out to meet his father. I am so worried about him, Mom. I feel lost without him."

Her mom held her even tighter as Justine just sobbed into her shoulder. "I am so sorry, Justine." She knew there wasn't anything she could say that would comfort her daughter so she just held her until Justine's sobs began to lessen. Then she kissed Justine on the forehead put her arm around her shoulders and the two started to walk toward the main staircase in the hall. "Maybe a hot bath will help you feel better." Justine nodded in agreement and they walked upstairs.

CHAPTER 24

JUSTINE FINDS
SOMETHING TO DO

'What am I going to do now that James is gone? I can't just sit here and mope the whole time. I need to keep busy. But doing what, I wonder?'

Justine knew if she didn't keep busy, she would just sit and worry about James. She decided to wander around the palace to see if anything popped out at her. She remembered that Princesses Madison and Bethany had a tutor every day. Maybe, she could help them with their studies. But that wasn't very appealing. Besides, how could she teach them anything that only pertained to the 1500s? There are way too many things that have happened since then and she would probably confuse them more than help them. How about her parents? She went to check on them to see what they were doing to keep from getting bored. She went to their room but no one was there. Where could they have disappeared to? Then she saw Luke coming down the hall.

"Hey, brother. What's up? Doing anything fun and exciting? Something I could do with you?"

"Looking for something to do, huh. Well, I've been invited to teach some of the soldiers how to do Karate and they are going to teach me how to fight with swords. You can join if you want."

"No, I don't think so, but thanks for inviting me anyway."

"If you change your mind, we will be in the inner courtyard in front of the palace."

"Thanks, I'll keep it in mind. By the way, have you seen Mom or Dad? I can't find them anywhere."

"Well, since Dr. Lange left to go with James, there wasn't anyone to cover his office, so Dad and Mom have stepped in to help with the sick."

"Oh, that was a good idea. I didn't even think of that. I'll go look for them there. Have fun!"

"I will."

So, Luke took off to meet the soldiers and Justine went in the direction of Dr. Lange's office.

As she drew nearer to Dr. Lange's office, her pace quickened as she heard a lot of commotion and groaning. When she got to the door, she saw where all the noise was coming from. Her father and mother were holding down a patient on the examination table who looked to be ten and the child's mother and father were standing nearby looking rather anxious. Justine stepped across the room to stand next to the mother who looked as though she needed some assurance that Justine's father knew what he was doing.

"Oh, Justine! So glad you're here. Will you please take this child's mother and father out into the hall so we can set this boy's broken leg?" her father implored.

"Yes, of course. Ma'am, Sir, will you please come with me? We need to leave so my father can attend to your son." And Justine escorted the parents out into the hallway and closed the door. "Your son will be fine. My father is one of the best doctors in the world. Your son is in good hands." Then trying to change the subject, "What are your names?"

"Hanna. My name is Hanna. My son will be fixed? Should I not be in there?"

"No, you should not. It is easier for the doctor to do his job when family is not involved. Where do you live, Hanna?"

"I live near the outer courtyard. We raise sheep."

"How did your son hurt himself?"

"He was standing on the fence trying to sort the sheep into the pens when a ram butted him and he fell. My husband heard him screaming and ran outside. The ram was scratching the dirt with his foot getting ready to run at my son again. We stopped the ram and then my husband grabbed our son and carried him into the house. That is when we saw his leg. I have never seen a leg bend like that. That is why we brought him to Dr. Lange. But when we got here, no Dr. Lange. Your father told us he was Dr. Ross and was watching over the office while Dr. Lange is gone."

"It is a good thing you brought him here. He would have been crippled if his leg was allowed to heal like that. Would you like me to tell you what will happen with his leg?" As Justine explained what she knew, the parents listened intently and seemed fascinated by her explanation. She told them he will have a cast on his leg and had to explain the word 'cast' to them. When she got done, they realized there were no sounds coming from the office.

"Has he died? I don't hear anything!" the mother cried in alarm.

Justine talked to her very calmly and explained that he was probably asleep. That would make it easier for the leg to be set without any pain. The parents were relieved to hear that and everyone just sat in the hall awaiting word from Dr. Ross.

Finally, Dr. Ross opened the office door and walked over to where the parents and Justine were seated. "Your son will be fine. The operation was successful. Your son has a cast on his leg. Do you understand the word cast?"

"Aye, Justine explained to us this word, cast," his father answered.

"Good, I will show it to you when you go in to see your son. He will need to wear the cast for about six months, half a year, so his leg heals completely. It was broken in several places."

"Will he be able to work? He is needed to help with the sheep," his father insisted.

"No, he will not be helping with the sheep. If he does too much work, he could break it again and then I would not be able to fix it. Do you understand?"

"We will make do, father. Our son cannot help now. The other children will need to do his jobs until he is better."

"I am sorry he cannot help. You do understand that it will be about six months before he is completely healed."

"Aye," the boy's parents nodded in agreement.

"I can take you in to see him now. He will just be waking up and will be in some pain for several days. I want you to give him this medicine for his pain, but not very often if you can help it." Then he turned to Justine, "Thank you so much for your help. You came along at just the right time. We may just need you again sometime!"

Dr. Ross ushered the parents into the office to be with their son. Justine smiled, "One good deed done!" she said to herself. "Now let me see what else needs to be done around here!"

CHAPTER 25

THE ROSS FAMILY FITS IN

Justine was feeling very proud of herself after she assisted her father with his patient. This could be something she could do each day to help the time pass while James was gone. She was tired and decided to go back to her room to rest before dinner. She had no sooner lain down when there was a knock on her door.

"Now, who could that be?" she mumbled. She got up off the bed, walked to the door, and opened it. "Cedric, why are you here?"

"The Queen has requested your presence in the Great Hall."

"Right now?"

"Aye. Please follow me."

Justine sighed and followed him reluctantly to the Great Hall. When they entered the hall, Justine noticed the rest of her family was also there already seated at the table. 'Now what,' she thought to herself.

"Ah, Justine, so glad you have joined us. I have something I want to propose to you and your family. Each one of you has special skills you could offer this kingdom while you are here. Therefore, I would ask each of you to assume a position in this court while you are with us for however long that may be."

"A position in the court..." Luke began.

To which Cedric whispered, "Sir, it is impolite to interrupt the Queen while she is talking. You must wait until she is finished and then ask permission to address the Queen."

"Oh, sorry."

"Thank you, Cedric. But I am not offended by his reaction. They are not of this time and not aware of our customs. We need to exhibit patience with them for now. These are the positions you will hold." Then she looked at Dr. Ross, "First, Dr. Ross, you will be our physician along with Dr. Lange. Our kingdom is too large for one physician to see to all the needs of those who need help. Next, Mrs. Ross, Stephanie, you will be my advisor when problems are brought before me. You have told me you worked in your world to solve problems and see to it that those who do wrong are punished. I think your experience would be a great benefit to us. Then, there is Luke. I have been told that you are learning to prepare meals to be a great cook. I would like you to work with those in the kitchen to create meals and introduce foods from your time. And last, there is Justine. You are to become a member of the royal family and as such, I think it is time you met your kingdom. I would like you to sit beside me whenever the people of the kingdom come before me. I would also suggest that you go outside the palace and visit the villagers, accompanied by some soldiers of course for your safety. It is important they see you as part of this kingdom, someone who cares for them and for Wiltshire. These are the positions I wish you to take to serve us while you are here."

"May I address your majesty," Dr. Ross asked.

"You may," the Queen replied.

"When you began, you made the statement, 'however long that may be' when referring to the amount of time we will be here. I don't think any of us are planning to remain here for an extended length of time. We have lives to return to back in England. I have a new job at the hospital there. Justine is to finish high school, and Luke with be attending culinary, or cooking, school. We can't just forget about all that!"

"Dr. Ross, I understand your concerns. We do not know what the future holds or how long your stay will be. What we do know is, no matter how long you remain with us, you will be returning to the day you left when you return home through the portal. You will not lose any time in your future."

"How can that be? Are you saying that even if we stay here for, let's say, a year, we will return to the original day we left and time in the future will have not moved at all?"

"Aye, that is the magic of the portal. That is how we have been able to keep our existence a secret all these many years. No one who visits and then leaves has ever returned as your family has done. And, when your family finally leaves us, you will not remember having been here and therefore our secret will continue to be safe."

Then Justine couldn't contain herself and blurted out, "That would mean, if I marry James and remain here with him that when my family leaves, they not only won't remember any of this, but they won't know where I am either?" As Justine started to think this through, questions began popping into her head that she hadn't thought of before. Her speaking became faster and faster as these thoughts began taking over her mind. "And what if I want to visit my family in the future and all of a sudden show up at the house? But they are only going to be in England for two years, what happens after that? And will we lose our memory of this place when we go through the portal, never to return? Will I even remember why James is with me after we go though the portal? And what if James doesn't want to go through the portal but I do?" Justine sat down and started crying.

"Honey, stop! You're getting carried away. You're upsetting yourself," her mom said as she hugged her daughter and tried to comfort her. "These are things that will need some answers, but not right now. We will need to set aside some time to discuss all of your concerns, which, I must say, are mine, too, now. But the Queen made it clear that no one other than our family and Dr. Lange has ever put this to the test. There is much to discover and we have time to address it while we're here. Let us settle in as the Queen has requested and serve this kingdom. After James has returned, our two families can sit down and explore the answers to all our questions."

"Thank you, Stephanie. You have advised your daughter well. Justine has made me aware of her concerns which I share as well and our families will need to talk about all of this at some point in the future. But let us think about the present now and live it the best we can. Therefore, it is my hope the Ross family will accept the positions I have mentioned so the kingdom might benefit from the gifts each of you has to offer."

"I think I can speak for the members of the family and accept your offer. We would all like to put our talents to good use as long as we are part of this kingdom."

"Thank you, Dr. Ross. Now, let us partake in our evening meal."

CHAPTER 26

JAMES AND THE ARMY ARRIVE

After riding all night and through the morning, moving as fast as possible, James and the army of soldiers found the King still camped at the River Stour. They rode into camp and dismounted. Hearing the commotion, King William threw open the flap on his tent and came out with his sword drawn. When he saw James, he sheathed his sword and greeted him with a hug.

"My son, I am surprised and glad to see you at the same time. I did not expect you to accompany the army and them not to arrive for another day. You have made very good time."

"The message you sent said to make haste, so we did. We rode our horses hard and they should be attended to as quickly as possible. They will need to be strong if they are to carry us into battle. We did not stop along the way unless it was necessary. Sir Gawain has been very helpful, Father. We would not have made it here without him."

"Sir George, please see to their horses and make sure the men are fed." Then to Sir Gawain, "Thank you, Sir Gawain, for delivering the message so quickly and returning with the army. I see you have included Dr. Lange and Gretchen in this group. Welcome to you both. I am pleased you are here as we may be in need of your services at some point.

"Your majesty, it was James who suggested they accompany us. I will not take the credit for bringing them."

"Thank you, James. But this leaves Wiltshire without a physician. Who is in charge now that you and they are here?"

"Father, Dr. Ross is seeing to the clinic and mother is very capable of handling anything that might come up. So, we have come to help."

"It sounds like Wiltshire is safe, for now. I need all of you to join me in my tent for we have much to discuss."

James, Sir Gawain, Sir George, Dr. Lange and Gretchen all joined the King in his tent. It was very large with enough room for their meeting. In the middle of the tent was a small table used when traveling. On the table was a map of Dorset which the King had brought with them so as not to lose their way while traveling. The King moved to the back of the table and the others formed a circle around it.

"Father, where are Arius and John? I did not see them when we arrived."

"They have not yet returned."

"Returned from where, Father?"

"I sent them to Dorchester castle to find the Captain of the Guard, Sir Gregory. It is hoped we can convince him King Henry has taken leave of his senses and needs to be removed as King or at the very least not allowed to order his kingdom into an unnecessary war. Sir Gregory was with King Henry in Wiltshire a year ago when the King made an unannounced visit, sure we were hiding something from him. I have since sent several messengers to the King asking to meet, but he has refused our requests. This obsession has consumed him for the past year and it needs to stop. That is why

I chose to take matters into my own hands and make the journey to Dorchester so we could meet face to face and resolve this. After we departed from Wiltshire, I decided to send Arius to spy on King Henry so we might know what we could be facing once we arrived at his castle. When Arius returned, he informed me that it was King Henry's intent to welcome us into his castle and then surround us and take us prisoner. Once I learned of this, I sent Sir Gawain to Wiltshire to gather the army together. King Henry will learn of their arrival from his spies and, I feel, will not be able to remain within the protection of his castle walls but will be compelled to confront us on the battlefield."

"Do you think this Captain will go against his King and order the army to stand down?" James asked.

"I do if Arius and John have had the chance to talk to him. They have been gone for two days and I am anxious for their return. For now, we just wait. But it is important, while we wait, to discuss our battle strategies so we will be prepared for two different possibilities. The first, to fight if they remain within the castle walls, and the second, if they ride out to meet us on the battlefield."

King William informed them of the plans he had already formulated and they all agreed, with some slight changes, the plans were well thought out and would lead them to a victory over King Henry's forces no matter which battle they were to fight. But they hoped the second one would be the one King Henry chose.

All of a sudden, they heard a loud roar and ran out of the tent to see what could possibly be making that sound. As they looked up, they saw a dragon hovering overhead. No one had seen a dragon in England for some 150 years. The horses started prancing and neighing in fear and the men looked surprised and scared at the same time. King William ordered the bows to the ready for he didn't know what to expect. The soldiers who heard the order grabbed their bows and knelt down with the arrows aimed at the dragon. Then they impatiently waited for the order to shoot. As James looked closer, the dragon seemed to have something or someone riding on its back.

"Father, don't shoot!" James yelled. "It looks like John is on that dragon!"

"John? That's impossible!" Then he looked closer, and it was indeed John! "Where did that dragon come from and why is James on the back of it?" Then he ordered the soldiers to stand down.

"I think we need to allow it to land so we will find out," James replied.

James ran to the clearing nearby where it appeared the dragon could land. He made sure he gave it plenty of space to land that massive body. The King stood next to James and many of the soldiers surrounded him in the event the dragon was not friendly. As the dragon drew nearer, James noticed that John was hunched over and try as he might, he could not sit up straight. He feared something had happened during the visit to Dorchester. But where did this dragon come from? James thought it looked like a silver back but wasn't sure since he had only seen pictures of dragons when he was younger. The eyes were a steel blue and the scales on its body sparkled in the sunlight. It had two horns extending from its head with gills located below them. There were spines on its neck but they extended no further. The massive wings created such a strong wind as it attempted to land that those on the ground had to use all their strength to not get knocked over. It landed rather clumsily, lost its balance and fell forward on its face. James, not thinking about his own safety, immediately ran over to help his brother disembark from the dragon's back. John yelled out in pain as he attempted to maneuver his body off of the dragon. Then he just fell into his brother's arms as he slid off the dragon. Several soldiers ran forward to help James carry him away from the dragon. Once there was some distance between them and the dragon, they knelt down to place John on the ground. Then, a strange thing happened. The dragon began to shrink and change shape. As it grew smaller and smaller, everyone realized the dragon was actually Arius.

"James," John said as he reached up to James, "Arius is the dragon and he saved me from King Henry." Then John collapsed and passed out.

"He is badly hurt and needs a doctor to attend to his wounds," Arius explained as he approached. "I got to him as soon as I could."

James looked up at Arius in wonder, "Arius, you changed into a dragon. I was not aware you could do that."

"Me, either! It was a shock to me, too!"

The King ran over to help with John. "I need some soldiers to carefully carry my son to my tent. Please put him on my bed."

"Father, John needs Dr. Lange!"

"I am glad you brought him with you. Sir George, fetch Dr. Lange immediately."

Four of the soldiers reached down, picked John up and carried him to the King's tent. John was clearly in a lot of pain for he yelled out as the soldiers carried him as he began to regain consciousness. They laid him gently on the King's bed. Arius, James, and the King followed close behind.

As they walked to the tent, the King looked at Arius astonished, "So, you can change into a dragon. This is certainly a new development. How long have you known you could do that?"

"About a day," Arius replied. "I am as much surprised as you, your majesty."

"I need to know everything, but let us see to John first."

Once Dr. Lange arrived, King William motioned to everyone to leave the tent. As they were leaving, King William took hold of Dr. Lange's arm, "Take good care of him. Inform me as soon as you know anything regarding his injuries."

"I will, your majesty."

CHAPTER 27

ARIUS EXPLAINS

"Arius, I must know everything. Every little detail. Do not leave anything out, good or bad. And I want to know more about the dragon!" King William stated.

So, Arius sat down on a log near them, sighed, gathered his thoughts, and began to recount the events of the secret visit to Dorchester.

"John and I left here and arrived at Dorchester castle outside the palace still invisible. There were few guarding the walls of the castle so we were not sure where the rest were nor did we know where to find Sir Gregory. We decided to search the soldiers' barracks and found many soldiers standing everywhere. It seemed to be during a duty change and some were preparing to leave for their assignment. We remained there for a while and listened to their conversations which we hoped might give us some insight as to any future plans. We did hear some talk about the animosity between the kingdoms and how they thought King Henry was overreacting to the appearance of a rider on the hill a year ago and how this has consumed him. After hearing this, we felt we had grounds to stand on when we talked to Sir Gregory. We knew he surely had to be aware of how his soldiers were feeling. We stayed there to see if we could learn the whereabouts of the Captain and heard he had been summoned to the palace by King Henry."

"We left there not knowing how long it would be before we could talk to the Captain on our own. We decided we would listen in on the conversation between Sir Gregory and King Henry hoping we might learn of any plans regarding Wiltshire. We were still invisible so it was impossible for anyone to detect our presence. We found the King and the Captain meeting alone in the Great Hall. However, we realized we had arrived at the end of the conversation for the King dismissed Sir Gregory right when we got there. So, we followed Sir Gregory, through the halls of the palace looking for the right time to confront him. He finally paused in an alcove near the Main Hall. That is when John and I appeared behind him. When he turned around, he saw us and started to pull his sword. When he realized who we were, he replaced his sword and asked us why we were there."

"Once we finished explaining our reason for being there, we told him we wanted to hear his thoughts. It took him a minute to respond. Then he told us he agreed with us regarding King Henry and his frame of mind. He stated that King Henry has been completely unreasonable for the past year, treating everyone in the kingdom with disdain, accusing people of crimes they had not committed. He wanted to see this all end but was afraid of the King and knew he would face certain death if he was not successful in his attempt to overthrow the King."

"Just then we heard someone approaching and realized it was the King looking for Sir Gregory. I was not close enough to Prince John so that I could grab him and we could disappear. When the King came around the corner, he saw Prince John standing there. Sir Gregory immediately drew his sword and told the

King that he had come across Prince John walking through the palace and was bringing the Prince to the King. The King demanded to know what Prince John was doing in his castle. The Prince stated he had come on his own to try to negotiate peace with the King in hopes that no blood would be spilled on either side. The King did not believe he had come of his own accord and assured him there could be no peace between our two kingdoms. Then he hit Prince John and knocked him to the ground. As the Prince stood back up, I noticed his nose was bleeding. The King hit him again, this time in the stomach and the Prince doubled over from the blow. The King ordered Sir Gregory to take the Prince to the Throne Room. I followed them hoping I could grab the Prince at some point and return here but at no time was the Prince alone. I heard the Captain whisper to the Prince that he was sorry but he had to follow orders. Once they arrived in the Throne Room, the King sat down on his throne and ordered the Prince to kneel before him. When he wouldn't, King Henry had the Captain force the Prince to kneel down. Then the King got up, walked over to Prince John, bent over, grabbed him by the hair forcing the Prince to look at him and spit in his face. He told the Prince that he was just dirt under his feet and needed to be cleansed. The King stood up and ordered one of the soldiers in the room to kick this 'dirt pile' until he told him to stop. So, the soldier kicked the Prince continually until King Henry was satisfied and told the soldier to stop. John just lay there on the floor groaning in pain. I was so mad at that point my body was shaking. I knew I had to intervene somehow. Then, I felt a power surging through me I had never felt before. I wasn't sure what it was but suddenly I felt I could do or be anything. So, I wished I had the power to become a fire breathing dragon to scare the King and carry Prince John out of there. Suddenly, my body began to change form and I grew into a very large dragon. I looked at the King and the Captain, opened my mouth and out came this large stream of fire. What a wonderful feeling that was! I felt invincible! They both yelled and tried to run out of the room. I blocked their exit every time. When more soldiers began to arrive, I knew I needed to grab the Prince and leave. I looked up and set fire to the ceiling. When I did, I could see daylight and knew we had a way out. I sprayed the room with fire, grabbed John with one of my claws, spread my wings and took off.

"I could hear the whizzing of arrows in the air around me as we flew away. Once I got a safe distance away, I carefully landed so I could check on Prince John. I let go of him, stepped back and waited. He started to move but very slowly. When he had gained consciousness, he looked up, saw me and yelled in fear. I told him not to move because he was badly hurt and then explained that the dragon was me and to not be afraid. He realized that the voice was mine and calmed down. I told him he needed to crawl on my back so I could fly him out of there and to your camp. I crouched down as far as I could so he didn't have far to climb. He got on my back, grabbed on the best he could, and I flew him here."

The small group of listeners just sat in silence as they listened to Arius talk about the events that had taken place in Dorchester. Everyone was stunned by the actions of King Henry and by Arius's transformation.

The King finally spoke. "I don't care how crazy King Henry has become; he should be beheaded for his treatment of my son. Knowing this, I cannot guarantee that even if Sir Gregory agrees to our plan that I can follow through on it." Then turning to Arius, "Thank you, my most loyal sorcerer, for returning my son safely to me. You put your own life in danger to pull him out of a most terrifying experience and for that, I will be forever grateful. And to think, you did it as a dragon! This is one thing I still find very hard to believe."

"I am as surprised as you, your majesty. I think, because we have been at peace for these many years, that my magic has only scratched the surface. Who knows what I am capable of doing. I also have never felt so mad and helpless at the same time and I think that was the trigger I needed to let the magic escape. I knew Merlin had unbelievable powers that up till now I thought had passed me by. I guess I was wrong."

"I am very thankful you discovered these powers right now and were able to save Prince John."

"Excuse me, King William, your son would like to speak with you," Dr. Lange stated as he exited the tent. "He is still very weak. He has some broken ribs, a broken arm and a lot of bruises but will be fine with rest. He is lucky one of his ribs didn't puncture a lung. I have set his arm and have bandaged his chest to prevent his ribs from moving, but he won't be able to do much for a while. I suggest, if possible, that he return to Wiltshire where he can convalesce with no temptations to move around too much."

"I agree with you doctor. But how...?" The King paused in thought for a moment and then turned to Arius. "Arius, could you fly my son back to Wiltshire? The queen would take good care of him. And Dr. Ross is there, too."

"I would be honored to, your majesty. I will fly him there as soon as he is able. I was informed that Prince James brought Gretchen with him. You will be in good hands while I am gone. I will alert the seekers who remain in Wiltshire of my arrival and they in turn can alert others. I do not want to scare the villagers, the soldiers, or the royal family."

"May I go in with you to see John, Father? I would like to see my brother."

"Aye, you are welcome to join me. Please excuse us. I need to see my son."

King William, James, and Dr. Lange proceeded to leave the small group and entered the King's tent where they found John awake with much of his upper body covered in bandages.

John attempted to get up and his father put his hand on John's chest to prevent him from moving.

"You need to stay in bed, son. You have some injuries that will keep you down for a while. Dr. Lange has said you are not to move since you have some broken ribs and a broken arm. I am expecting you to follow his orders."

"I am sorry, Father. I did not intend to be captured. I have ruined our chances of a peaceful resolution to this problem with King Henry."

"I am not worried about that right now. You are more important to me and I need to attend to you at the moment. I have asked Arius to take you back to Wiltshire when Dr. Lange says you are up to traveling."

"No, Father. I want to stay here with you."

"John, you are not well and would do me no good if you stayed here. I would only worry about you and I need to concentrate on King Henry at the moment. James will be here and will fight alongside me if it comes to that."

"Father, Arius turned into a dragon. A dragon!" And then he laughed. "Ow, that hurts. He must have scared King Henry to death!"

"He was not the only one who was scared," James interjected. "You should have seen how quickly this camp grabbed bows and arrows and took their positions. Then, I saw a person sitting on the back of the dragon and Father yelled to everyone to stand down. When we realized it was you, we allowed the dragon to land. You were able to slide off and then Arius changed back into himself. I will never forget that moment."

"If the presence of a dragon does not deter King Henry from his quest to go to war, then he truly is obsessed and we will need to defeat him in battle. Sir Gregory may still come through for us. Time will tell. Now you rest, son. You do not need to worry about anything right now except letting your body heal."

"I will stay with him, your majesty, and let you know when I think it is safe for him to travel."

"Thank you, Dr. Lange. Come, James. We need to let your brother rest."

CHAPTER 28

BACK IN DORCHESTER

"What just happened?" King Henry yelled. "There was a dragon in my palace! How did it get here? Where did it come from? Why is there a hole in my ceiling? Where are my daughters? I want someone to give me some answers right now!"

"Your majesty, I have soldiers seeking the answers to your questions at this very moment," Sir Gregory replied. "We have found your daughters and they are coming here as we speak. I think I have an answer to where the dragon came from, but I do not think you will be pleased."

"Tell me right now if you plan to live any longer!"

"My thought is that the dragon may have been Arius, your majesty."

"Arius?" Then King Henry laughed. "That old wizard. He is not capable of turning into a dragon. He is no Merlin. Is that your answer? You had better come up with a better explanation and soon!"

"Think about it, your majesty. Who else does magic and would be concerned with the safety of Prince John?"

"Arius?" King Henry repeated his name several times as he was thinking. "You may be right. There are no other wizards in England, especially one who would be looking out for the Prince. So, Arius can become a dragon. That doesn't change anything! They want us to be frightened of their dragon. Well, we will not be turned into scared little rabbits," he stated snidely.

"Your majesty, if I may speak."

"You may not! I want you to gather the army together and be ready to march toward the River Stour by tomorrow. They will not be expecting us! We will have the advantage. We will defeat King William and his army, dragon or no dragon, and then move to take over Wiltshire! We will have victory!"

"Your majesty, your daughters have arrived."

"I did not request to see them! Get them out of here!"

"But, your majesty, you asked to see them but moments ago."

"Well, I do not wish to see them now! I must prepare to go into battle! But first, I need food!" Then the King yelled at his servants, "Where are my servants? Will someone bring me some food? All this talk of a pending battle has made me hungry!"

One of his servants cautiously stepped up, "Your majesty, food has been prepared and is awaiting your presence in the Great Hall."

"Finally! At least someone around here knows how to get something done! Sir Gregory, why are you still standing here? I ordered you to prepare the army! Now leave!"

The Captain bowed to the King, turned and walked out of the room.

As he was leaving, he grabbed his second in command and whispered, "Walk with me."

Once outside the palace, Sir Gregory stopped, looked around for a private spot to talk, and signaled to his second to follow him.

"What is it that you need, Sir Gregory? Why the secrecy?" Sir Abbot asked.

"Have you noticed how the behavior of the King has deteriorated over the past year? And gotten even worse over the past week?"

"Yes, his thoughts seem to be consumed by King William and what he might find in Wiltshire. But during this past week, he has been acting crazy!"

"I agree. He wants me to assemble the army and be ready to leave tomorrow morning. He wants to leave the protection of the castle and meet King William on the battlefield. I do not know what is in his mind! And now, King William has a dragon, a fire breathing dragon! I truly think the odds are against us and I fear many will die in this battle."

"I agree, but what can we do? If he orders us to go, we go. He is the King."

"That is true, but I think if we order the men to stand down, they will do it."

"The men trust you, Sir Gregory, and if you give that order, they will know it is for a good reason. So, what is your plan?"

"I will amass the army as ordered and we will ride out to meet King William. The King will think he is on his way to a battle. After the soldiers move to their positions, I will give the order to stand down and the men will take a knee indicating they will not fight. I realize this will make the King very angry. As Captain, I will state we feel the King is no longer capable of making rational decisions and needs to be confined in the palace until such time that the palace physician feels he is of sane mind."

"That is a very bold plan, sir. Do you think it will work? Will there be any in the army who would not follow your orders and continue to follow the King?"

"Aye, there may. But I think that would be very few if any. It is my hope once the majority of the soldiers take a knee they will follow. We must not make anyone aware of this plan for I fear word would get back to the King."

"You are certainly counting on the loyalty of the men to do as ordered without any prior warnings."

"That, I am. But there is one more thing. I need you to ride to the River Stour where King William is camped and tell him our plan. If this is to work, his army cannot attack us after I tell our soldiers to stand down. I am asking you to do this as I cannot leave. King Henry would suspect something if I am not here to lead the army."

"But, sir, his soldiers will try to kill me if I attempt to ride into their camp."

"Prince John was in the palace to talk to me about establishing peace between our two kingdoms when King Henry saw him. So, I know King William will be awaiting my decision. However, he may not be very happy to see you due to the treatment his son received at the hands of King Henry. You should leave tonight under the cover of darkness. Do not stop for any reason. You must reach King William before our army arrives at the river."

"I will not let you down, sir. I will take one of the fastest horses and leave by a side gate."

"God speed to you."

CHAPTER 29

SIR ABBOT DELIVERS
A PLAN

Sir Abbot left Sir Gregory hoping the plan would work and King William would not kill him when he arrived at their camp. He went to the stables and saddled the horse he knew had the stamina to make the trip, grabbed the reins and walked stealthily through the town. He located the side gate but as he tried to open it, he found the gate was locked. He checked the hook beside the gate where the key was kept, but it wasn't there. It must have fallen off the hook. He searched the grass and bushes near the gate hoping to find it. It had to be there. He kept looking and just when he was about to give up, he saw something shining in the moon light. It was the key! He quickly picked it up and unlocked the gate. Once the gate was open, he maneuvered the horse through the opening and shut it behind him. He continued to walk the horse away from the castle. When he was out of ear shot, he climbed on the horse, gave it a hard kick, and horse and rider took off at a gallop.

Sir Abbot stayed on the road through the night since he figured he would not encounter any travelers. But, as soon as the sun was up, he took to the fields so no one would see him. The only time he stopped was to allow the horse to drink water and give it a short break. Both he and the horse were very tired by the time they neared the River Stour. He wasn't sure where King William was camped so he followed the river to the north for awhile. When he caught the whiff of fires burning, he knew the camp wasn't far away. He continued on until he finally located the tents in a small clearing on the other side of the river. He looked for a shallow place to cross the river and then proceeded cautiously at a walk toward the camp. He was halfway across when he heard a soldier yelling to the camp that a rider was approaching. He heard the rustle of soldiers running and then quiet. Since he knew they had seen him, he decided to dismount and walk his horse the rest of the way hoping he would not look intimidating.

As he neared the camp, he was surrounded by several soldiers. He raised his hands in a gesture of peace to show that he meant no harm.

"I request an audience with King William. I have a message for him. I am here at the request of Sir Gregory, the Captain of the Guard for King Henry." Then he saw the soldiers on one side of him part and noticed King William was approaching.

"Stand down. We have nothing to fear from this man. I have been awaiting word from Sir Gregory and am eager to hear what he has to say." The King walked over to Sir Abbot. "What is your name and your position?"

"I am called Sir Abbot, your majesty, and I am second in command to Sir Gregory. He has sent me here to deliver a message to you."

"Please follow me to my tent where we can talk." The King proceeded to his tent followed by the soldiers who were escorting Sir Abbot.

Upon entering the tent, King William gestured to Sir Abbot to sit on one side of the table. Sir Abbot remained standing until the King was seated and then sat down himself.

"You are here with a message from Sir Gregory so please deliver that message."

"I must begin with an apology from Sir Gregory to you and your son. King Henry has been possessed by demons and ordered one of his guards to torture your son. Sir Gregory knew it to be against the covenant between our two kingdoms but was afraid of what King Henry might do if his orders were not carried out. He tried his best to spare Prince John from the beatings. But King Henry stepped in and kicked the Prince several times. He is most sorry for that."

"Prince John is recovering and will heal over time. I cannot forgive King Henry for his treatment of my son, but I accept Sir Gregory's apology. It has become very clear over the past year that King Henry has lost his mind. That is why Prince John went to Dorchester. He was to talk of this with Sir Gregory in hopes of averting the battle that was to come, save many lives and thus restore peace between our two nations."

"Your son was successful in his plea and did convince Sir Gregory something needed to be done. This is his plan to which we must have agreement if it is to succeed."

"I am listening."

Sir Abbot laid out the plan from beginning to end for King William. He then finished with, "We hope this is agreeable with you and our two kingdoms can again live in peace as we have these many years."

"Thank you for putting your life at risk to deliver this message. I agree to this plan and to one day restoring peace in England. What will become of King Henry and his daughters when you return to Dorchester?"

"King Henry will no longer sit on the throne and he will be confined for the remainder of his life. He will not be placed in the dungeon and will receive the care befitting a King. His daughters will be able to visit with him but only under guard. His eldest daughter would be next in line to rule the kingdom in his stead."

"He should live out his life in a dungeon for what he did to my son, but I will respect your wishes. It is important he be kept under guard at all times for his influence may be more widespread than you realize. King Henry can be very charismatic when he needs to be and could deceive his kingdom into believing he is sane and being wrongly persecuted. You must be vigilant as long as he is alive."

"I have witnessed this first hand many times, your majesty, and know what you say to be true. I will leave you now and return to Dorchester where I will deliver your response to Sir Gregory. We will meet you on the battlefield within the week."

"Very well. Godspeed to you as you travel back home."

Sir Abbot bowed out of respect for King William and departed the tent. Once outside, he mounted his horse and galloped toward Dorchester. King William beckoned to the guard at the entrance to the tent.

"Please summon Sir George, Prince James, and Arius to my tent immediately."

Within minutes, all three were inside the tent.

"Sir George, please assign one of your fastest riders to follow Sir Abbot, at a distance so Sir Abbot is not aware of him. He is not to engage anyone unless it is necessary. His purpose is to ensure Sir Abbot arrives in Dorchester without incident. After you have done so, please return to my tent so I may present our new battle plan."

"Yes, your majesty."

"Arius, I think John should be able to travel and I need you to take him back to Wiltshire where he can continue to recover from his injuries. Dr. Ross is there and will be able to attend to him. I have sent a messenger to the Queen to inform her of your new appearance in case your message to the seekers did not get through. She in turn can warn the kingdom of your arrival. After you have seen to it that John is safely home, I need you to return. We will be meeting King Henry's army on the battlefield within the week. I will explain everything upon your return."

"If that is what your majesty wishes, then I will do as you command. I have sent word to the seekers who remain in Wiltshire that I will be arriving with Prince John and that I will be a dragon. I told them I would explain later. I also told them that it was imperative they alert the soldiers. I would not appreciate seeing arrows whizzing by me upon my arrival."

"Thank you, Arius. Now that we have each sent messages, there should be no problems once you arrive at the castle. James, you will assist Arius and travel with your brother."

"What? Me? But, Father.... Ride on the back of a dragon? How does one do that?"

"By holding on, I assume. James, I need you to hold John so he does not fall off of Arius on the flight."

"What is to keep *me* from falling off? We have many soldiers here who are more capable and stronger than I am. Assign one of them to this task."

"I am asking you to do this. You may return with Arius and I will explain everything then. Now, you two are dismissed."

"Aye, Father. But I am not happy about this."

"Understood."

Arius and James left to prepare John for the flight home.

CHAPTER 30

IT'S NOT EASY TO
RIDE A DRAGON

"John, we are taking you home. Arius is waiting outside. And yes, he has changed into a dragon, and yes, Father has asked that I accompany you."

"What?" John exclaimed as he tried to sit up in the bed. "Oh, that hurts."

"Here, let me help you." James reached over and helped his brother achieve a sitting position.

"I can hardly sit up much less ride a dragon. What is Father thinking?"

"Not sure right now. I have been advised there is a new battle plan of which I am not aware but will learn more upon my return. That means I am privileged to be able to ride Arius twice!"

"Well, I certainly do not envy you for that. How are we to both ride on his back?"

"We did not have much time, but some of the soldiers and I were able to devise a sort of harness to hold you in place. We cannot have you falling off now, can we? We fashioned it out of some tent material and whatever else we could find. It was hard to get enough of anything to go around that large belly on the dragon! Arius declared he would have come up with something more substantial had he been given more time."

"Little brother, you surprise me sometimes. But remember, I can still get the better of you, not now of course, but when I am recovered."

"Aye, first you need to get better. Dr. Ross will be attending to you in Wiltshire. Dr. Lange will remain here."

"I suppose you will stop and see Justine while you are there."

"Maybe. But for right now, I need to get you up and out of the tent. Guards, we need your assistance," James yelled.

Two guards entered the tent along with Dr. Lange.

"What do you think you're doing?" Dr. Lange inquired of James. "He's not well enough to move! I have not signed off on this!"

"I am following the orders given by my father. He wants Arius to carry John home. When John gets there, Dr. Ross is to attend to the injuries he has."

"How are you to travel? John has some broken ribs that could become dislodged if bumped."

"We have devised a harness for Arius that will hold John while he is traveling. I will sit behind him to help keep him stable."

"I need to come along right now to supervise and inspect this harness." So, James and the two guards were able to lift John and carry him to where Arius, the dragon, was standing. The guards were rather apprehensive as they approached even though they knew the dragon was Arius.

"I thought you two were lost. Where have you been?" Arius asked.

"You can talk?" John blurted out and the guards almost dropped him.

"Of course, I can talk. Do you not remember me stopping after I saved you and inquiring as to your condition? You were surprised then, too. But it seems you have no memory of that. I merely took the form of a dragon but I am still me," Arius replied indignantly. "Now, please get on my back so we can get you home. This is how it will work. Climb on my elbow and I will hoist you up on my back. Once you get there, you will notice a makeshift harness we devised to help you ride without hands. James will help hold you in place so you can remain as still as possible. But no guarantees on my part. This is all new to me!"

The four of them maneuvered John up onto Arius' elbow and Arius slowly lifted him to where he could grab the harness. John, lying on his back, slowly pulled himself up, his face grimacing in pain as he did. He stopped when he was on top of Arius and couldn't go any farther.

"John, don't do any more pulling." Dr. Lange ordered. "James will do the rest."

"John, I am coming up to help you," James announced. "Wait for me before you do any more."

Then the guards lifted James onto the elbow and he was lifted up towards Arius' back. He grabbed the harness and crawled into place behind John. Then carefully he maneuvered John into place and positioned John's legs through the harness up to his waist while John was lying down. Next, when he grabbed John by the waist, John groaned in pain but did not yell out. James helped him to a sitting position in front of him. Then James slid his own legs under the harness above John's and wrapped his legs backwards around John's which he hoped would secure John in place.

"Sorry, John, if that hurt. I am doing my best to move you so I have a good hold on you. Please let me know if you experience any pain while flying and I will try to reposition you."

"James, right now, you are squeezing me too hard!" John whispered because he couldn't breathe.

"Sorry, I just don't want us to fall off!" James responded as he released his grip.

"James, make sure you hold him below his ribs or by his shoulders so you don't break any more." Dr. Lange yelled.

"Did you hear Dr. Lange; you are not to break any more ribs." John added.

"I understand, brother. Now, Arius, not sure if we are ready for this, but I guess we will find out. We are ready to go."

Arius extended his massive wings, dropped his head, and sprang into the air. James and John both looked down and saw the ground disappear below them.

"This is ridiculous! I cannot believe we are flying!" James yelled with excitement. "This is great!"

Just then, a wind gust caught Arius by surprise and his body surged upward and sideways. James and John hung on for dear life with James trying very hard not to bump his brother. Arius was finally able to get control of his body and leveled out once more.

"What was that?" Both boys yelled at the same time.

"Very sorry, Princes. A large gust of wind caused me to momentarily lose control. But I think I am beginning to figure this whole flying thing out! So, I hope it will not happen again." Arius surveyed his surroundings and looked down. "I have never seen the earth from this vantage point. This is fantastic!"

Arius decided to try some new moves and momentarily forgot he was carrying two boys on his back. He dove downward for a short distance and then shot back upward and leveled off again.

"Arius!!! I cannot hold John steady while you are busy trying out your flying skills!" James yelled at the top of his lungs.

"Very sorry, again. I got carried away."

"Well, try out your wings another time. After we get John home."

"Understood, Prince James."

James could feel John's body tensing up from pain. He tried to move him around a little to see if that helped.

"Thank you, James. Now my chest does not hurt so much."

James couldn't believe how fast Arius was flying. At this rate, they would be back in Wiltshire before nightfall. James relaxed into the motion of Arius' body and found it was easier to ride the enormous dragon. He felt John relax, too, as he responded to James' body movements. The air was so crisp and cool at this altitude. The wings along with the speed created a lot of wind which made it difficult to see at times. But James noticed Arius was flying through the clouds, sometimes above them and sometimes below. They were so light and fluffy as they soared through the sky.

After some time had passed, James looked ahead and could make out the walls of a castle. It was Wiltshire.

"John, I see Wiltshire in the distance. Hold on a little longer. We are almost home."

John lifted his head to see but was in too much pain to be excited.

"Arius, please hurry. I think John is in a lot of pain."

"Will do, young prince."

Arius picked up speed and the ride became a little bumpier. James tried as hard as he could to hold John steady. Finally they neared the castle walls. As they drew closer, James could hear the faint sound of people cheering. Then it got louder and louder and as Arius flew over the walls, he could see people in the courtyards cheering and soldiers cheering on the tower walls. When Arius reached the inner courtyard, he landed as gently as he could. People started to rush over to help bring John down off the dragon's back. James saw his mother coming toward them followed by Dr. Ross and Justine. His heart jumped. He was so excited to see her he momentarily forgot about John.

"Make way for the Queen," some of the townspeople shouted. James shook his head and again concentrated on his brother. When he looked down, he saw his mother standing near the dragon.

"Mother, John seems to be in a lot of pain. We need to lift him off very gently."

Arius got as close to the ground as his body would let him. Then Dr. Ross started shouting orders.

"I need some men up on the dragon's back who can lift John to the ground. I need that stretcher over here immediately. James, gently release John from that harness. As soon as he is on the stretcher, I need John carried to Dr. Lange's office."

The scene became one of organized chaos. They all knew what they were to do and did their job with precision. John was lowered with ropes under his armpits. When he was close to the ground, some soldiers gently placed him on the stretcher. His mother made her way over to the stretcher and grabbed his hand and held it tightly.

"You are home now, my son. Everything will be fine. Dr. Ross is a wonderful doctor and he will attend to you." She let go of his hand and walked with the stretcher all the way to the office.

James was just sitting on top of Arius thinking about everything that had just transpired when he heard a voice stir him from his thoughts, faint at first.

"James, James. Are you okay? John will be fine. My dad will take good care of him. James. Are you coming down from there?"

"He most certainly is. I am not staying a dragon forever, you know."

"Arius, you can talk?" Justine said stunned.

"Why does everyone keep asking me that? Of course, I can talk. Now, James, if you would kindly slide down off my back, I will transform back into the real me!"

"What?" Then he looked down and saw Justine. "Justine! Where did you come from?"

"I have been standing here calling your name but you didn't respond."

"I am sorry," James answered. "So much has happened that I was lost in my thoughts."

"Your highness, Prince James, will you *please* get off my back?" Arius repeated.

"Oh, oh aye, I will slide down if you will offer me your elbow to slide to."

"That I can do."

So, Arius lifted his elbow up towards his back. James moved to the top of the elbow and was lowered to the ground. Almost immediately, Arius transformed back into himself. The harness fell on top of him and he had to push it off before he could move.

"Wow! That was fantastic!" Justine marveled as she watched him change. "I can't believe you can actually become a dragon!"

Then she felt a hand grab hers and she turned her attention back to James. She looked up at him and then sprang at him with a huge hug. "I have missed you so much," she whispered.

James replied, "I missed you, too." He relaxed his hold on her, moved her in front of him, and kissed her passionately.

"Prince James, I am sorry to break up this happy reunion, but we need to return to your father's camp." Arius said sheepishly.

Justine stepped back and looked at James in astonishment, "You have to go back, now? But you only just got here!"

"Father wanted John out of the camp away from anything that may happen."

"What's going to happen?"

"I do not know what my father is planning, Justine. That is what I will find out when Arius and I return."

"Why didn't Arius just zap you and John home like he does when we are transported to the portal? Why a dragon?"

"Aye. Arius, that is a question I had but didn't have time to ask."

"As for the whole dragon thing, it was a surprise to me, too. I was not aware that I could transform into anything for that matter. I have never needed to before now."

"What changed?" James asked.

"When we were in Dorchester castle, John and I had found Sir Gregory, the Captain on the Guard, and were talking to him in a hallway. All of a sudden, King Henry came around the corner and I barely had time to disappear. He saw John standing there with Sir Gregory and it seemed like something snapped inside him. He became enraged and ordered Sir Gregory to strike the Prince and then take the Prince to the Throne Room. There, he made the Prince kneel before him and spit in his face. He ordered one of his guards to beat Prince John. Prince John fell to the ground, and the soldier continued to kick him. John curled up into a ball to protect his body from the blows. Anger started to swell inside me and I found myself wishing to become something big and powerful so I could stop John from further hurt and be able to carry him out of there. I felt my body start to change and grow. I saw the ground disappear beneath me. Then I realized

I had become a fierce, fire-breathing dragon and was no longer invisible! I set fire to the hall, scared the King and Sir Gregory and they ran for cover. That is when I grabbed Prince John with one of my great claws, blew a hole in the ceiling, and flew off. The soldiers on the wall of the castle saw me and began to shoot arrows at me. But I was too far up in the air for them to hit me or John. So that is what happened, and why I can now transform into a dragon."

"Does my father know of this treatment? This cannot go unpunished. I will have his head for this. I want to meet King Henry on the battlefield and be the one to take his life!"

"King William has been told and knows that this was by the hand of someone who has lost his mind. There is a plan in the works to deal with King Henry which will be shared upon our return. For now, young Prince, you must be patient until our return." Arius knew the enraged feelings Prince James was experiencing because he, too, had felt it.

"I will wait to see what my father has planned, but know that King Henry will pay for this."

Trying to change the subject, Justine brought up an earlier question, "But why did John and James have to ride you back to Wiltshire when you have the power to transport people from one place to another?"

"The distance was too great for that spell to work. King William knew that, and so he requested I take John home as a dragon. Now if you will excuse me, I need to check on John so I can report back to the King."

"It seems like a mere thank you is not enough, Arius, for saving my brother. But I will say it anyway. Thank you."

"You are welcome, young Prince."

Suddenly Arius vanished.

"I cannot leave here before I know how John is doing either. We need to go, too."

James grabbed Justine's hand and led her toward the palace. Once inside, they climbed the stairs and ran down the hall to the office. His mother was standing outside the door along with Arius and his two sisters.

"James," his sisters both shouted at the same time. They ran to him and hugged him, one on either side of him.

"We are so glad you are home," and Bethany started to cry. "Dr. Ross is still checking John for any injuries. We have not heard from Dr. Ross about how John is doing since he was taken in there."

"My dad is a great doctor and surgeon. John is in good hands," Justine assured the girls as she tried to comfort them.

Just then, the door opened and Dr. Ross entered the hallway. All eyes immediately turned in his direction.

"Queen Marianne, your son has no more injuries than the ones he sustained prior to this last trip. James, you did a great job keeping your brother from hurting himself any further. And Arius, great flying. You must have been gliding very smoothly."

Under his breath, "You have no idea," James chimed in.

"But he does need to rest. Dr. Lange did a great job using what he had on hand to create a cast but it was not strong enough to hold his arm in place. The break in his arm had become separated and I needed to reset it. The ribs are still broken, but his lungs are fine, no punctures. He is confined to bed rest for at least a week to allow his ribs to heal. I will reevaluate his condition at that time and decide if he needs to rest further."

"Thank you, Dr. Ross. Your presence here is appreciated more than you know. This is the second time you have stepped in to help members of my family and I am very grateful to James for bringing you here."

"Thank you, Mother. I am glad he is here as well. You have delivered good news concerning my brother, Dr. Ross. I will relay this information to my father upon my return to his camp."

"You are to return, James? I almost lost one son. I am most fond of all my children and do not want to be without any of them. But if your father has requested you return, I cannot say any different. Promise me, you will be careful."

"I promise, Mother. And I have Arius there to protect me! I can ride a dragon now, and together we will be formidable!"

"I will do my best to protect the royal family, your majesty. James, we must return to the river. We cannot waste any more time."

James hugged his sisters, then he hugged his mother. "Do not worry, Mother. I will be back very soon with Father and the rest of the army."

Then, James grabbed Justine's hand, "Walk me out."

When they reached the inner courtyard, Arius had already transformed into the dragon and was ready to go. They walked over to where he was standing.

"Arius, I have just one question. How am I to stay on you now that the harness is no more?"

"No problem, young Prince. As we were flying, I could feel your body shifting on my back which helped me invent in my mind something I think will work. I have fashioned a harness I think you will like better than the last. Take a look!"

James dropped Justine's hand and walked around to Arius' side.

"That is fantastic! That almost looks like a saddle we put on a horse."

"It is based on that design. But I have made some adjustments. Climb up and see how it feels."

"Be right there."

Justine walked over to James.

"I guess I have to say good bye again. But I know you will be back; I can feel it. So, no crying this time. Just good bye for now and I can't wait for your return."

"I know I will be back. We are supposed to get married. I do not want to miss out on that!"

They kissed goodbye. Arius offered his elbow to James. James climbed on and was pushed upward till he could climb on Arius' back. He surveyed the new harness to see what Arius had created. It did have a saddle base to it so he had something to sit on, but the stirrups were very different. There was a place to put his foot, but there were several smaller straps that attached around his legs. There was a strap in front of the saddle which gave him something to grip so he wouldn't fall off.

"This is impressive, Arius! I definitely think this will work much better than that old harness. This is going to be fun!"

"I am glad you approve, your highness. I have also made the belly strap much more comfortable. And, this new one can be used more than once!"

James sat down, attached the straps around his legs, grabbed the strap in front of him and told Arius he was ready to go. Justine sadly walked back to the door of the palace to watch as they took off. Many of the townspeople came out to watch and stood around the courtyard. Arius spread his expansive wings, put his head forward, started to flap and took off. The two were gone in an instant. Justine continued to watch the sky and finally caught a glimpse of them flying through the clouds past the castle walls. She told herself she wasn't going to cry, but she couldn't help herself. Her fiancé was flying away on a dragon into another kingdom and a possible battle where she had no idea what the outcome would be. But in her heart, she knew he would be okay. She finally opened the door and went back into the palace to await his return.

CHAPTER 31

ARIUS AND PRINCE JAMES RETURN

"This is unbelievable, Arius. This is beyond any dream I have ever had. We are up here in the heavens looking down on the earth below, flying in the clouds, souring over mountains and through valleys. And this new harness is wonderful! I feel very safe up here and do not think I could fall off!"

"I am glad you like it, Prince James. That was the purpose of the design. Now, let us see how well it works!"

"What do you mean by thaaaat? Arius!!!"

James held tightly to the strap in front of him with both hands as Arius plunged toward the ground. He leaned back in the saddle to keep from sliding off and gripped with his legs. He was thankful for the leg straps Arius had included. When Arius drew near to the ground, he leveled off and James let out a huge sigh of relief. But his relief was short lived for Arius shot up toward the clouds.

"Oh no! This is ridiculous!" Yet James started laughing and hollering as Arius climbed. "I can do this! I am truly riding a dragon! Is that all you can do, Arius," he offered as he dared Arius to perform other moves.

Arius began to fly as fast as he could and dart sideways, up or down at a moment's notice. At one point, James seemed to pop up out of the saddle but didn't let go of the strap and was able to hang on.

"Whoa, that was close."

"Hold on, Prince James," Arius ordered. Then, as he was flying through the air, he attempted a body roll. Before he could get upright again, James completely came out of the saddle, the straps holding his legs came undone and he was hanging from the saddle. He yelled because he knew he was going to lose his grip. His hands started to hurt so badly that he couldn't hold on any longer and he let go. He began to hurl toward the ground. He couldn't believe how fast he was falling. This is it he thought to himself. Just then, Arius swooped in underneath him and picked him up. James was sitting backwards and had to turn himself around. Then he immediately grabbed the strap in front of the saddle, hoisted himself back into the harness and reattached the leg straps.

"I guess we need to work on that one," Arius surmised.

"You think? Could we just fly straight for awhile? No more fancy flying." James needed the rest. His muscles had never felt as sore as they did now. But he couldn't help but grin when his thoughts turned to everything he and Arius had just accomplished together. He knew with a little more practice he would be able to handle anything Arius had to offer. The two of them made a great team.

"Aye, no more practicing for now. But that was fun testing out my new me! I had no idea what this body could do. However, we do need to return to the camp. Your father is awaiting our arrival."

The two flew off toward the River Stour where King William was camped. It was night now but Arius didn't seem to have any trouble seeing in the dark. James just sat on his perch and watched as the moonlight bathed the surface of the earth. He couldn't help but marvel at it all. There was so much beauty he had never had the chance to witness before!

The soldiers could hear the wings flapping before they could see anything. Then the massive shape of a dragon appeared in the moonlight and began to descend to the earth. King William awoke and stumbled half asleep out of his tent. He looked up and saw Arius approaching the ground but James was nowhere to be seen. He waited until Arius landed before he walked over to greet him.

As he drew nearer, he noticed James sitting astride the dragon in what appeared to be a saddle.

"James!" his father exclaimed. "I could not see you atop the dragon and thought you had not returned. Your arrival surprised me as I did not expect you to return so soon. It seems you were able to deliver John to the palace since he is not with you."

"Father," James yelled down from his perch, "you would not believe the feeling I get from riding up here. There is nothing like it! And, as you can see, Arius invented a harness that affords me the ability to ride without falling off! However, I did fall off one time. But Arius swooped under me and caught me so everything worked out just fine!"

"You fell off!"

"Aye, Father, but Arius and I were learning together about all the ways he can fly and what I need to do to stay on. We need to practice some more, but I think I have almost mastered them all."

"Prince James, you can converse with your father after you slide off of me. I would like to change back into myself again."

"Oh, aye, sorry."

James undid the straps around his legs and as he did so he said, "Arius, I think these leg straps may need some work." Then Arius offered him his elbow and James was lowered to the ground. Once there, he hugged his father, and the two backed away so Arius could transform into himself.

"Arius, you do not look any worse for the wear! You seem to be able to become a dragon with ease," King William noted.

"Aye, it seems so."

"Now, I want to hear about John and how he is doing."

James and Arius informed the King about the problems with the original harness and how hard it was for James to keep John stationary throughout the trip. They described the reception they had received from the people of Wiltshire and how helpful those people had been once the three of them landed. They explained Dr. Ross took over and gave specific orders as to how to handle John as they removed him from Arius' back and took him to Dr. Lange's office. They stated Dr. Ross was pleased John had been returned to the palace and had no new injuries. John would still need time to convalesce.

"That is very good to hear. I knew it was the right thing to do and we had the means to do it thanks to Arius. Now, you two retreat to your tents and get some much-needed rest. I will see you in the morning."

"Aye, I am very tired, Father. It has been a long day."

"Aye, that it has," Arius added. "Sleep will be most welcome right now."

Once in bed, it didn't take long for James and Arius to drift to sleep.

CHAPTER 32

JOHN'S RECOVERY

James and Arius had been gone for several hours after delivering John to Dr. Ross. John was now resting quietly on a bed in the office after having to have a bone reset and his chest rewrapped to protect his lungs from the broken ribs. He was still a little groggy from the sedative Dr. Ross had given him.

"How is our patient?" Dr. Ross asked as he entered the office. "I see you are finally waking up after your surgery."

"Surgery?" James inquired sleepily.

"Yes, you had to have a bone reset in your arm and your chest rewrapped. The ride on that dragon didn't help your broken bones very much. Although, I dare say, you could have been worse if James hadn't held on to you like he did. And I do think Arius played a big part in that, too, trying to fly without jolting you too badly. I think we need to leave you in the office until at least tomorrow and then maybe we can move you to your bedchamber where you would be more comfortable. I want you to stay in bed for the next week and then I'll examine you again. I'll have Luke and Justine take turns checking in on you from time to time. For your first meal, I would like you to have some broth and bread. I'll check with the kitchen to make sure they have some on hand. Then, it should be fine for you to eat whatever you would like."

"Thank you for taking care of me." John said as he drifted back off to sleep.

Dr. Ross made sure the cast on John's arm was still in place as were the bandages around his chest and then he left the office so John could sleep. He was on his way to the kitchen when Cedric stopped him in the hallway.

"May I help in any way, sir. You look as though you are looking for something."

"Yes, Cedric, that would be great. I was on my way to the kitchen but now I can just tell you. I would like some broth and some bread brought up to Dr. Lange's office for John to eat, please. He has fallen back asleep so there's no rush. I'll have Justine go sit with him while he sleeps and she can help feed him if need be."

"I will see to it right away, sir."

"Thank you, Cedric."

Since Cedric was taking care of John's meal, Dr. Ross went to find Justine. He thought he knew where he might find her: the garden. Whenever she had a spare moment, that was where she went. He entered the garden and walked toward the gazebo. He saw her there, sitting on a bench reading a book.

He thought it would be fun to see her jump from surprise so in a loud voice he said, "Hey there, daughter. What are you up to?"

Justine jumped a mile and Dr. Ross just stood there and laughed.

"That gets you every time!"

"Dad, that wasn't nice! I was quietly reading!"

"Yes, hence the loud voice to scare you!"

"Well, now you've scared me and I've stopped reading. Is there a reason you're here, in my nice quiet garden?"

"Ah, let me see? Why did I come here?"

"Dad......"

"Oh yes. I remember now. I want you to go sit with John for a while, please. He was sleeping when I left the office. Cedric will see to it that John receives his dinner, and I think John may need some help feeding himself since he broke his dominant arm. So, if you could assist with that, I would appreciate it. I will have Luke relieve you after dinner."

"Sure, Dad. I can do that. I've been enjoying helping you out in the clinic while Dr. Lange's been gone. I like working with the people and getting to know them. This will be more practice for me. Is there anything I need to know in case something happens?"

"Just have him keep his arm immobilized for now and in the sling. Also, the bandages around his chest need to remain snug but not too tight. If he complains about that, come get me."

"Okay, will do, sir!" And Justine saluted him.

"Okay, okay, I said please! Now off with you. We need to keep an eye on him since he is still waking up from the surgery."

Justine closed her book with a snap, got up and walked past her father toward Dr. Lange's office. When she arrived, she slowly opened the door so as not to wake John. First, she checked him to see if he was still asleep, which he was, and then she sat in the chair located near the bed. She opened her book and sat quietly and read.

John gradually opened his eyes and tried to focus on his surroundings, still feeling the effects of the sedative. He turned his head and saw Justine seated next to the bed quietly reading a book. He didn't say anything but just lay there and watched her, the curves in her face, the way her hair fell on her shoulders, how she was sitting, and the daintiness of her hands. She was sitting so close he could almost reach out and hold her hand. But he wouldn't. He didn't have the courage to tell her how he felt a year ago for James beat him to it. She had only been there for a short time, but she made her way into his heart anyway.

She looked up from her book and noticed he was awake.

"Oh, good. You're awake. How do you feel?"

"Still tired, but better. Even though I just woke up, I feel like I am gaining some of my strength back."

"That's good to hear. My father will be happy about that."

"What about you?"

"Me? Of course, I'm happy. You are improving which is a good thing."

"Aye. A good thing."

"Your dinner should be arriving soon. Dad said you are to have broth and some bread. He ordered it for you from the kitchen."

"What are you reading?"

"This? Oh, just something I found in your library. It looked interesting. But it's not what I thought so not sure if I'll finish it or not."

There was a knock on the door. Justine got up to see who it was and opened the door. It was one of the servants with John's dinner.

"Thank you very much for bringing the broth. I can take it from here."

Justine brought the tray in and placed it on a table next to the bed.

"Your dinner is here. I hope you feel like eating. But you obviously can't eat lying down. I'll help prop you up a little so you can eat. Here, grab my arm with your left hand and I'll try to pull you up slowly."

John did as he was told, but Justine found this task harder than she thought it would be. As she tried to pull him up, John couldn't help but groan from the pain. So, Justine carefully laid him back down.

"Well, that's not working. Maybe I should get someone to help me."

"Oh no, I feel that will not be necessary. I am sure we can do this. We can give it another try."

Justine thought for a moment and then said, "I have an idea. As I start to pull you up, I'll put a pillow behind your back and keep doing that until you are high enough that you can eat.'

"I like that idea. But instead of my holding on to your arm, may I hold your shoulder instead?"

"Right, I guess we can try that. Maybe if I get on my knees?"

Armed with several pillows at her side and kneeling on his right side, John put his left arm around her shoulder and Justine began to lean backward. She pulled him up just far enough so she could place a pillow behind his back. This time he didn't groan which made her happy her plan was working. Finally, John was high enough that he would be able to swallow with no problem.

"Yay, we did it." She said as she began to pull away from him. As she did, she looked over at him and paused momentarily. She noticed John looking right at her and it made her nervous. Then he leaned his head toward her and kissed her. She was caught by surprise, not because he kissed her, but because she kissed him back. She immediately pulled away, stood up and walked to the other side of the room.

"What are you doing?" she asked frantically. "I am promised to James! We are in love! You can't kiss me! That's not right! What were you thinking?"

"I was thinking how beautiful you are. You were so close I could not help myself. And you kissed me back!"

He paused for a moment and then said, "I want you to know I am in love with you!"

Justine stood there in shock. She stared at him in disbelief for several minutes and then she was finally able to respond.

"What?" she whispered.

"I am in love with you," he repeated. "I fell for you the first time you were in Wiltshire, but I never said anything. Then you and James grew close and I stepped aside. When James left to find you again, I never dreamed you would be returning. I thought you were out of my life forever. But when I returned from patrol, there you were, more beautiful than I remembered and I fell all over again. That is why I kissed you. What I want to know now is, why did you kiss me back?"

"Because, because I miss James and needed that kiss. When I closed my eyes, I could picture James here with me and it made me happy!"

"Is that the only reason? Maybe deep down you have feelings for me, too."

"I can assure you that is not the case. I am in love with James. I am going to marry him and that's all there is to it. I do not love you. So, please, don't try that again or I can't help take care of you. I will refuse to help. And I don't want to disclose to my father why that is."

"I understand, I do not like it, but I understand. I will not try to kiss you again or show anyone around us that I have feelings for you, especially James. It will be as before."

"Thank you. I appreciate that. Now, I will go get Luke to help you with your dinner because I can't be in this room right now."

Justine opened the door and left.

CHAPTER 33

THE BATTLE

King Henry amassed his great army, left the protection of the castle walls and began the march toward the river with Sir Gregory and Sir Abbot at his side.

"Are you sure this is what we should be doing, your majesty? Leaving the protection of the castle for open fields?" Sir Gregory pointed out.

"You dare to question my decision?" King Henry declared.

"No, your majesty. I merely wanted to make sure I was understanding your orders." Sir Gregory replied trying not to upset the King.

"Do not question me again or you may find yourself beheaded!" King Henry threatened.

Sir Gregory figured they would reach the river within two days. There the army would cross the river downstream from King William's camp and set up camp. He knew King Henry would not dare attack at night for he was afraid of the dark. He kept a close eye on the King as they traveled, constantly reassuring him the battle plan they had discussed was a solid one.

They finally reached the river at the end of the second day as he had expected. He set out to find a safe place to cross which wasn't hard since the water in the river was low. The army crossed without any difficulty and as the soldiers were setting up their tents for the night, King Henry motioned to Sir Gregory to approach him.

"Do not light any fires tonight. I do not want King William to know we have arrived. That will give us the advantage of surprise. We will establish our battle lines in the early morning and then charge his camp. I want the foot soldiers to advance from the front and those on horseback come at them from both sides."

"We will be ready, your majesty," Sir Gregory replied.

"We must get our rest now. We will be successful tomorrow and then I will be able to enter Wiltshire as its new King!"

Sir Gregory bowed and left the king in search of Sir Abbot who was overseeing the setup of the camp. Sir Gregory knew, as he left the King that he dare not even mention the fact that King William has two sons who would ascend the throne after King William's death. King Henry has been consumed with acquiring as much power as he can and does not care what or who stands in his way. Stir Gregory knew there was no logic to his thinking anymore.

"There you are, Sir Abbot. I have been looking for you everywhere."

"I have been doing what you asked me to do, Sir."

"Aye, sorry. Please tell the men there are to be no fires lit tonight by order of the King."

"But, Sir, how are the men to eat? There has to be a fire to cook the meat."

"I understand. But they will have to find something to eat that does not involve cooking."

"This order will not make the men very happy."

"I know. But it came straight from the King."

"Is there anything else?"

"Aye, he wants to set up battle lines at first light in order to take King William by surprise. But that will not be possible since I saw King William's spies in the fields following us. I did not make King Henry aware of that though. So we will do as we have been told but then stop the battle before it begins."

"I will tell the men about not lighting fires and inform them of the plan for the morning."

"I will see you in the morning then."

As the sun began to make its appearance, King Henry emerged from his tent wearing his armor and ready for battle. He noticed the rest of the camp did not seem to be stirring yet so he started toward Sir Gregory's tent to demand an answer as to why his soldiers were not ready. As he neared the tent, he saw Sir Gregory in the distance dressed and already giving orders to the men.

"It is a good thing you were not in your tent sleeping!" King Henry bellowed as he approached.

"No, your majesty. You specifically stated we should be ready at first light."

"Aye, I did. I did indeed. Are all three groups lined up and ready to advance?"

"Aye, your majesty. They are."

"Where is Sir Abbot? I do not see him anywhere."

"He is ready to lead the men on horseback, your majesty."

"I cannot wait to see the look of surprise on the faces of King William and his army. This will be my finest hour! I, King Henry, will soon be the ruler of two kingdoms! Next, all of England!!! Now, let us get this over with."

"There is one problem: a morning fog has settled over the field making visibility almost impossible."

"That will not stop us. We must attack despite the fog."

"I would suggest that we wait till the sun begins to burn some of it away so the men can see where they are going. We will be successful, I assure you, but not if we cannot see our hands in front of our faces. It will not take away the advantage we have of surprise if we give the fog time to dissipate."

"It had better not! All right, we will wait, but not for very long!"

Sir Gregory rode his horse up and down through the soldiers to tell them to line up across the field and be ready to charge when given the signal and asked Sir Abbot to have the horse soldiers remain near them for now. The soldiers moved into their positions and waited.

King Henry began to grow impatient and was ready to order his army to proceed when he noticed something on the other side of the field. He moved a little closer to get a better look and realized King William's army was there in front of them not three hundred feet away. The fog had given them the cover they needed to advance on King Henry's army and now they stood there in front of him. Then he heard a loud noise coming from above him and saw a dragon and rider fly over the field and settle down near King William's army.

At first, he was stunned. King William had caught *him* by surprise. How could this have happened? It was supposed to be the other way around! He turned his horse and began riding through the soldiers yelling at them to attack. But they didn't move! Then he heard a horn blowing in the distance and every one of his soldiers took a knee and placed their weapons on the ground.

"What are you doing? You are supposed to be fighting! I order you to fight! Get up and fight! This is my battle to win! You cannot take that from me! I am supposed to rule all of England!"

Then Sir Gregory rode up on his horse.

"What is this? I am King and I order you and your men to attack!"

"We will not, your majesty. We find your majesty unfit to rule Dorchester and are removing you as King, by force if necessary." Sir Gregory stated as he stood his ground for he knew if he had been acting alone this would be treason. But he had the whole army and the people of the kingdom behind him.

"You do not have the authority to remove me as King. It is my right! It was passed down from my father! I was his only son!"

"I do have the right granted to me by the laws you have put in place. You have proved you are not of right mind and would have sent many of your men to their death for your own glory. This has been witnessed by the men in your army as well as the people of your kingdom. We have all seen it. You are no longer our King and your eldest daughter will now become Queen. You will be confined at the castle until your death."

"I will not stand for this! You cannot take my crown away from me! I will have Wiltshire and England at my feet!" And with that, King Henry rode his horse as fast as it would take him through the line of soldiers and toward the army on the other side of the field yelling, "England will be mine!" He drew his sword, held it up in front of him and charged. He ran his horse into the front line of soldiers swinging his sword from side to side. The soldiers parted and let him through. Once through the soldiers he looked around and saw King William sitting on his horse. He started to charge King William yelling, "Your kingdom will be mine!" Suddenly, seeing that his King was in danger, one of his knights let go of an arrow which struck King Henry in the heart. King Henry fell from his horse to the ground.

King William dismounted and walked over to where King Henry had fallen. He checked to see if he was still alive, but he was not. He then shouted, "He was a King and should be carried back to his army. I need eight soldiers for that honor."

Eight soldiers stepped forward and took up a position on both sides of King Henry's body, lifted him and proceeded to walk across the field. King William mounted his horse and followed the soldiers to where Sir Gregory was standing.

Once they arrived, Sir Gregory announced to his army, "He died a soldier's death and will be buried as befits a King. We will carry his body back to Dorchester." At that point, the soldiers stood up and saluted Sir Gregory with a fist pound on the chest of their armor.

"When will a successor be named?" King William queried.

"We cannot leave Dorchester without a ruler and will crown his daughter soon after we return. However, I am not sure how this will be received by the lords of the kingdom. They may not be willing to follow a queen. That remains to be seen. There will be a period of mourning after which I would like to meet with you regarding the future of our two kingdoms. This was for the best and ended as it should. You were in danger and one of your soldiers shot him to protect you. King Henry would never have submitted to confinement for the rest of his life. I want to thank you, King William for working toward peace and preventing unnecessary bloodshed on this field. We will not forget. Now, we must return to Dorchester and bury our King."

"I look forward to our next meeting with you and your new Queen. We will return to Wiltshire and hope to observe many more years of peace between our two kingdoms."

The two bowed to each other out of respect and King William turned to leave along with his contingent. King William then bowed toward the body of King Henry, mounted his horse and returned to the other side of the field where his army was waiting.

CHAPTER 34

THE TRIP BACK TO WILTSHIRE

King William ordered the camp be dismantled and the army began the trek home. James, however, had convinced Arius to allow him to ride home on his back, as a dragon of course. Also, James thought this would give King William intel from the sky as they soared above. King William agreed and James was excited to be able to ride on the back of a dragon again. The King knew when Arius was near for the sound of his wings could be deafening at times. He thoroughly enjoyed watching the two disappear through the clouds and then reappear moments later. It was hard to believe Arius never knew he could shape shift. But then again, there had never been a moment when he had needed to as the kingdoms had been at peace for the past one hundred fifty years. There were writings and pictures from long ago that showed sorcerers had been able to take many forms, but no one was sure it was a skill that passed down through the generations until now. Arius seemed just as surprised by the transformation as anyone. The King was sure news of this had already traveled throughout England by now. The King knew he would definitely be able to use this to his advantage and should be a major deterrent to any further incidents in the future.

"Arius, what do you think about staying a dragon? You could fly wherever you wanted and I could go with you! Who knows how far we could go and what we could see? We could travel over other countries and continents and..."

"Prince James, I do not have to permanently remain a dragon for that to happen. I can change any time I please and soar off when I want. I do not have to always have you with me, either. But there are some impediments to your plan."

"And what may those be?"

"For one thing, I am in service to your father, the King. If he requests my presence, how am I to comply if I am out flying all over the countryside. And for another, you are newly engaged which will not allow you the freedom to just leave Wiltshire."

"Very good points, Arius. As for being newly engaged, it is my feeling it will make no difference for I think Justine will be excited for me. She would not deny me the opportunity to travel near and far. Also, if I should ever be King, our travels would be of benefit as I would know more about those who live in other places. To your first point, we have just established peace among kingdoms again and if my father intends to maintain that peace, I think checking on those around us on a regular basis would be very beneficial. Sending you and me into other kingdoms rather than relying on horse and rider, would be more expedient."

"Prince James, before you or I make any plans, we must have the approval of your father, the King. Without his blessing, there will be no more dragon unless absolutely necessary. As much as I have truly enjoyed this newfound power, I still serve the King."

"Arius, do not worry about my father. I know I can convince him of the benefits of having a dragon around. By the way, can you become anything else? Maybe if we dig out the old writings concerning your ancestors, we might learn something."

"We have lost sight of your father and the army. We need to focus on the task at hand for now. We can look into this further once we are back in Wiltshire."

So, Arius dove below the cloud deck and caught sight of the army moving rather slowly, it seemed to him, through the valley in the direction of Wiltshire. The sun was setting by this time and he knew the army would soon be stopping for the night. Before setting down, Arius had an idea. He had never seen the sunset as a dragon and decided to soar back through the clouds.

"Arius, what are you doing? I thought we were to land for the night."

"I want to see the sunset from up here first."

As Arius came up through the clouds, they saw the sky above them begin to glow in bright pinks and oranges, and the clouds around them took on the colors of the sunset. Then they witnessed sunbeams spread out through the sky emanating from the sun in front of them. Arius hovered in mid-air as the pair took in the glorious sight.

"Never seen anything more beautiful," James murmured as he sat there in awe of what they were witnessing.

"That was certainly better than I had anticipated. That has filled my body and soul with peace. Now, I am ready to land for the night."

Arius let his body drop straight down and finally flapped his wings so he could land on the ground below.

King William was waiting for them.

"Please explain to me why you hovered overhead as if you were to land and then suddenly disappeared back through the clouds, only to come out sometime later."

"The sunset." Arius replied.

"The Sunset? I am confused."

"Arius wanted to take in the sunset, Father, for the first time from up in the sky. It was breathtaking. The colors were so vivid up there. We watched until the sun disappeared below the horizon. Once that happened, Arius was ready to land for the night."

James slid down from his saddle and Arius, the dragon, transformed back into himself.

"That must have been a beautiful sight, indeed. Someday, I would like to see that... But right now, we need to think about returning home. We will get an early start tomorrow and I want you two back up in the sky to keep watch. So, eat something and then rest well for we have another day ahead of us."

"We will, Father."

The next morning, everyone was up bright and early, excited they were to be home that day. After a quick breakfast, the King ordered everyone to tear down the camp so they could be on their way as soon as possible.

"James, since we are not far from Wiltshire, I think you and Arius should sweep the area when we depart and if you do not see anything suspicious, then you two may continue on to Wiltshire. We will not be far behind you," King William instructed his son.

"I am relieved to be able to put this all behind us and return home. At some time in the future, I look forward to meeting the new Queen," James replied.

"As do I. It will be important to establish a rapport with her early on in her reign. But we will wait until the period of mourning is over and then pay her a visit."

Arius suddenly appeared before them and startled them both.

"Your Majesty caused my heart to stop beating, Arius. Please stop doing that. Good morning, Arius. What do you need?" the King asked.

"Your Majesty and Prince James. I am assuming we are to arrive back in Wiltshire today, are we not?"

"That we are. As I have instructed James prior to your arrival, you and he are to fly overhead to ensure there is no danger as we begin our departure this morning."

"I am to become a dragon again?"

"Aye, you are. You offer us the advantage of seeing things from above. You, as a dragon, have been a true asset for our kingdom and will continue to be from now on. Your powers were limited before, although I very much appreciated the feats you could perform. But now, as a dragon your powers are truly remarkable! We must take the time to discover whether or not you have other talents unknown to you up till now. But not right now."

"And I am lucky enough to be able to ride on your back! Four eyes are better than two!" James offered excitedly.

"Now off with you two. Inform me if you observe anything we should know about."

James and Arius left the King to do as they were commanded. Soon, the great wings of the dragon could be heard flapping in the wind as the massive body lifted into the air and took off. A yell of excitement spread through the air and all knew James was aboard the dragon.

The two of them soared back and forth over the army as they broke camp and began the trip home. Once the army was on their way, Arius enlarged the area over which he was flying to determine whether there were any threats below them.

"Arius, look! Over there to our right, in the tall grass. I see two riders! They look to be following the army. However, they are both wearing cloaks with hoods and I cannot discern who they are. What do you think?"

"Well, two riders would certainly pose no threat to our army, but it is curious as to why they are there and I do not see anyone else in the area. We must alert the King and he can decide what course of action to take now."

The two flew north until they located the army. When they spotted the King, Arius flew toward the ground and hovered over the King's position. King William saw them and immediately stopped his horse. Sir George was also nearby.

As they hovered, James yelled, "Father, there are two riders approaching our position. They do not look to be a threat, but we wanted you to know. I do not think they saw us as we were too far up in the sky. What do you want us to do?"

"The only thing you can do now is to guide Sir George to their location. He can take it from there. We will remain here until Sir George returns."

"Aye, Father."

Then he turned to Sir George and instructed him to gather five trusted soldiers, follow Arius, and ascertain who the riders were and why they were following the army.

Arius continued to hover until Sir George was ready.

When they saw Sir George signal, they climbed even higher so their presence would go undetected. Sir George would be the one who would confront the two riders and determine if they posed a threat. Once Arius and James spotted the riders, Arius hovered overhead to indicate the riders' position. They watched from above as Sir George and his men approached. The riders got off their horses as did Sir George. Sir George did not draw his sword nor did his stance appear rigid, but relaxed. Then the three mounted their horses and the small band of eight riders rode off in the direction of King William and the army.

Arius and James followed them now very curious as to the identity of the riders. The riders reached the army and located the King. They watched as the two strangers dismounted. Both dropped their hoods but James still could not figure out who they were since he and Arius were still too far away. Then James saw one of them curtsy in front of his father. That was strange for that meant one had to be a lady. His curiosity had now gotten the better of him.

"Arius, one of the riders is a lady! We need to get down there and find out who that is!"

So Arius dropped toward the ground and landed as close to the King as he was able without knocking anyone over. James descended to the ground and moved as quickly as he could to stand by the King's side. He was glad to see Sir George standing near his father with his hand on the hilt of his sword. As he approached, he realized the lady looked to be one of King Henry's daughters. What she was doing there was anyone's guess.

"James, this is Catherine, the eldest daughter of King Henry. They have been trying to catch up to us ever since the battle."

"I do not understand, Father. Was she at the battle site?"

"She has not had time to apprise me of the situation, so I will let her explain to us both why she is here. Lady Catherine, or should I say Queen Catherine, please enlighten us regarding your presence here."

"Thank you, King William. My story is long and I will tell it to you in due course, but first, my main reason for being here is that I need your help. My kingdom has become one of ruthlessness, lies, and deceit while my father was king. I mean to change that and bring order back to Dorchester and Dorset. Although our two kingdoms have enjoyed peace these many years, there are those in power who look to change that and remove me from my seat as Queen."

"What can we do to help, my lady, that would not cause more harm and possibly create animosity between your people and mine?" King William posed to her.

"I am here to propose a joining of our two kingdoms through marriage, sire. I would like to marry one of your sons and that son would become the King Dorchester needs. Together he and I would restore the kingdom to its former self and thus maintain peace with the other kingdoms in England."

James turned his back toward the Queen and addressed his father. "Father, may I speak to you, alone?" James insisted.

"James, do not concern yourself with this proposal. As I told you, if agreed to, you would not be the one I would choose for this union. It would be your brother, John."

James sighed with relief as he would not be able to give up Justine for any reason. Then he turned back toward Queen Catherine.

"I understand, with the sudden death of your father, you may have some obstacles to overcome. But why have you followed us and proposed this now before you have even returned to Dorchester?" King William asked.

So, Catherine proceeded to explain how her father's condition had deteriorated over the years, and led him to rule his kingdom unfairly. His mind had become poisoned by those around him into believing lies about King William, his own kingdom, and the other kingdoms around Dorset. She was informed of Prince John's visit and how he had been sorely mistreated by Sir Gregory and her father. Then she learned of the battle into which her father was leading the army against King William. She knew it was wrong and hoped to convince Sir Gregory not to go through with it, unaware of Sir Gregory's plan. She also knew of the men who were supposedly King Henry's trusted advisors who were secretly hoping King Henry would meet his death during this battle. That would give them the opportunity they needed to seize the throne for themselves. So, she followed the army and kept to the trees and tall grasses so she wouldn't be seen in hopes to persuade Sir Gregory not to enter into battle, and thus saving her father from, she feared, certain death. But the opportunity never presented itself and she had to remain hidden. Then, she watched as Sir Gregory raised his arm, and her father's army took a knee refusing to fight. She was so excited that she let out a yell. But it seemed to go unnoticed as right then was when her father rode off toward King William's side of the field threatening the King with a sword. She witnessed her father be struck by an arrow and killed. She said she dropped to her knees at that moment and wept. One of the soldiers heard her and came running through the trees toward her with his sword raised. When he realized who she was, he sheathed his sword and knelt before her. He escorted her to Sir Gregory who was standing by the dead body of her father. Upon seeing her approach, Sir Gregory and the soldiers immediately knelt before her for they understood she was now Queen. By that time, King William had already left and his army was seen marching toward Wiltshire. She knew then what she had to do. She ordered Sir Gregory to accompany her on her journey to find King William and instructed Sir Abbot to return her father's body to Dorchester and prepare for the funeral. She told Sir Abbot that he was in charge until she returned.

"I have recounted the events as they happened. I appeal to you, sir, to consider my proposal for I know I will surely be relieved of my position as Queen and my sister and I put to death, thus ending any successors to King Henry's throne. But, if I were to return with a King by my side and the power of your kingdom behind me, I would certainly be considered a threat to those who seek to overthrow me."

"I will think on it as we return to Wiltshire. Will you be traveling with us or returning to Dorchester?"

"Sir Abbot has been charged with overseeing the kingdom until my return. He must keep those who would take the throne for themselves at bay and will protect my sister. That will enable me to travel with you to Wiltshire in hopes that you will agree to my proposal. I assume my betrothed might be one of your sons, and I would suggest that we be married soon. Sir Gregory will remain with me."

"So be it. Sir George, inform my soldiers that we are to continue our journey to Wiltshire accompanied by two important guests. James, you have the task of flying above us as before. Inform me if you observe anyone following us."

"Aye, Father. We will monitor the area."

James and Arius took off into the air and the army continued on toward Wiltshire. They did not see anyone within miles of the army as they flew overhead. That meant that Queen Catherine had been telling the truth and no one was following her.

'I wonder what John will think about all of this. I am sure it will be as much of a surprise to him as it was to me! John, King of Dorchester, what an......' Then out loud he bellowed, "That means that I will be the next

King of Wiltshire! How can this be?" Then his fist came down in defiance.

"Ow, that hurt!" Arius yelled. "So, you just now realized that you are next in line for the throne! And then you hit me because of it?"

"I am so sorry, Arius. I was just pondering how John will react to this when the thought came to me that I would be next in line after John. Arius, what am I to do? I am to marry Justine. I thought we could travel back and forth through the portal in order to remain close to both families. I never considered that I might ever be king. That was supposed to fall to John, not me!"

"Prince James ..."

"That would mean Justine would be Queen! She would have to remain here with me forever! Which is fine with me, but will it be fine with her? I do not want to ask her that question for I am afraid of the answer!"

"Prince James," Arius loudly interrupted.

"Sorry, Arius, I did not hear you. What is it you have to say?"

"You were speaking aloud and I heard everything! John is aware this may happen as it was discussed with him prior to your departure from Wiltshire. Your father saw this as a way to unite our two kingdoms thus maintaining the peace that has existed for many years. John was not in favor of the idea for he knew his first priority as son of the King was to the people of Wiltshire. There was also the issue of bringing someone from the outside to live in Wiltshire. This would solve that problem as they would take up residence in Dorchester. And now that you have since proposed to Justine, it most certainly makes him the only prospect for this marriage."

"My father mentioned this to me upon my return to Wiltshire but I did not take him seriously. I was not aware of how dire this situation had become."

"Aye, he knew King Henry had grown worse over the past year and hoped, with this marriage, that John might be a positive influence over the King and his people."

"Wow, as Justine would say. He will certainly be surprised when we return with his soon-to-be-bride. I am sure he had not planned for this to be happening so soon! That was very clever of Father to act like he had not considered the proposal made by Queen Catherine and told her he would think on it."

"I do not think it would have been prudent on his part if he had not acted as though this was an original idea proposed by Queen Catherine."

"Very true, Arius. It remains to be seen. Do you think we could delay going back to Wiltshire for a little while? We are so far removed from all the problems of the world up here. I am not ready to face what is coming."

"The dye is cast, young Prince. There is nothing you can do now."

"Thanks, Arius. You know how to spoil a perfectly good dragon ride!"

CHAPTER 35

A WARM WELCOME

The army traveled without incident all the way back to Wiltshire. As they approached the castle, they could hear the trumpets announce their arrival. The massive gates opened and King William and Queen Catherine were the first to enter followed by Sir George and Sir Gregory. They entered the inner courtyard to cheers coming from the villagers who had gathered there. King William dismounted as did the knights on horseback. The King then headed toward the palace steps where he saw Queen Marianne and Justine standing outside the palace doors along with Madison and Bethany. John could not attend since he had been confined to bed rest. Dr. Ross, Luke and Mrs. Ross remained inside the palace.

"Where is James? I don't see him anywhere." Justine pointed out to Queen Marianne.

Then, overhead, they heard the loud flapping of wings. They looked up and there hovering over the courtyard were Arius and James. There was a loud cheer as the crowd also looked up to see their Prince atop a massive dragon. The villagers backed up leaving a large area for the dragon to land. Arius spread his legs as he neared the ground to lessen the impact of landing in the stone courtyard. Even though he was very large, he had finally mastered the technique of landing and was able to touch down without much of a thud!

"Very impressive, Arius!"

"Thank you, Prince James. I think I have figured out this whole being-a-dragon thing."

James dismounted from Arius' back and soon after, Arius turned back into his normal self. He said a chant and the harness disappeared leaving only the two of them standing inside the landing area. The villagers started to approach the two but were stopped by the voice of the King. James and Arius joined the King on the palace steps along with Dr. Lange and Gretchen. Justine was ready to move to be next to him but he shook his head signaling that she should remain where she was for now.

"Thank you, people of Wiltshire, for that warm welcome you gave me and my soldiers. We are very pleased to have returned and happy to report that there were no deaths on this journey but one, King Henry. He showed himself to be very brave on the battlefield and he died a warrior's death. Now, we have made peace with the kingdom of Dorset and welcome his daughter to our fair kingdom. She is now Queen of Dorset, Queen Catherine." King William waved his arm toward her as he introduced her to his kingdom.

A cheer erupted in the crowd and the chant, "Hail, Queen Catherine," could be heard rising up from the ranks of the people. The King put his arm up to signal to the crowd there was to be silence again.

"It has been a long journey and we are all very tired. I ask that my soldiers return to their homes and rest. It is well deserved. My family and I will now take our leave of you and retire to the palace. Thank you again, my people, for welcoming us home."

King William turned to enter the palace followed by the rest of his family. Cedric was there to hold the door for him and welcomed him back to the palace.

"Thank you, Cedric. It is good to see you. Would you please have a lady in waiting attend to Queen Catherine, take her to a bedroom upstairs, and see to her needs?"

"Aye, your majesty. It will be done."

"Now, I would like to see John. We have much to discuss." He looked around for Dr. Ross. "Dr. Ross, you have again helped this family through some hard times. Dr. Lange, where are you?" He asked as he looked around him.

"I am here, your majesty," Dr. Lange stated as he moved up through the family members to stand next to the king.

"Due to the care John received from you in the camp and the continued care from Dr. Ross once John returned home, my son was able to not only survive the horrible beating he received in Dorchester, but will soon be back to normal. And, Arius, where are you?"

"Here, your majesty."

"Arius, I do not know how it happened, but I am most gracious to you and your dragon for preventing further injury to John and delivering my son to me in the camp. And if that was not enough, you and James carried John back to Wiltshire where he has been safe in the care of Dr. Ross. I will be forever grateful to all of you. Now, Dr. Ross, please lead me to my son. Dr. Lange, I would like you to come as well."

Dr. Ross responded, "I would be very happy to. I will explain his condition along the way. He is healing very nicely. If he is careful, he should be up and able to move around soon. He is no longer in Dr. Lange's office, but has been moved to his bed chambers, as you say here."

"That is good to hear."

The three left the main hall and ascended the stairs to go to John's room. Cedric ushered Queen Catherine to the room she would be occupying for now. Queen Marianne gathered her daughters and Mrs. Ross and Luke and moved them to the Great Hall which left James and Justine standing alone in the Main Hall. They stood quietly for a moment, just staring at each other. Justine finally broke the silence.

"I'm so glad you're back. I missed you terribly."

"I missed you, too." Then he looked at her very seriously. "I was not aware I would be bringing you through the portal to this. Nor your family. I put all of you in danger. I was thinking only of myself and how happy I was that you would be with me in Wiltshire again. It was not fair of me to bring you here and I will see to it that Gretchen escorts you home, if that is what you want."

"That is not what I want! You had no way of knowing that this was going to happen when we came here. Listen to me, James. If I hadn't wanted to follow you back to Wiltshire, I wouldn't have come. I wanted to be here with you as much as you wanted me here. I loved Wiltshire from the first moment I visited it. I found it breathtaking and your family very warm and caring, and then there was you. You, who looked at me the first time through those dark brown eyes and I was hooked. I wanted to be with you from then on, no matter where you were. If I need to live here with you, then so be it. So, no, I don't want to go home."

James stood there stunned for a moment for he now realized she would follow him to the ends of the earth if need be. They would always be together. In Wiltshire, in modern day England, it didn't matter. She just made that very clear. Bringing Justine back to Wiltshire was not a mistake. He put his hand out toward her and she put her hand in his. Then he pulled her to him, their eyes met, and he kissed her with such passion that she practically melted in his arms. They stood together in the main hall locked in each other's arms for quite a while. Then he backed away slightly, looked at her and they walked arm in arm out of the main hall toward their favorite place in the palace, the garden.

CHAPTER 36

JOHN HEARS THE NEWS

King William, Dr. Ross, and Dr. Lange all converged on John's bedchamber. Dr. Lange knocked on the door, opened it, and announced the arrival of the King. John was sitting in a chair by a window overlooking the inner courtyard. He continued to stare out the window as if no one was there. Dr. Lange announced the King in a much louder voice which caught John's attention. He stood up ever so carefully when he realized he was to receive his father. King William walked over to John wanting to hug him.

"Will it hurt him if I give him a hug?" King William asked Dr. Ross.

"A gentle one should be fine," Dr. Ross replied.

So, the King wrapped his arms around John barely touching him and whispered, "I am so proud of you." Then in his normal voice, "John, please sit down. I give you permission to sit in the presence of the King."

"May I get you a chair, your majesty?" Dr. Ross asked.

"Please. I would like to talk to my son alone. But before you leave, Dr. Ross, please apprise me of his condition and how long will it take for him to recover."

"Since I have been with him for the past week, he has done a remarkable job of healing. His ribs are knitting back together..."

"Excuse me, Dr. Ross, what do you mean by knitting? I do not understand this term," King William asked.

"Oh, sorry. It means the broken bones are going back together the way they should. And his bruises are much better, too. I think he should be able to move around the castle in a couple of days. I will just need to keep his chest wrapped so he doesn't break anything again. He should be right as rain in a month." Dr. Ross noticed the puzzled look on the King's face and added, "I mean, he should be good to go for light activity in about a month. But he will need weekly checkups with either Dr. Lange or me for about six months."

"Thank you, Dr. Ross. I am so glad he is healing and will be able to resume some duties soon. Now, I would like to speak to John alone."

Dr. Ross and Dr. Lange exited the room and walked down the hall together. Dr. Ross discussed John's condition with Dr. Lange so he was up to date on everything.

"John, how are you feeling?"

"I am fine, Father. I know Dr. Ross is looking out for me and I am very grateful. My chest is not as sore as it used to be. I think I will be able to get up sooner than Dr. Ross said."

"My son, you will listen to the doctors and do as they say. I will not have you injure yourself further. When I came into the room, I saw the look of anguish on your face and know you are not healed. There is nothing to be done now that the battle is over and we have returned home."

"Father, since I could not be there in person, I was watching out the window as you and the army entered the inner courtyard. I noticed a young lady riding up front with you and then it looked as if you introduced her to the crowd. Who was that? Also, please tell me how the battle ended since you sent me home before it took place."

"Before I answer the first question, I will tell you about the battle. Then I will follow that with the answer you are seeking regarding the young lady."

King William proceeded to inform John of the series of events that took place the day of the battle. He told him that even though John had suffered injuries at the hand of King Henry, that the conversation with Sir Gregory was successful. If that had not happened, many lives would have been lost at the whim of a madman. He explained how the foot soldiers had taken their positions on the battlefield and were ready to charge when ordered to do so. But when King Henry gave the order to his men, Sir Gregory gave his order, and the army took a knee on the field.

"At that point, King Henry was so upset he was being disobeyed, that he took off on horseback toward us and eventually toward me. Because that put me in danger, one of the archers let go of an arrow and pierced King Henry through the heart. He died instantly. I had several of our soldiers carry the body back across the field to where his army was waiting. I talked to Sir Gregory for a moment and then left the field. His army escorted the body of the King back to Dorchester.

"King Henry is dead? What does that mean, Father?"

"Now, I will answer your first question. The lady beside me was King Henry's eldest daughter, Catherine, who is now Queen of Dorset."

"Lady Catherine? But why is she here? Why is she *here* and not in her own kingdom overseeing the funeral of her father?"

"I need to explain that and hope you will agree to what I am about to propose to you."

"Am I to be married? Is that why she is here? I think I should have a say in this. We only just discussed this. It was never set in stone. I never thought it would actually happen. I am not ready for this!"

"Aye, you are more ready than you think. I need to explain what happened after King Henry died so you realize how this all came about."

"Aye, please explain. I would love to hear how I ceased to be the successor to the throne in our own kingdom," John stated in an agitated tone.

"I understand you are frustrated, but I think you will see this differently after I have explained how Catherine came to be here."

King William then told John about how she followed her father's army and hid in the trees so as not to be seen.

"She was not in favor of the battle and wanted to talk to Sir Gregory about not following the orders given by her father. Before she had that chance, she saw the army take a knee and refuse to fight. She saw her father ride off at a gallop, holding his sword out in front of him as he charged the foot soldiers. Then she saw him fall to his death. She then witnessed my soldiers carry his body back across the field where I was able to pay my respects to the fallen king. She remained hidden until after the body was delivered and our soldiers had left. She told me she then approached Sir Gregory who immediately knelt in her presence as well as every soldier in the army as she was now the Queen of Dorset. She took Sir Gregory aside and explained she could not return to Dorchester. She knew there would be those in the court who would see her dead so they could assume the throne. They saw her as weak. Sir Abbot returned to Dorchester to look after her sister, Victoria, and oversee the kingdom until her return. She, along with Sir Gregory, pursued our army and finally caught up with us. She told me it was her hope to join our two kingdoms through marriage. She is confident, with me and my army beside her, the Lords in her court would not dare question her right to be queen. She and her sister would be safe from harm."

"As you are now aware, it was not my offer to join our two kingdoms but hers and hers alone. I have not agreed to her proposal. I told her I would approach you with the idea and we would let her know. This is not a new idea to you as we did discuss this possibility prior to our leaving Wiltshire. I find her very thoughtful, caring, smart, and very pretty. I think this would be a good marriage for you. You do not have any love interests and have not been seen with anyone in our kingdom for a long time. You would be a great king one who is fair and just. Now I am asking you as I promised Catherine. What do you think of her proposal?"

"What if I have found someone here in our own kingdom? Someone I have grown more fond of this past week, would that make a difference?"

"Someone here, in Wiltshire? This past week? Who has been here in the palace that has not been here before?" The King stopped, looked at John in disbelief as he realized who he meant. "You are not referring to Justine, are you? That will not happen and you are not to say anything to your brother for any reason. Has something happened between you two?"

"No, father, nothing happened. She has been helping to take care of me this past week. My feelings for her have grown stronger as I have gotten to know her better. You may not be aware of this, but James was not the only one to fall for her when she was here a year ago. However, he was the one who pursued her before I could say anything. So, I stayed in the background and did not speak up. I am speaking up now before it is too late."

"It is too late, John. She is promised to James. He has proposed and they will be married. You are now promised to Catherine and will be married within the month. I will not hear any more about this. You will not cause division in this family. Whatever was said in this room, stays in this room. Do you understand?"

"Aye, Father. I understand."

CHAPTER 37

JOHN MEETS CATHERINE

After his father left, John sat in the chair staring out the window and sulked. How could he have been so stupid? He told Justine how he felt while James was out of the picture and he thought he might have a chance with her. How can he marry Catherine when he is in love with Justine? At least if he moves to another kingdom, he won't have to look at her every day and wish she was his.

'Come on John, what are you thinking?' he said to himself. 'She loves James and you have a duty to your kingdom even though you will not be its king. She has never declared her love for you so stop pining for her and get on with your life. James must never know how I feel!'

He stood up, very carefully, and decided then and there that he needed to move on. Justine was no longer an option for him. He would soon be the King of Dorset with a new queen by his side. That was his new reality and he needed to accept it. He also decided that he would no longer be confined to his room. So, he got himself dressed, which wasn't an easy task, straightened up as well as he could and walked toward the door. Just as he reached for the handle, the door opened and there stood Dr. Ross.

"I was just coming to check on you and it's a good thing I did. Why are you dressed and leaving your room?"

"I cannot stay in here any longer, Dr. Ross. The walls are closing in on me. I need to get out and see what is going on in the world. I am still sore, but I was able to dress myself."

"I see that. How do your ribs feel? Are they still in place?"

"My ribs are fine. Well, not fine, but better. You have taken good care of me, Dr. Ross, and I promise I will be very careful if you let me leave this room."

"Alright, you may leave, but I will continue your check-ups twice a week. I want you to promise me, if you experience pain in any area, you must tell me immediately. No exceptions."

"I promise, Dr. Ross. Now, may I go downstairs?"

"Yes, and I will accompany you just to make sure your first time out is without mishap."

"Thank you, sir."

John walked out into the hallway and gave a happy sigh. Dr. Ross and John moved down the hall slowly at first, and then as his confidence grew, he started to walk at his normal pace.

"So far so good, John. When we get to the stairs, I want you to take them slowly at first."

"As you wish. You are the doctor."

When they finally reached the bottom stair, John breathed a sigh of relief and the two proceeded into the Parlor which was right off the Main Hall. Catherine was sitting in the corner quietly reading. When he saw her, his mind flashed to Justine.

"Justine, still reading I see."

"No, your highness, I am not Justine. I am Catherine from Dorchester."

"I am sorry. You are right. I do not know why I said that."

"You have been ill, your highness. It is understandable that you could be confused."

"That is true. This is my first time venturing out of my room. It feels so good to be moving around again."

Then Dr. Ross interjected, "I can see why you said that. She does look a little like Justine. Well, if you will excuse me, I need to check on some things with Dr. Lange. You will have someone come get me if anything happens, right?"

"Aye, I will be most careful, sir."

John then looked at Catherine more closely and noticed her features were very similar to Justine's. He hadn't seen her for some time and only from a distance. Now that he saw her up close, she was much prettier than he remembered.

"May I escort you somewhere, your highness."

"Thank you. That would be nice. I would like it very much if you would walk with me outside to the garden. I do not want to be in the palace any longer."

"The garden it is then. But you will have to direct me as I have not been there as yet."

John pointed with his good arm in the direction of the garden and the two walked slowly out to the garden. He was surprised by her poise and demeanor. That someone like her could have had King Henry as a father. But then again, King Henry had not always been mad.

When they reached the garden, Catherine located a bench upon which to sit.

"You look tired, your highness. Maybe we should sit for a while."

"That is a good idea."

"Let me help you." She put her arm out to brace him and with his left arm on hers, he eased himself onto the bench. "There, that was not hard. I will take my leave of you, sir, if that is what you wish."

"I do not wish. Please, sit beside me. I would like to get to know you better."

Catherine sat down and the two remained silent for a time. Then John spoke first.

"I was sorry to hear King Henry had died. He was a good king."

"Thank you for your kind thoughts, sir, but we both know he has not been a good king for a long time. The father I knew died years ago. He was not the same after my mother died."

"I am so sorry. You have had two great loses in your life. That must be hard. How did your mother die?"

"She caught a fever from one of the servants and never recovered. My father was devastated. He loved her very much. So I was left to raise my younger sister while I watched my father get worse with the passing of time." Then, changing the subject, "I was not aware of the treatment you received at the hands of my father. Sir Gregory told me that a soldier had been ordered by my father to beat you and then my father decided to beat you further by his own hand. He was not at all concerned or cared what happened to you. Sir Gregory wants you to know he is very sorry for the treatment you received. Sir Gregory also informed me that Arius saved you by transforming into a dragon and carrying you away."

"I realize Sir Gregory was faced with either doing what King Henry had ordered or face his own death. I was also lucky Arius was there; otherwise I might not be here now. No one knew he could transform into a dragon, not even Arius! He grew so large the room was almost too small to hold him. I remember seeing those steely blue eyes and the fire that erupted out of his mouth! He was able to blow a hole in the ceiling. Then he picked me up and flew me back to where my father was camped. After that, he flew me here to Wiltshire so I could heal. When my father and the army returned from the battle, I was not allowed to attend but was able to observe from the window in my bedchamber. I saw him introduce someone to the crowd and discovered later that it was you. Then I inquired as to why you were here and not in Dorchester. He explained the series of events that led you to be here. He told me you followed your father and the army to the battlefield and when they made camp, you hid in the trees and watched from a distance. Why did you do that?"

"Because I wanted to stop the battle from taking place. I knew it was wrong and I was prepared to step in and try to convince my father not to confront King William."

"That was a very brave thing to do. But you might have been killed had the battle actually taken place."

"I knew it was a risk, but I had to try. I was not aware Sir Gregory had already devised a plan, which I later learned was because of you. I witnessed the whole army take a knee on the field and refuse to follow the orders my father had given. He became so enraged that he rode his horse straight through his own army across the field and headed right for your father. That is when he was struck in the heart by an arrow to save the life of your father. I saw it all happen and was so very sad to see my father killed. I continued to stay hidden until after the body of my father was delivered to us on the battlefield by your father and a small contingent of soldiers. Afterwards, your father returned to his army and they left the field."

"Why are you here in Wiltshire and not back in your own kingdom? You are now their rightful queen." Even though his father had explained the reason she was in Wiltshire, he wanted to hear it from her own mouth.

"There are those who wish to see the heirs to the throne killed. There is also a law in our kingdom that a queen may not reign without a king by her side. That is why I am here. I felt if I had the chance to talk to your father, I could propose that our kingdoms join together through marriage. I think if I return home as not only its queen but with a king by my side, it would quell the ambitions of those who would claim the throne and there are many. They feel they should be the ones to rule. I am not sure who would be the victor if chaos erupted in my kingdom, but I am certain there would be many who would die because of it. However, there is one who has looked after my sister and me since the death of our mother. It is Lord Chauncey. He is loyal to us and is respected by the other lords. If I were to return with a King by my side, Lord Chauncey would work diligently to ensure the other lords respect the transition of power. There would be no fighting. Dorset could then be restored to its former glory where law and order would be the norm."

"I understand why you are here and made the choice to not return to Dorchester at this time. I also commend you for your desire to do what is right for the people of your kingdom. I did not know such a law existed in your kingdom, and even though you are its rightful heir, without a king, you would not be given the opportunity to rule and could possibly be put to death. I have not had much time to think on this proposal for my father approached me with this thought soon after his return. I, too, want what is best for both of our kingdoms so that we continue to live in peace."

Prince John slowly stood up and took a few steps away from the bench on which they were sitting. This was not an easy decision for him. His whole life he had been groomed to follow in his father's footsteps as King in their own kingdom. And now, because of circumstances beyond his control, he is being asked to marry someone he has just met and move to Dorset as their king. This idea wasn't new to him since his father had suggested it several weeks ago. But he thought it would be James that would be the likely choice. Now, he was angry with James for proposing to Justine, which meant he had no chance to pursue that relationship. And, James' proposal also meant that he had to be the one to step up and marry Catherine. She did seem very nice and she reminded him of Justine in her looks and her personality. His father and mother were an arranged marriage and in time they grew to love each other. Maybe that would happen for him, too. He needed to put his personal feelings aside and be the person he was raised to be: a king.

Queen Catherine stood up and placed her hand on his arm. "Prince John, are you in pain? May I be of some assistance to you?"

He turned around and faced her. He saw her staring at him with those bright blue eyes and a look of concern on her face.

"I am fine, thank you for asking. I was thinking about your proposal and what my father said when he first mentioned it to me. He told me I will be a great king no matter what kingdom I may rule over and he is very proud of the man I have become. He also said that it would give him great comfort if I were to be King in a bordering kingdom. Therefore, for the sake of both our kingdoms, I will accept your proposal and will sit by your side as your King. Together, we will work to achieve your dream and mine thus preserving the peace that exists."

There was a look of surprise on her face for she did not expect to have a decision so soon. She reached up and kissed him on the cheek. "Words cannot express the joy I feel right now, your highness! I will make you very happy. We will have a good life together, you will see. You will not be disappointed."

"I think you mean what you say and that is why I agreed to be your king. I would not have said as much if I thought you were deceitful and not have a good heart."

"You have made me so happy!" Catherine put her arms around him and started to hug him when he groaned in pain. "Oh, my goodness! I forgot about your injuries! I am so sorry for that."

"Please, you do not owe me an apology. May I suggest that instead of a hug, that we seal this with a kiss?" He leaned over and kissed her gently on the lips. Then, he looked at her and kissed her again. Even though they had just met, he knew in his heart they were meant to be together. They sat for a while, she with her head on his shoulder. They continued to talk until late in the afternoon and finally rose from the bench and went back into the palace.

CHAPTER 38

THE DECISION IS SHARED

Prince John and Queen Catherine walked into the palace looking for King William and they located him in the Throne Room talking to Arius.

"Father, we would like to talk to you if you have a moment."

"John!" His father said in surprise. "You are up and walking around! Where is Dr. Ross? Has he given you permission to do this? And you are with Catherine. You have interrupted me and I would finish my conversation with Arius first. Then, you must respond to my questions."

John and Catherine backed away and waited for the King to finish. He continued to talk to Arius but their voices were so low that neither John nor Catherine were able to discern the topic being discussed. So, they waited patiently for King William to finish. And then suddenly, Arius disappeared.

"Now, that I am no longer occupied, you must respond to my questions and then you may tell me what is it you two young people would like to talk to me about."

"Aye, Father, Dr. Ross knows I am up. I am to alert him if I feel any additional pain. He assisted me when I walked down the stairs and into the parlor. Catherine was there reading. I mistook her for Justine for a moment, and then she informed me of her name. She offered to escort me as I walked. We went outside into the garden for I could no longer stay inside. Catherine and I have been sitting in the garden for several hours just talking and getting to know each other. I have learned a lot about her past and her plans for the future of her kingdom. Even though I have only known her for a short time, I feel closer to her than I have felt with anyone. We have many of the same hopes and dreams for our kingdoms and for our lives. I feel we are of one mind. I want you to know that I have agreed to this marriage, not just to unite our two kingdoms, but because there is a connection between us I cannot explain. I do not claim to love her but know that will come with time."

"My son, this is very good news, very good news, indeed! I feel the ceremony must take place soon so you and she may return to Dorchester as the rightful rulers. Sir Abbot will only be able to keep the peace in the kingdom as long as he can convince the Lords that Queen Catherine will be returning. I am sure they will soon tire of his promises and begin to stir up trouble. You shall be married within two weeks."

"Thank you, Father. I did not think it would be this soon, but I understand the concerns you have. I have not fully healed and hope Dr. Ross and Dr. Lange will allow me to travel."

"Thank you, King William. I am most grateful for allowing me the honor of marrying your son. He will be a wonderful King and most loving husband. I could not ask for more."

"There will be much to do these next two weeks. I will talk to Dr. Ross and Dr. Lange on your behalf. Also, I think it necessary to inform the Queen of this upcoming wedding. This news will be very much a surprise! She will not have much time for preparations to take place. I will be the one to tell her. Then at dinner this evening, you two can announce your upcoming nuptials to the rest of the family. Until I tell the Queen, there will be no mention of it to anyone."

"Aye, Father. We understand. We will stay out of sight until dinner is announced."

"Now, I need to locate the Queen. I will see you two again at dinner."

Prince John and Queen Catherine bowed to the King and left the room leaving the King to ponder the best way to inform the Queen.

'There is no good way to tell her, so I guess I'll just come right out and say it,' he thought to himself.

He found the Queen in her boudoir next to their bedchamber stitching on her needlepoint.

"There you are, my beautiful wife! I have been looking for you."

She looked up from her needlepoint and looked at him suspiciously. "My beautiful wife, is it? Now I am afraid to ask why you were looking for me. But I will. What may I do for you, my husband?"

"Remember my mentioning to you the reason Queen Catherine is here in Wiltshire?"

"Aye, I do."

"Well, Prince John has just informed me that he has agreed to the marriage."

She put her needlepoint on the table beside her and stood up, "Are you telling me that our son is going to marry Catherine? They hardly know each other. And how did they come to tell you this? John is still healing and not to be up walking around. When did they make this decision? Did you pressure him into this?"

"John did this on his own. Dr. Ross gave him permission to be up and helped him walk to the parlor. That is where he met Catherine. They spent the whole afternoon together. He told me that in the short time they have been together he has learned a lot about her and is ready to be her husband. They will announce it to the family this evening at dinner."

"This evening! It is a good thing you informed me of this beforehand."

"Aye, that is why I am here. There is one other thing you should know."

"And what might that be?"

"The wedding will take place in the next two weeks," the King announced as he winced a little waiting for her reaction.

"Two weeks!" Queen Marianne blurted out. "Two weeks!" she exclaimed again. "How do you propose we prepare for a royal wedding within a two week period?"

"Because I know you and it will be done. Now I must see how close we are to announcing dinner."

He kissed her on the cheek and left her standing there with a look of shock on her face. She stood there for a moment and then had to sit down since her knees were shaking. 'How are we going to accomplish this in two weeks?' she mumbled to herself. Then she heard the bell ring that announced dinner. She gathered herself together and departed for the Great Hall.

When she arrived, everyone was standing around the table for they could not sit down until the King and Queen were seated. She walked over to her seat and together, she and the King sat followed by the rest of the family. The servants began placing the plates of food in front of each person and as soon as they were done, the King stated Prince John had an announcement. So, John stood up and faced his family. He took Catherine's hand and had her stand next to him.

"Catherine and I are to be married."

"Married?" Madison and Bethany chimed in together.

"I am happy for you, my brother," James said as he stood, walked over to his brother and gave him a gentle hug. Then he hugged Catherine, too. "When is the big day? I suppose you need some time to get to know each other better and I know Mother will need time to plan the wedding."

"It will be within two weeks," John replied. "With the death of her father, Catherine is now the Queen of Dorset and needs to return to her kingdom. No kingdom should be without a ruler for very long."

All of a sudden Mrs. Ross heard herself exclaim, "Two weeks?" Then she followed it with, "Oh, I am so sorry. I did not mean to say that out loud. Please forgive me."

"Stephanie, those were my feelings exactly. No need to apologize," Queen Marianne stated. "But I may ask for your help."

"Please, ask away!"

One by one, each person at the table got up, hugged John and Catherine and offered their congratulations on their engagement. Justine reluctantly approached John, gave him a quick hug. Then turned and hugged Catherine.

"Congratulations to you both. Catherine is a very lucky person," Justine said as she backed away and returned to her seat. James followed her.

"Are you okay? That was a very impersonal hug you gave John, almost as if you were afraid of him."

"I'm sorry. I didn't mean for it to look like I didn't care. It just didn't feel right to hug him when I know they just met. Is there a reason he is getting married so soon and to someone he hardly knows?"

"Justine, I'll explain later. For now, just be happy for them."

Justine couldn't help remembering how just a week ago, John had kissed her and proclaimed that he loved her. How could he now turn around and say he is marrying someone he hardly knows? She really didn't care who he decided to marry because she was in love with James. But this whole thing just didn't make sense. She had a hard time looking in his direction for the rest of the meal, and when she did, she noticed him looking back. Something was up, and she couldn't wait for the meal to be over so she could talk to James.

As soon as the meal was over and everyone stood up to leave, Justine grabbed James by the hand and pulled him toward the parlor.

"Okay, spill the beans."

"Beans? What beans? Oh, I get it, it is another one of your 21st century sayings. So, what do you really mean?"

"Tell me what's going on with this marriage. Why Catherine and why now?"

"You seem rather interested in why John is getting married. Is there a reason for that?"

"No, no specific reason other than they just met and now they're getting married. Don't you find that a little odd?"

"No, I do not. There is a reason for it."

"What could possibly compel him to marry someone he doesn't even know?"

"Because the lords in her kingdom want her dead. Then they could decide who would rule in her stead. That would destroy the peace that has existed not only with us but with the surrounding kingdoms. The kingdom has turned against her because of her father and his mad behavior. She is nothing like her father, and I know that because I know John. He would not agree to marry her if he felt otherwise. Now she will return to her kingdom as Queen and a King by her side, John. This will ensure her kingdom has two rulers who are just and fair, and can maintain peace."

"The lords in her kingdom want her dead? I can't believe they would kill their own Queen. I think I understand now why he accepted her proposal so quickly and why they will soon be married. So that means he will be living in Dorchester, away from his family, and be King of Dorset. It will be hard to have your brother so far away.... Um, I just thought of something. If John is now leaving Wiltshire to be king somewhere else, that would mean..."

"Aye, I will be the heir to the throne in Wiltshire as I am the second son."

"Then that..."

"Aye, you would be my queen after we get married."

"Oh my gosh," Justine whispered astonished. "Oh no! I am not queen material. I have not been raised to be a queen. I don't know the first thing about it. What if I mess up?" she cried.

Then James put his hand up to her mouth and talked in low tones, "Justine, I love you. You have a big heart with no mean bone in your body. You are exactly who I want beside me, always. Whether it be just as my wife or as my queen. I was and would be lost without you. You will make a great queen someday. But I expect my father to live forever so put all of your fears aside. We will face it together if that day ever comes." Then he pulled her close to him, she threw her arms around him and they kissed.

"I'm sorry, James. Wherever you go or do, I will be there. Nothing can tear us apart now. I'm sure I will have time to learn how to be a Queen and if that day ever comes, I would gladly sit beside you."

CHAPTER 39

THE WEDDING

The next day, the palace was abuzz with activity as servants began to prepare the palace for the wedding. Flowers needed to be gathered, dresses made, food prepared, rooms cleaned, tables set, invitations sent, minstrels hired, and the priest notified. Everyone's help was enlisted. Even the Ross family was put to work. The wedding was to be in the garden with the reception in the Great Hall.

Two weeks went by very fast and finally, it was the day of the wedding. Whatever hadn't been done by then was forgotten. Catherine was able to wear Queen Marianne's dress. Navy blue accents were added since that was Catherine's favorite color, along with some alterations so it suit her. The skirt and the bodice were made of blue velvet. The bodice had a square neck trimmed in a gold embroidered satin ribbon and full-length sleeves trimmed in gold embroidered navy blue satin which extended into pendant sleeves. The poofy skirt parted on both sides revealing a gold brocade under skirt. In front, the skirt was floor length but extended for several feet in the back as a train. Her silk veil extended down the back of the dress and was attached to a circular crown.

Justine, Madison, and Bethany were the bridesmaids. They were each wearing a dress of red velvet trimmed in the same gold material as in Catherine's dress.

Until now, Justine had worn loose fitting clothes and had dressed very casually since she wasn't a member of the royal court, at least not yet. So she was taken aback when she was being dressed by her lady in waiting, Anne. She could hardly breathe when the corset was tightened around her waist.

"Please, could you loosen that a little bit? I'm beginning to feel faint."

"Aye, my lady, but we need to be able to do up your bodice. I will loosen it a little."

Then she stepped into the skirt and Anne was able to lace it up. Next, she put her arms into the bodice which laced up in front. She was surprised at how low it was in front and how, as her lady laced it up, it pushed her breasts up, like a push up bra.

"Does this have to look like this in front? I feel exposed!"

"Aye, this is how the tops fit all the ladies."

"I've noticed! But I didn't think I would have to wear one!"

"You look beautiful. Like a princess. Now I need to fix your hair. I need to put it up, but I will keep it simple."

"What do you mean by that? I thought I could just wear it down."

"Not for a wedding, my lady. Even Madison and Bethany will be wearing their hair swept up." Then after about ten minutes, "There, I am finished. You must look at yourself in the mirror."

Justine rose from her chair and approached the mirror. She closed her eyes as she moved in front of it. She counted to three and then opened them. A grin appeared on her face, small at first but then widened into a smile.

"This is me? Boy, do I look different!" Then she turned from side to side and tried to look at the back of her. "Wow, if my friends could see me now!" Then she paused and her eyes began to tear. "My friends...I miss my friends. I don't have any friends here. No one to talk to, to share what's happening to me right now." Then she started to cry and turned away from the mirror.

"My lady, you must not cry right now. Your face will be all red and puffy and the wedding is to start soon."

"I'm sorry. I was just feeling lonely and sorry for myself. I'll be okay."

"I will get you a cold towel to place on your face to help take down the swelling in your eyes." She found a towel, placed it in some cold water and returned to give it to Justine. "Here, my lady, hold this on your face."

"Thank you for the cold compress." Justine put it on her eyes and held it there. "I'm better now. How do I look?"

"Perfect, my lady. Now we must go downstairs."

"I hope I can walk in this thing. The skirt is so big!"

Justine walked down the hall followed by Anne and started down the stairs. She descended to the landing and when she turned to start down the main staircase, there, at the bottom of the stairs was James. He glanced in her direction turned away and then immediately turned back.

"Justine? Justine!" He couldn't believe it was her. She looked so different. So grown up! As she reached the bottom step, James reached out to her with his right hand, placed his left hand behind his back and then bowed. "My lady, may I walk you to the garden."

"You may," Justine replied shyly.

Then she put her arm in his and they started toward the garden.

"Do you like my new look, sir?"

"You are breathtaking. I did not believe it was you coming down the stairs. You look so different now that you are wearing the proper clothes of our time."

"Better, worse, what?"

"Not better, not worse, different. You are beautiful no matter what you are wearing. I love you in your regular clothes and I love you dressed as you are. But I must say, this outfit does reveal a little more of you and I find you very sensual right now."

Justine popped him one on the arm.

"What was that for, I just gave you a compliment!" James said startled that she had hit him.

"I know, but I wasn't ready to hear it."

"Well, you had better be ready, for you are. I have just never said it before. Sometimes, I have a hard time keeping my hands to myself when you are around."

Justine felt her face becoming beat red and that was just as they were coming into the garden area.

"Justine, are you okay?" Mrs. Ross asked as she turned to see her daughter standing there. "Your face is bright red! Almost the color of your dress! But, oh my goodness, look at you. You look stunning, and so grown up! You're not my little girl anymore. Drew, look at our daughter."

"Justine? You don't look like yourself. You do look stunning as your mother said. Where has time gone? Just yesterday I held you in my arms and rocked you to sleep. Now look at you."

"I am still your Justine, just bigger!"

Cedric approached Dr. and Mrs. Ross, "I will show you to your seat now. It is up front behind the royal family. Prince James, you must join your brother at the gazebo."

"See you at the reception, Mom and Dad."

James kissed Justine, "I will see you at the gazebo where we had out first kiss."

"Go on; you'll be late."

The prelude started and Catherine, Madison and Bethany all walked over to where Justine was standing.

"You look so beautiful, Catherine! I love your dress. And Madison and Bethany, we three look like triplets! All in red! Catherine, I have never asked you, but I was wondering how old you are."

"I am nineteen, one year younger than John. Why do you ask?"

"I wanted to know how close we are in age. I'm seventeen. I hope we can be friends even though we will not be living very close."

"I would love that. I do not have any friends in Dorset. People were afraid to be around my father and therefore us, too."

"Well, consider that changed. And now that Arius can transform into a dragon, the distance between us may not be as great!"

Then they heard the minstrels play the music for the processional, and they all took their place in line. Bethany was first, then Madison, and Justine, maid of honor, was last. They made their way down the aisle through the garden. It smelled so beautiful as they walked past the flowers on either side of the guests. It reminded Justine of the first time she walked in the garden and saw James in the gazebo. She looked ahead, and there, standing in his spot, was James. Her gaze caught his and they continued to look at each other until she reached her spot at the bottom of the stairs.

Then they all turned to watch as Catherine began her walk down the aisle. Justine looked over at John and noticed his gaze was focused on Catherine. It wasn't a look of, "Oh no, here she comes. Let's get this thing over with.' But a look of awe, and excitement as he watched her come closer. They had spent every waking moment together the last two weeks. Maybe he actually cared for her. She knew that love at first sight was real since that's what happened to her the moment

James walked into her bedchamber the first time her family came to Wiltshire.

The wedding was wonderful, and both Catherine and John lovingly stated their vows to each other. She couldn't help but look over at James during the ceremony knowing that someday that would be them standing there. Then she heard the words, "You are now married in the sight of God," and the wedding was over. The priest didn't say, "You may now kiss the bride." Maybe they didn't do that in the 16th century. Well, no matter. They were married and together they walked down the aisle to cheers from the guests.

As they walked, Catherine noticed a familiar face seated among the guests. It was Lord Chauncey from Dorchester. That would mean... Then, seated next to him, she saw her sister, Victoria! She stopped dead in the middle of the aisle.

"Catherine, is there something wrong?"

"John, my sister, Victoria, is here! She is seated right next to Lord Chauncey. They came to the wedding! How did they..."

At that moment, Victoria slid out of the row of guests and hugged her sister.

"Catherine, you look so beautiful!" Victoria stated as she stood in awe of her sister. "The ceremony was wonderful and I am so glad Lord Chauncey and I were able to make it in time."

"Victoria! I cannot believe you are here! How did you come to be here? You have made me so happy." She reached out her arms toward her sister and gave her another hug.

"Your majesties," Lord Chauncey stated as he joined them. Catherine extended her right hand and he bowed and kissed it.

"Catherine, I am afraid the guests are still waiting for us to finish our walk down the aisle. You must continue this conversation in the Great Hall," John insisted.

"Oh, I am sorry. I forgot for a moment where we were." Then to her sister, "Let us go to the Great Hall and you must tell me everything?"

John and Catherine finished their walk down the aisle and proceeded to the Great Hall. Lord Chauncey and Victoria followed them out of the garden.

"Your majesty, it is so good to see you and to know you are safe," Lord Chauncey began. "As soon as we learned from Sir Abbot of your upcoming wedding a few days ago, we traveled night and day to ensure we would be here on time. Victoria, of course, had to see her sister get married and me, because it was important for someone from Dorset to witness the marriage. There are many in Dorset who would not believe you are married. But we have now seen and can attest to the fact that you and King John are united."

"Thank you ever so much for making that long journey. My heart is filled with joy. Please relax and enjoy the feast King William and Queen Marianne have laid out for our guests. Come, Victoria, I want you to meet your new sisters."

Together, King John and Queen Catherine walked with Victoria to find Madison and Bethany. They introduced the girls to each other and left Victoria with them so the three could get better acquainted.

Finally, after several hours of visiting with the guests and eating the wonderful food, John grew very tired since he was still recovering from his injuries. He decided it was time for Catherine and him to leave. They stood at the end of the Great Hall and announced they were ready to retire for the night. They thanked everyone for coming and then left the room. Once they had departed, the King announced to the guests that the wedding festivities had ended and they were to return home.

"Lord Chauncey, we have arranged for you and Victoria to spend the night in the palace." King William shared as he approached the Lord.

"Thank you, your majesty, that is very kind."

"Can Victoria sleep in my bedchamber, Father?" Madison implored for she knew if she pleaded with her father, he couldn't help but say yes.

"No, I want her to sleep with me," Bethany insisted after she heard Madison's request.

"I think it would be nice if the three of you slept in the same room. It would offer you the opportunity to learn more about each other. But you may not stay up all night talking."

"Aye, Father. Thank you, Father," they both said. The three girls walked away chatting and giggling as girls do sometimes.

"That was very kind, sir," Lord Chauncey acknowledged. "Catherine and Victoria have only had each other to talk to for a long time. This will be good for Victoria to be with other young ladies her age."

"I can only imagine what that room will be like tonight knowing Madison and Bethany. I will have Cedric show you to your room. There will be breakfast in the Great Hall in the morning whenever you awaken."

Cedric led Lord Chauncey out of the Great Hall and up the main staircase. King William looked around the hall to see if his wife was still there. He found her sitting on a chair in a corner of the room.

"You seem to be lost in thought, dear wife."

"I was just recounting the events of the day. How well everything went given we didn't have very much time to plan this wedding. And how lucky we are to now have someone like Catherine married to our son."

"Everything was wonderful today. Thank you, my dear, for organizing this whole event. Our son looked very happy indeed. I think this will be a good marriage. Our son will be a great king. He learned from the best!"

"The best being you, my love?"

"Absolutely. Who else?"

"I am very tired. I think it is time for us to retire, my husband."

"I agree."

Meanwhile, James and Justine had returned to the garden to get away from the crowd of people and just be alone together. James was tired of answering questions about Justine, and Justine was just tired of talking to everyone.

As they were walking hand in hand toward the gazebo, Justine asked, "Why so many questions about me, us? I have been here for some time now and many in the village have seen me. I have actually talked to some of them when they came to Dr. Lange's office. I don't think it's a secret anymore that we are a couple."

"Justine, many of the guests were not from our kingdom and wanted to know who you are, where you came from, how we met? All the usual questions. Of course, I never divulged your real identity. They would not understand and that would put the existence of the portal in danger. They do not need to know all about you. Who I love is of concern to me and not them." Then he pulled her to him so they were facing each other. "You are what matters to me, nothing else. I was lost after you left and I could not think of anything else but finding you again. I had Gretchen looking for you whenever she went through the portal. My father kept introducing me to young ladies in the kingdom but I wanted nothing to do with them. They were not you. You! You are my life now. I do not want to be without you ever again." He grabbed her and kissed her so hard she almost passed out. Then he caught his breath and kissed her again. They felt as one body standing in the middle of the garden. And suddenly, they lost all sense of where they were and fell to the ground among the flowers, him on top of her. Their love was driving their emotions now as James tried to lift Justine's skirt.

"James," Justine uttered breathless, "we can't, we need to stop."

"Stop?" he said as he tried to get hold of himself. He sat up next to her and turned away for he was having a hard time relaxing.

She reached for his hand as she lay there. "I'm sorry, James. I was afraid that if we let it go any further, we wouldn't be able to stop. I want you. I want you so badly it eats me up inside. But not right now."

Then James lay down next to her and continued to look up at the sky for he couldn't look at her now.

"I think I understand. But do you know how hard it is to be near you and not have you! I think we should set the date for our wedding as soon as possible. I wish we were the ones who had gotten married today."

"Please be patient with me, James. I need some time."

"I will wait for you as long as it takes. But may I ask one thing."

"Yes."

"Please do not take too long. For now, I will be the perfect gentleman and only hug or kiss you when you ask me to. But we *will* set the date for the wedding."

"We will talk about it tomorrow. For now, just hold me, please." He pulled her to him, she put her head on his chest and the two drifted off to sleep.

CHAPTER 40

NEW INFORMATION COMES TO LIFE

The next morning, James and Justine were still lying in the garden. James opened his eyes and looked around him and realized they had slept there all night. He looked over at Justine, marveling at her features. He loved the curve of her nose and the color of her hair. Her hair wasn't as neat and tidy as it had been the night before. He lay there quiet, waiting for her to wake up. Finally, she started stirring and opened her eyes.

"Good morning, sleepy head."

Justine looked at him and suddenly realized where they were and immediately sat up. She looked around to see if anyone could see them. Then James stood up, brushed himself off, and extended a hand to Justine.

"Do not worry about anyone seeing us out here. We are still both fully clothed so it is obvious nothing happened. And to tell you the truth, I actually liked sleeping out here under the stars with you. It was very relaxing. It was probably the best sleep I have had for a while."

Justine looked up at him, "Me, too. Waking up next to your warm body was so nice," she said dreamily. Then she caught herself, "I mean, I had a good night's sleep, too. The garden has such a calming effect on me."

"The garden was it. Well, then, maybe we should try sleeping out here more often since we both slept so well."

"Yes, that may be a good idea," she stated without thinking about her answer. "Oh, good grief. I need to be quiet. I just keep digging myself in deeper and deeper, don't I?"

"Aye, but I like your answers." James helped Justine stand up. "For now, I think we should go into the palace and change out of these clothes. I am sure breakfast will be served soon."

"Yes, that's a good idea. I need to get out of this corset."

"Need any help?"

"No, thank you for the offer, but I think I can handle it. Besides, I have Anne to help me if need be."

"That is true, but I could probably do a better job than she."

"Yes, I bet you could," she added. "Come on. We need to go inside."

She grabbed his hand and led him into the palace and into the main hall, up the stairs to the landing.

"Here is where I take my leave of you, my lady. Though we be parted for a short time, I will think upon you and remember this moment until we meet again." Then James kissed her hand.

"Hahaha! That was really good! Until we meet again, my love."

They went their separate ways, she up the left staircase and he up the right. Justine went to her bedchambers and found Anne sleeping on a chair. She banged some things together to see if she could awaken her. Anne jumped with a start, saw Justine and immediately stood up.

"I am so sorry my lady. I came to your room after the feast to help you undress and you were not here.

I waited for you, and I must have fallen asleep in the chair."

"It's fine. Please don't apologize. I'm the one that should be sorry. I had no idea you would be waiting for me. Well, I'm here now and I need to get out of these clothes."

"Aye, my lady. I will help you with that."

Meanwhile, it didn't take James long to change and he was out of his room in no time. He needed to work off some nervous energy so he decided to go for a ride before breakfast since it was still early. He bounded down the stairs, went outside and began to walk toward the stables. He heard a voice from behind him calling out his name. He stopped, turned around, and there was Gretchen trying to catch up to him. So, he waited for her not sure why she needed to talk to him this early in the morning. He hadn't seen her since the army had returned from Dorset.

"Prince James," she said out of breath. "Please forgive the early morning intrusion. I have something of most importance to tell you."

"I am listening, Gretchen."

"Your highness, the portal."

"Aye, what about the portal? Has something happened to it?"

"No, sire. But I have uncovered some new information which we were not aware of until now. You must listen to me carefully."

"Gretchen, you have my attention. What do you need to tell me?"

"Since our return from the battle, I have been looking through some old documents Arius has carefully preserved that date back over 150 years, to the time when Merlin was still the sorcerer of Wiltshire, or rather Camelot back then. Merlin left explicit instructions regarding the portal and some warnings regarding the use of it. I never really paid attention to any of it before now. I thought it best to look for information since we have been using it more now than in the past. In the past, only seekers would be able to travel through the portal and back. That stopped with Dr. Lange when he decided to remain in Wiltshire. For him, time on his side moves as it does for us and he no longer returns to the day he left. We have always made sure he traveled with a seeker through the portal so he wouldn't lose his memory of us when gone."

"Does this have something to do with Justine and her family?" he asked concerned.

"Aye, it does, your highness. I will explain. Merlin stated the portal will return someone to the moment they left only once, which we knew. Here is what we did not know since we were not faced with this before. Justine and her father had their one time when they left and returned after the King had surgery. That determined the moment of return even though Mrs. Ross and Luke had only traveled through the portal once. No one in the family can return to the life they left at the moment they left it now. From this point on, they are "travelers.""

"Travelers? What does that mean, Gretchen? What are you trying to tell me! I need to know!"

"Merlin stated that a traveler is someone who goes through the portal more than once. In their case, time for them will move as it does for us. A seeker is a traveler."

"Does this mean that Justine and her family cannot return to the day they left but it will now be several weeks after that day? And if they stay here any longer, the same amount of time will have passed for them in the future?"

"That is what I am saying, Prince James. I, as you, thought that the family would be returning to the very moment they left England because it had been a year since they left. But that is not what Merlin tells us."

"Gretchen!" James yelled as he began to panic. "What will Justine say when she finds out? What will her family say? They all thought they were safe and could return to their life in modern day England with no problems. And to make matters worse, they will not remember ever having been here!"

"Prince James, there is something else."

"Something else? How could there be something else? What are you going to tell me now?"

"That they will not lose their memory of this place," she stated quietly. "Dr. Ross and Justine traveled through the portal twice and that is why the two of them remembered bits and pieces of their time here. I thought it was the necklace, but maybe it was a combination of both. It appears a traveler will have full memory of their time here after they have traveled at least two times. But when they all left a year ago, Mrs. Ross and Luke had only gone through once so they could not remember having been here. Now, that has all changed. All are now travelers. Merlin stated that once a person becomes a traveler, they can never return to their life as they knew it in the future. They had to remain in Wiltshire and were only allowed to leave for short periods of time. They had to be accompanied by a seeker, not because they might lose their memory, but to ensure the traveler did not tell anyone about our existence."

"I need to sit down. My head is spinning." He walked over to a bench located under a tree near him. Gretchen sat down beside him. "What am I going to tell the Ross family?"

"I am so sorry, your highness. I did not know any of this until I started to investigate. Your father requested I locate more information regarding Arius and what he is capable of doing, and of the portal. We have never been faced with any of this before. We had a reason to seek someone, brought them here, and then returned them. No complications with that. Then Dr. Lange and Dr. Ross. We did not know the effect the Ross family would have on us. What happened between you and Justine was not expected, and therefore we were unprepared. Dr. Lange chose this life of his own free will. The Ross family will now be part of Wiltshire whether they like it or not. This is good information to know, is it not? If I had not located those papers left by Merlin, the Ross family would have returned weeks or even months after they had left with knowledge of Wiltshire. That could have been devastating."

James put his head in his hands for several minutes and then looked up. "Thank you, Gretchen. This is important information that will need to be shared with my father and with the Ross family. I would like very much for you to be the one to tell my father about this. I must find the right time and place to tell Justine first, and then her family. For me, this is great news for I will be able to have Justine with me always. But for her family?"

CHAPTER 41

DEVASTATING NEWS

James sat on the bench for a long time after Gretchen left. He was glad he didn't have to talk to anyone and could just sit in the quiet of the morning. He knew Justine had already said she would be with him anywhere he was, and if that meant staying in Wiltshire, she would do that. But her family?

They had just moved to England and were ready to begin their new lives there. Then he and Justine took them through the portal and were assured they would be able to return to their life where they left off. But that has all changed now that they aren't just visitors anymore. They had a new title, travelers. Once his father learned this new information regarding the portal, would he even allow them to leave? And if they did, they would be returning to a world from which they had just disappeared. People would ask questions and want to know where they had been. The family members would know why they had been gone, but would they be able to remain silent and not tell anyone? It seemed to work for Dr. Lange, though. He just travels back and forth whenever he needs supplies or asks Gretchen to do it for him. However, he does travel with a seeker whenever he leaves. The only thing James knew to do now was to wait for Gretchen to talk to his father and find out how his father wanted to handle this. Until then, he would need to keep this new information to himself.

He reluctantly got up from the bench and walked back to the palace. When he entered the main hall, he could smell food and hear conversations coming from the Great Hall so he knew everyone was at breakfast. He took a deep breath and walked into the Great Hall. He looked around to see who was there and saw Justine and her family were there and most of his own family. John and Catherine had not arrived yet and his father wasn't there either. Maybe that meant Gretchen and his father were discussing the documents she had located. He decided it would be best if he just sat down, acted as if everything was normal, and ate breakfast.

Justine noticed him standing in the entrance to the Great Hall and saw the look of concern on his face. He didn't see her approach and when she spoke it startled him.

"James, you look worried. Is everything okay?"

"What!? Justine, it is not good to sneak up on someone."

"I didn't sneak. How could anyone sneak up on someone on these wooden floors?"

"Everything is fine. I was just coming to join everyone for breakfast. I am starving! Let us sit and enjoy our meal."

"Okay. If you need to talk about something, I'm here for you. You know that, don't you."

"Aye, if something was bothering me, I would let you know."

They sat down at the table and joined in the breakfast conversations about the wedding. After breakfast was over, James excused himself from the table and told Justine he had something that needed his attention and he would see her later. As he was leaving the Great Hall, he saw Gretchen waiting for him. She told him that she and the King had talked and he now wanted James to meet with him. He straightened up, ready to face whatever his father had to say, and walked with Gretchen to the Throne Room. When they arrived, James saw Arius standing next to his father.

"Father, Gretchen said you wanted to see me."

"Aye, my son, I do. I think you are already aware of the topic to be discussed."

"I am, Father. Gretchen explained everything to me early this morning."

"I have consulted with Gretchen and Arius and have read for myself some of the warnings left by Merlin regarding the portal. I have decided that I cannot let the Ross family leave Wiltshire to resume their life in their own time. They must remain here with us. Like Dr. Lange, they may travel through the portal with a seeker by their side for short periods of time but may not remain. For now, I will allow them to retrieve any belongings they may need from their home in Oxford and then return here."

"I knew deep in my soul that this would be your ruling even though I wished it would be something different."

"I think it best if I tell them of my decision and not you. I do not want this to come between you and Justine, but I know the family will be devastated. I will summon them this morning. Be ready, my son for whatever the members of the family may say to you in anger. It may take them some time to accept this as their new reality."

"I understand, Father. If I may, I will take my leave of you now and go for the ride I was to take this morning when Gretchen found me. I need to clear my head and not be around anyone for a while."

"Aye, you may. Please know that this decision was not made in haste, and if I could have decided differently, I would have."

"I know, Father. I would have made the same decision you did. Please excuse me."

James left the Throne Room keeping to the back hallways so he wouldn't run into anyone. He walked to the stables, saddled his horse, and rode off through the front gate into the hills surrounding the castle.

King William knew that no matter when he broke the news to the Ross family they would be upset, so he decided it would be best to do it sooner than later. He had Gretchen gather them together and meet him in the Throne Room. He asked Gretchen and Arius to remain in the room with him and help explain the reasoning for his decision.

He sat on his throne awaiting the arrival of the family pondering how best to break the news to them. He decided it would be Gretchen who would tell them for it was her suspicions surrounding the portal which led her to the archives and her findings. Then, when she was done, he would ask Arius to reflect on this information before informing them of his decision.

Gretchen soon returned with the Ross family. He asked them to be seated in the chairs in front of him. King William began as he had planned and asked Gretchen to share the information she had. Their faces changed from being curious as to why the King had summoned them, to disbelief in what they were hearing, to a look of shock when Gretchen told them they were now travelers instead of just visitors to the kingdom and the difference between the two. The King then asked Arius if he had anything to share but he declined for this was all new to him, too. King William then shared his thoughts and told them his decision that they were to remain in Wiltshire for the remainder of their lives. All became irate and Dr. Ross began yelling at the King. The King then summoned the guard and Dr. Ross had to be escorted out of the Throne Room followed by the rest of the family.

"They must realize they cannot talk to me as they did for I am the King and my decision will not be questioned. Now that they know, they will need time for this information to sink in. I expect you, Gretchen, to talk to them in my stead and help them understand. But they must not question my authority on this matter ever again."

"I understand, your majesty."

"Arius, I need you to locate James and apprise him of what has happened here. He needs to know what he will be facing upon his return."

"Aye, your majesty. It will be done."

"Now leave me alone, please. And no one is to enter this room for a while."

Gretchen and Arius both bowed to the King and then exited the room leaving the King alone with his thoughts.

"I know where to find the Prince. I can see him sitting by a lake outside the castle walls. I will go and talk to him while you go find the Ross family. You will probably find them all together. Oh, wait, I see them. They are in the bedchamber where the parents sleep, with the door closed. They look to be very angry. Justine appears as though she is trying to calm the parents who I think are most unhappy. I cannot read the reaction of the son, however. I do not get the impression that this news was as upsetting to him."

"Thank you, Arius. This is good information to know before I approach them. I will see you later."

They each went their separate ways to do as the King had commanded. They both knew their task would not be an easy one, Gretchen more so than Arius. The distance to James was not very great and Arius could disappear and reappear right where James was located.

"Arius, could you please announce yourself next time," a surprised James implored. "And, why are you here anyway?"

"Prince James, going from invisible to visible always startles people. It would take the fun out of it if I had to announce myself. Also, I think you know why I am here. Your father has notified the Ross family of his decision. Dr. Ross was so angry he started yelling at your father, which one does not do since he is the King, and had to be escorted from the Throne Room. Gretchen now has the task of trying to calm them down and help them to look at this as a good thing. I am not sure how she is going to do that, but that is her problem, not mine. However, I was sent to talk to you to let you know how the news was received, and then discuss a strategy for your return to the palace for the family will most certainly confront you."

"Thank you, Arius. This is most comforting news," the Prince replied sarcastically. "I think I should never return to the palace. I fear the Ross family may find it hard to forgive me since Gretchen and I were the ones to bring them here. However, at first, Justine was the only one who was to return with me. But Luke heard us talking and said he thought the whole family should go and visit Stonehenge again. Dr. and Mrs. Ross then said that would be a good weekend trip and they could meet my parents. What started out as me bringing Justine back to Wiltshire per her request, turned into a family trip! So, I am not the one at fault here," he stated inspired by this revelation. "I can blame Luke for the family being here!"

"Your highness, Luke would not have had the chance to suggest the trip had it not been for you making the journey to modern day England to find Justine."

"Aye, but..."

"Young Prince, it really does not matter how they got here. The fact is they are here and because of our lack of knowledge regarding the portal, will now need to remain here. The blame falls on us all for putting to use a portal about which we knew very little. We will certainly continue to read the documents left by Merlin so we are not surprised again by something we did not know. But there is a bright spot in all of this."

"And what could that possibly be?"

"The members of the Ross family may still visit their time as Dr. Lange does, but they just cannot remain there."

"I am not sure they will see it that way. Dr. Ross had moved to Oxford to begin a new job and the family came along with him for the two years he was to live there. Luke was going to learn how to be a cook, Justine was to finish school, and Mrs. Ross left her job in America. Now, they were just told they must give all that up to live here, centuries behind their own time."

"I wonder... Maybe there is a way they can still do that?"

"What? How? My father has decided, and that would mean he would need to change his edict."

"Gretchen and I have not read everything Merlin wrote about the portal. There could be something hidden in those words that would allow them to finish what they started. You must not despair yet, my Prince. I will return to the palace to tell the King about this idea, and then Gretchen and I will set about reading the documents."

"That is great, Arius, but what do we tell the Ross family while we all wait to hear from you or Gretchen?"

"Nothing. They must not think their fate is any different than what the King has already decreed. We do not know if Gretchen and I will be able to find anything different. They must not be given false hope.

But, if and when we learn something new and if the King is amenable to change his ruling, then we will inform the family."

"Please do this with haste, Arius. For if Justine is angry with me, I will find living in the palace unbearable until I can make this right."

"Understood." Arius disappeared leaving the Prince alone.

What was he to do now? He couldn't let Gretchen be the only one to receive the brunt of the anger the Ross family must be feeling. He would have to return and face the music so to speak. He had to make things right so he wouldn't lose Justine over this. He mounted his horse and galloped off toward the palace not knowing what he would be facing when he arrived.

CHAPTER 42

JAMES EXPLAINS THE PORTAL

As he neared the castle, James stopped his horse on the bluff overlooking the main gate. Should he go into the palace and confront this head on, or should he disappear until it all blew over and let everyone else handle it? Although the second one sounded very appealing, he thought better of it and decided to confront this issue head on. Who knows? Maybe he would be the one to help the family accept this new future and that would be the end of it. However, he knew it wouldn't be that easy. He would rather go into battle against some angry foot soldiers than be confronted by the Ross family right now.

He took a deep breath, gathered some courage, rode through the main gate and the outer courtyard to the stables. He told the stable boys he wanted to take care of the horse himself. He was just unsaddling the horse when he heard a familiar voice behind him. He closed his eyes and waited for the explosion. When he didn't hear anything, he opened one eye and then the other. He looked around and there was Justine standing with her arms folded across her chest. She wasn't saying anything and that made him nervous. They just stood there looking at each other for what seemed to him an eternity, and finally Justine opened her mouth to speak and then closed it again.

She took a deep breath and said through clenched teeth, "How could you have done this to my family? I don't mind that you did it to me since I already told you I would be with you no matter where you lived, but my family?" Then she got louder, "They are devasted. They thought this whole time they would be able to return to the moment they left and be able to continue living their normal lives. But that all came crashing down this morning when Gretchen told us about the documents she had uncovered written over 150 years ago that disputed that! They are so angry I can't even be near them. My mom is seeing red!"

"Whatever does that mean?" he asked.

"Red is the color associated with being really angry, when you get red in the face as you yell at everyone. That is seeing red!"

"Aye, I understand that now. May I..."

"No, you may not. My dad just started a new job, one he had always dreamed of doing, teaching, and that dream has been shot to pieces. My mom quit her job to come to Oxford and she was going to do some volunteer work. My brother was going to go to culinary school and learn to be a chef, and now his dreams are all gone. As for me, I was going to finish high school and I don't really care about that especially since I won't be going to college now. And you, you had to come find me," and her voice got quiet, "which I'm glad you did and personally I wouldn't change a thing. But how am I to ever face my parents and brother again?" and she dropped her arms slumped forward. "How?" and she started to sob.

James walked over to her, wrapped his arms around her, and just held her until her sobbing slowed and finally stopped. She looked up at him, and he began to wipe the tears from her face with his thumb.

"We will get through this together. I will go with you now to meet with them. I heard from Arius that

Gretchen was to try to console them. Did she have any success?"

Justine moved away from James, turned and replied, "She was talking, but I don't think they heard what she said. They were too closed off to really make sense of any of it."

"I am sorry I was not here to help her with that. She should not have had to do that by herself. We were both to blame for the misinformation your family was given."

Justine put her hand on his arm, "But you didn't know. Gretchen only just learned about it herself. How were you to know that things would be different if you go through the portal more than once? So, don't blame yourself for something you had no control over." She dropped her arm and apologizing said, "I'm sorry I yelled at you. They were angry, I was angry, and I needed to take it out on someone and you happened to be the lucky recipient."

"Please do not apologize. I really did not know! I only just learned all of this this morning. After I talked to my father and learned of his decision, I jumped on a horse and rode out of here so I did not have to face anyone. That is how brave I was. I must find a stable boy to take care of my horse and then together we will go talk to them."

They walked up to the palace and in through the front door. Standing there, in the main hall looking forlorn was Luke.

"Luke, what are you doing?" Justine questioned. "You look lost!"

"I am. I don't know what to do. After Gretchen left, we started talking about this new situation when suddenly Mom and Dad asked me to leave their room. So I did, and now I don't know what to do. Justine, we can't go home, ever!"

"Luke, that is not true," James blurted out. "You can; you just cannot go back to live."

"What? Are you sure? That isn't what your father said. He told us we are to remain in Wiltshire, to live here."

"That is true, but it is obvious you have not considered all the information presented to you. Justine and I are going there now to talk to them, and I would like it if you would come as well. Maybe there is some good news to share that will help them accept this."

The three of them ascended the staircase to the second floor and walked down the hallway to the bedchamber where Dr. and Mrs. Ross were. They knocked on the door.

"Who is it?" Dr. Ross grumbled.

"Dad, it's Justine. I'm here with Luke and James. May we come in?"

The door opened rather abruptly and Dr. Ross stood there staring at them. "Yes, you may come in. I'm not sure I want to let James in, but at the same time, I'm very interested to hear what he has to say about all this."

The three entered the room and sat down in the sitting area off the bedchamber. Justine started to speak, but James put his hand on her arm to stop her.

"Since they want to hear from me, then I shall tell them everything I know right now. I would ask one thing: that I not be interrupted until I finish what I have to say. Agreed?"

"Agreed," Dr. Ross acknowledged.

"Agreed," Mrs. Ross and Luke stated together.

"And you, Justine? You will be silent, right?"

"I will. At least I'll try."

Now that James could relay the information as he knew it without any interruptions, he began. He explained the history of the portal since it was discovered around ten years ago and how it had been used. There were no documents they knew of at the time to explain the portal and its use. So up till now, everything they knew about it came through trial and error. He told them that the only people who were allowed to travel in and out of the portal regularly were seekers. Seekers were assigned to travel to the future. Their task was to find something or someone needed in the kingdom and, if it was a person, to return him/her. There was no need to know any more about the portal since it was always used in the same way, until Dr. Lange. After his initial visit, he made it known he wanted to remain in Wiltshire for the rest of his life. Sometimes, he would travel back to his own time to gather needed medical supplies and return. But he was always accompanied by a seeker because it was thought Dr. Lange would forget everything about Wiltshire once he left and then never return. It was not known that he had become a traveler and could traverse the portal by himself if he had wanted. However, Dr. Lange may still need to travel in the company of a seeker to ensure he doesn't unknowingly disclose the whereabouts of the portal to someone on the other side. As he talked, James noticed the facial features seemed to soften on Dr. and Mrs. Ross as they listened to his explanation. Finally, he told them this new information came to light because Gretchen noticed that things had changed with the arrival of Dr. Lange and now them. She began to search through the archives for information concerning the use of the portal back when Merlin created it. After much digging, she finally located the information Merlin had written down for future generations to follow in case he wasn't around. Gretchen had only informed him of all of this that morning. She then went to the King with the facts because the King would be the one to rule on their fate. The King decided he would be the one to relay this information and his decision to the family. When he finished it was so quiet, you could hear a pin drop. Finally, Mrs. Ross spoke up.

"May we ask questions now," Mrs. Ross inquired.

"Aye."

"This morning when your father talked to us, he told us we are to remain in Wiltshire and never leave. But you just said Dr. Lange is allowed to leave."

"Mrs. Ross, I was not in the room at the time my father explained all of this to you, so I am not aware of his exact words. But what I do know is that Dr. Lange needs to replenish his medical supplies and when he does, he lets my father know, my father assigns a seeker to accompany him, and together they go and come back through the portal. Time passes for him in his time as it does in our time. It might be many months before he must go for supplies. But you must remember: Dr. Lange has chosen Wiltshire to be his home, and therefore he returns of his own free will."

"Prince James, his exact words to us were that we were to remain in Wiltshire for the rest of our lives," Dr. Ross affirmed. "He gave no further information, just that. I grew angry and was forcibly removed from the Throne Room. From that point on we didn't hear from anyone except Gretchen who had already presented her findings in the Throne Room. I'm afraid, after all that, we weren't very hospitable when she was here."

"Thank you, Dr. Ross, for sharing that information for, again, I do not know what my father said. I think what my father may have meant was that Wiltshire is now to be your home, as Dr. Lange has chosen it to be his home. I do not want to speak for my father, but I would think you would be under the same rules as Dr. Lange in that you may leave Wiltshire for short periods of time, but you are to always return. As to your being removed from the Throne Room, you must remember this is 16th century England and he is the King. You may not under any circumstances question his authority or raise your voice to him. That is forbidden, no matter how well you think you know him."

"I am truly sorry for that outburst and it won't happen again. I am still not happy about all of this. But you have explained the circumstances under which we find ourselves very well. It is clearer to me," and Dr. Ross reached over and grabbed his wife's hand, "to us, that neither you nor Gretchen were aware of this when you brought us here. This was out of your control, and I don't blame you for any of this. Your only crime was that you love my daughter so much you searched for her for a solid year and when you heard she had returned to England, risked everything to come find her. Justine, I can understand why you are to be together despite what life has thrown at you two. I think it will be important that I apologize to your father for my behavior and ask to discuss further the idea of venturing out of this kingdom for short periods of time. Thank you, Prince James, for having the courage to face us and for loving our daughter as you do."

James reached over and grabbed Justine's hand, "Dr. Ross, I was lost until your family returned to England. Now I am whole again and never want to be parted from her again. I understand this news was not what you wanted to hear, but for Justine, knowing that her family will always be here after we are married makes living here with me that much better. I will take my leave of you now."

James bowed to them, and pulled Justine with him out of the room. As soon as the door was closed, he kissed her and squeezed her so hard she almost popped!

"I think that went well, don't you," she said to him trying to breathe again.

"I am so glad that is behind me. Now, as your father said, he needs to have a conversation with my father about the rules surrounding the use of the portal. I think all will soon be peaceful around here again. Also, knowing that your parents will always be here, we can now set the date for our wedding!"

"Yes, I suppose we could." Then she cupped his head in her hands, looked at him lovingly, and kissed him.

CHAPTER 43

MERLIN'S WARNINGS AND ADVICE

Gretchen went to the tower where Arius stored all of the relics left by his predecessor. It was important to learn as much as she could regarding the portal if they were to continue to use it. It could no longer be just a portal for the seekers to use but could serve a broader purpose. When she reached the tower, she saw Arius sitting in front of a pile of old dusty books and rolls of paper. He didn't notice her come in.

"Arius, I see you are interested in the old manuscripts Merlin left, too."

"Huh, oh aye. I wish I had read through these before now. These things have been sitting up here for years, but I never paid them any heed until now. You would not believe how much information is contained in all of these books. Merlin documented many of his spells and also told why he needed to use them, who his enemies were, and what he did when he encountered them. Some of the enemies he faced were other sorcerers! I was not aware there were any besides Merlin. Turning into a dragon was the impetus I needed to discover who I really am. There must be more to me than I know and I intend to find out!"

"Good for you, Arius. I always thought you were meant for greater things than just disappearing and transporting others from place to place. Just like the portal. We only knew the basic information regarding the use of it and that is what we have done for these ten years. But things have changed and we need to know more."

The two sat and read through pages and pages of information. Much of it documented the history of Wiltshire.

"I hope there is a spell in here somewhere that will help me preserve all of this. Many of these books are so old they are beginning to fall apart."

"Just keep reading and maybe we will come across it," Gretchen encouraged.

Gretchen noticed Arius starting to experiment with some of the spells he was reading. He would turn his hands a certain way while saying unfamiliar words. One of the spells enabled him to create fire. He figured out how to throw it at something and almost hit Gretchen.

"Watch what you are doing! You could destroy some of these documents and hurt me in the process if you are not careful."

"Sorry! My fault! I got carried away! Will not happen again."

"Arius, I found it!"

"Found what exactly?"

"The information we need about the portal. Here it is!"

"Great! Now you read your book and let me get on with my spells."

"Is there any paper that is not written on in this room? I need to copy this."

"Oh, wait a minute. I just came across that spell you just mentioned earlier. Now where did I see it? Here it is! What do you want me to replicate? Oh, aye, I remember. I can do this!" He started to utter a spell, closed his eyes, waved his hands back and forth over the book and suddenly right next to it another one began to appear. When done, he opened his eyes. "What do you know! It worked! Now let me see what else I can do." He went back to reading his books.

Gretchen closed the old manuscript she had been reading and was now able to read through a newer one that wasn't so fragile. As she read, she came upon the title 'Travelers' and knew this was what she had been looking for. Much of the information at the beginning was what she already knew and had relayed to James and King William. But then she found actual accounts from the past of what Merlin had encountered when using the portal. She also discovered the reason Merlin had closed the portal and why it had remained hidden for so many years. On one occasion, a new seeker had been sent to find a doctor who was needed at the time, 'just as she had been sent to bring Dr. Ross to Wiltshire,' she thought to herself. This doctor needed to make several journeys to Wiltshire and was designated a traveler. The young seeker accompanied the doctor each time he left and returned. But on one occasion, because the doctor retained his memory of Wiltshire, the seeker overheard the doctor explaining to his colleagues where he went on his journeys and offered to take them with him the next time he was summoned. He had not been bestowed with the ability to silence him at that time. Not knowing how to handle this situation, the seeker returned without the doctor and immediately informed Merlin of the doctor's comments. Merlin knew he could not undo what the doctor had said. Fearing for the safety of his kingdom, he had to erase any trace of the portal. He permanently closed it and no seeker ever journeyed through it again. Wiltshire remained cut off from the outside world from then on. Then there was this warning from Merlin:

'If future generations happen to rediscover the portal and it is opened again by a sorcerer, it is important that those who are summoned only visit the kingdom once and never return. If this visitor does return, that person is now designated as a traveler and must never again be allowed to live in their own time period for this will put the kingdom in danger. It may become necessary for the traveler to 'tie up loose ends' before permanently settling in Wiltshire. If the traveler does need to leave for some reason, that person must be accompanied by an experienced seeker who has been given the power by the sorcerer to silence the traveler when necessary. This is the only way a traveler would be granted permission to leave Wiltshire. The traveler must not be put in a position where they may encounter someone they know and feel the need to explain why they have been gone. Afterwards, the traveler will return to Wiltshire. There must be no exceptions to this rule.'

Gretchen had found the information regarding the Ross's and Dr. Lange that she needed to know. Dr. Lange had been allowed to leave but the seeker who accompanied him did not have the power to silence him. They were lucky he had kept his promise to never share information. She also had to inform Arius of the special power a seeker would need when accompanying a traveler. She hoped he knew that particular spell or could find it. And how was Dr. Ross to explain his sudden departure from Oxford if he returned to gather their belongings? The phrase, 'tie up loose ends,' stuck in her head. Maybe the only way Dr. Ross could do that would be to finish his two-year commitment in Oxford. Afterwards when he was to return to America, he would instead return to Wiltshire. This would mean at least two seekers would have a two-year assignment, one for Dr. Ross and the other for Mrs. Ross. Luke's fate was still undetermined at this point. The members of the family would have to understand that the seeker would be with them 24/7, invisible at times. Now, she needed to inform Arius of this latest information and ask if he knew or was aware of the spell he needed to cast to create experienced seekers. If he didn't know it or couldn't find it, then there was no chance for the Ross family to return or for Dr. Lange to continue to travel through the portal, and her solutions would be of no use to anyone.

"Arius, I need to talk to you."

"Wow, this stuff is so interesting. I never knew I was capable of performing so many spells! I need to start practicing..."

"Arius, pay attention!"

He turned and noticed the serious look on her face. "You have my undivided attention. What do you need to tell me?"

"Do you know that there are two kinds of seekers?"

"What do you mean, two kinds?"

"That tells me you do not know. Merlin states there are seekers who are learning and those who are experienced."

"Like you."

"Aye, like me. But there is one spell meant for travelers that I am not able to cast and did not know about it until now."

"What is that?"

"I have to be able to stop a traveler from talking if they begin to mention their time in Wiltshire to someone in their own time period. Merlin said that is very important so they do not put the kingdom in danger of being discovered."

"And I am supposed to know how to enable a seeker to do this?"

"Aye. Do you know of such a spell or have you come across it in your reading?"

"No and no. I have only learned or tried pretty simple spells. I have not had need of many other ones."

"Then start looking. We may need to look for some new seekers since the ones we have will now need to become experienced. According to Merlin, we will need to have at least five seekers who will be able to cast that spell to travel with the Rosses, that is if they all leave here, and one for sure to travel with Dr. Lange whenever he goes through the portal."

"If you are not careful, I may use that spell on you!"

"I do not appreciate this attempt at humor, Arius. I am only telling you what Merlin warned us about."

"Understood. I will let you know if I locate such a spell. And even if I find it, I will need to practice it on someone so I know it works."

"That would be me, then. But we would need another person to make sure it works; you cast one on me, and then I should be able in turn to cast it on another."

"Very true. Now you go finish what you need to do. I have more manuscripts to explore."

CHAPTER 44

THE TEST IS SUCCESSFUL

Arius poured over the pages of information left by Merlin and finally found the 'silence' spell. He read through it and decided it sounded pretty simple. Now, he just needed to try it on Gretchen.

"Oh, Gretchen," he hollered. "I need you for a moment."

She looked up from her reading, "What is it? I am reading so I hope it is important."

"I found the 'silence' spell and I need to try it out. Remember, you volunteered."

"Aye, that I did." She made her way across the room and stood next to Arius. "I am ready."

"Let me read this one more time. All right, I think I have it. Here goes!" Then Arius said the spell which was to enable Gretchen to silence a traveler. "There, that should do it. How do you feel?

"Fine. Am I supposed to feel something?"

"No, not really. I was just checking. Now, we need to test it out. Who should we try it on?"

"Justine is a traveler and I think she would be amenable to us trying it on her."

"I sense her presence in the parlor with James. See you there." Then Arius disappeared. Gretchen could be invisible but could only transport herself from place to place on the other side of the portal. So she just had to walk to the parlor.

Arius reappeared in the parlor right next to James.

"Arius, I appeal to your better nature to not do that anymore."

"I will try, your highness. I need to talk to Justine. Gretchen should be here very soon. She will explain why we have come."

Gretchen finally arrived in the parlor. "I am here now. Arius, why did you leave without me? Oh, never mind that now. Greetings, Prince James and Justine. I need to try something on Justine but we are not sure if it will work."

"What are you planning to do, Gretchen?" Justine asked concerned.

"This will be harmless. It will only render you silent. We hope you will not be able to talk."

"I like that spell!" James commented as he laughed.

"Very funny, James. I'm not sure why this is necessary, but tell me what I need to do."

"I need you to start talking to James as if you were back in your own time and telling him about Wiltshire."

"Okay. James, you wouldn't believe where I have been..."

Then Gretchen cast the spell to silence Justine and waited. Nothing happened.

"May we try again?"

So Justine started talking about Wiltshire again, and again nothing happened.

"Let me try," Arius asserted. "If the spell works at all, I should be able to make her be quiet."

So, they tried again but even Arius couldn't make the spell work.

"What are we doing wrong?" Arius stated in frustration.

"I need to think," Gretchen muttered. She sat down on one of the chairs in the parlor and was quiet for some time. Then she looked up with a look of surprise on her face. "I think I know why the spell is not working. We are in Wiltshire."

"I think that is rather obvious," Arius shared.

"No, I mean, we cannot make her be silent about Wiltshire because she is still here. The spell is to work on a traveler after they have gone through the portal, not while they are still here in Wiltshire."

"I see what you mean, Gretchen. Then we need to test it outside the portal." Just then the four of them vanished and James and Justine suddenly found themselves standing next to the portal.

"Arius, explain yourself," James demanded.

"We cannot know if this spell will work unless we travel to the other side of the portal. So that is what we are doing."

"You might have warned us first. And why is this spell so important?"

"We will explain upon your return. Now you three must go through, but you will be invisible on the other side. I cannot go with you. Let me know if it is successful."

So, Gretchen, James, and Justine walked through the portal, or doorway, and stopped once they were on the other side. They looked around to see if anyone was in the vicinity and saw no one.

"We will remain invisible, but the voice will be heard; that is why we need to ensure no one is near." They looked around again and seeing no one, Gretchen asked Justine to repeat what she did in the parlor. Gretchen said the words to the spell and immediately Justine could not say anything related to the portal or Wiltshire. "It actually works!" Gretchen said excitedly. "Now try talking about something else and then mention Wiltshire."

While Justine was talking about other topics, her voice was fine, but when she mentioned Wiltshire, she couldn't say another word.

"This is beyond my expectations," Gretchen declared. "We need to go back through the portal and inform Arius of our success.

The three moved through the portal and Arius was waiting on the other side. "Arius, the spell worked," Gretchen shared. "Once I said the spell, Justine could not talk about Wiltshire at all. Justine, try it now since we are back home."

Justine started talking about many topics and then started to talk about Wiltshire but nothing happened.

"You see. I was right. The spell will only work once we have gone through the portal."

"You will need to teach me that spell in case I need it sometime," James insisted. Justine socked him on the arm. "You thought I was serious?"

"No, but I just like to bop you one every now and then."

Then suddenly they found themselves back in the parlor. "Arius, you did not warn us we were moving," James stated.

"Okay, we're back, so tell us why we are doing this." Justine implored.

So Gretchen and Arius told them about the additional information learned from the manuscripts Merlin left about the 'silence' spell and of its importance. They said that Arius had to locate the spell since he had never performed it or even knew it existed. But Gretchen didn't tell them the other information she had learned since she needed to present that information and her idea to the King first.

"Now I see why we had to test it out on the other side of the portal. And this spell is to keep travelers from disclosing any information about Wiltshire and the portal?"

"Aye, Justine. You are now a traveler and we needed to find out if it would work on you," Gretchen shared.

"What is next?" James asked. "What will happen now?"

"Now Arius and I need to go to your father with this information, and he will decide what is to be done, if anything will change. I cannot tell you any more than that. Thank you for your help. And Arius, this time, we need to travel together, please."

Gretchen and Arius disappeared at the same time and left James and Justine alone in the parlor.

"I wonder what this all means, even for Dr. Lange," Justine pondered.

"I cannot say, but I am sure we will find out soon enough."

Gretchen and Arius reappeared in the Throne Room where they usually found the King during the day. But he wasn't there.

"Did you not check to see where the King was before we vanished?"

"It sounded like you were in a hurry, so I transported us to where I thought he would be."

"Well, use your mind this time and figure out where he *is*."

"Ah, I see him now. He is examining some new horses at the stable."

And before Gretchen could make a comment, they disappeared and reappeared near the stables.

"It would be nice if you warned a person before you performed the disappearing act!" Gretchen told him. "I see the King over there by all those horses." Arius and Gretchen proceeded to where he was and bowed.

"Your majesty," Arius began, "Gretchen and I have learned some new information regarding the portal, and it is important we share it with you."

"I will meet with you both in a moment. I need to finish my business with this merchant first."

"Of course, your majesty. We will wait by that bench over there."

When the King had finally decided which horses he wanted to purchase, he went to see what Arius and Gretchen needed to tell him.

"I hope this is important."

"Aye, it is," Gretchen assured him.

Gretchen told King William about the information she had just read, about the warning from Merlin, about the reason Merlin had closed the portal, about the seekers accompanying a traveler, and about the 'silence' spell. She told him they had recently tested the spell on Justine but it only worked after having gone through the portal.

Then Gretchen decided she needed to test the waters and explain her thoughts regarding the phrase, 'tie up loose ends." After she had finished, there was silence from the King. He looked as though he was deep in thought. Maybe she had overstepped her authority, but she was sure all she did was to merely make a suggestion.

"That is a very interesting proposal, Gretchen. I must think on it and will let you know my decision soon."

"Thank you, your majesty," Gretchen nodded.

"Aye, thank you," Arius chimed in.

Then the two of them disappeared leaving the King to ponder the new information and the suggestion Gretchen had made as he returned to the palace.

CHAPTER 45

A CHANGE OF HEART

Once Arius and Gretchen had gone, King William needed to be alone for there was much to think about. He decided to walk through the garden where it would be peaceful with no interruptions. He instructed the guards who were always with him to stay at the door to the garden and make sure no one entered.

He strolled among the flowers and stopped occasionally to take in the various scents wafting by him in the breeze. His demeanor was much calmer now, and he felt his mind clear of all the worries troubling him. He took a deep breath and continued walking. He ascended the stairs to the gazebo, turned and looked out over the expanse of color all around him. He had brought peace to the kingdom and now needed to feel that peace within him. Standing there alone, he began to feel as if a weight had been lifted off his shoulders and the mental stress he had been feeling for weeks finally dissipated. Now he was ready to consider the fate of the Ross family with a clear head.

He sat down on the bench near him and began to mull over in his mind the pros and cons of allowing the Ross family to return to their life in Oxford for the next two years. It would allow them the opportunity to tie up loose ends as Gretchen had stated and then return to Wiltshire. However, they could also return to Oxford for the next couple of weeks, get their affairs in order, and then return to Wiltshire. He thought it might be beneficial if he discussed these options with Dr. Ross prior to making his decision. That way he would avert any disagreements that might arise again. He was ready to leave the calm of the garden and return to the stresses of his role as King.

He walked out of the garden with a renewed sense of purpose. He asked one of the guards at the door to fetch Dr. Ross and usher him to the Throne Room. On the way he encountered James who had been waiting for him. The guards had not allowed him to enter the garden as the King had instructed.

"Father, I have talked to Dr. Ross and Mrs. Ross at length regarding your decision that they remain in Wiltshire. I also understand that Gretchen has come to you with new details regarding the use of the portal that may allow them to return to Oxford for a longer period of time. Is that true?"

"Gretchen and Arius approached me earlier to update me on the information that she had just located in the notes Merlin left. There is much to think about, and before I make any decisions regarding the future of the Ross family, I must talk to Dr. Ross and hope we can come to terms on this."

"May I be part of that meeting?"

"No, you may not."

"That is your wish, Father?"

"It is. I will announce my decision to all involved soon."

"Thank you. You are a just and fair King and I have always admired you, Father. I know you will make the decision that is best for all."

"Thank you, my son." The King left James and continued on his way to the Throne Room.

He walked into the Throne Room and stopped. This was where he had made so many important decisions while he was King. He wasn't proud of all of them, and he had made some mistakes, but he knew he had done his best to be a wise and thoughtful ruler to his people. Now he was faced with another decision that would affect the lives of a whole family who had not chosen to come to Wiltshire. On top of that, James had fallen in love with Justine which complicated this even further. And to add an unknown to this equation, the family were now considered to be travelers who would retain their memories of Wiltshire no matter how many times they journeyed through the portal. But there were some bright spots in all of this. One being, a seeker would have the power to stop a traveler from talking about Wiltshire to others on the outside, and two, the kingdom would have an experienced heart surgeon in their midsts which would benefit all. He finally walked over to the throne, sat down and awaited the arrival of Dr. Ross.

He was deep in thought when the guard knocked on the door.

"Aye, enter."

"I have brought Dr. Ross as requested, your majesty."

"Thank you, please have him enter."

Dr. Ross walked into the room cautiously not knowing what to expect.

"Ah, Dr. Ross. I am pleased you have arrived for I have some new ideas to discuss with you."

"King William, I would like to apologize for my behavior this morning. I was out of line. I know that now. In America, where we are from, we may speak our mind freely without punishment. That was what I was doing, forgetting I am in 16th century England now with different rules and laws."

"You are forgiven, Dr. Ross. I also must remember that you are not from our time and not familiar with our customs."

"But it appears I will need to learn them since we are to reside here."

"That is why I summoned you here. There is much we need to discuss. Please have a seat at the table and I will join you. Guard, please bring us some ale."

King William left his seat on the throne and moved to a seat at the table on the side of the room. Cedric entered the room with the ale and placed the cups and the decanter on the table. Then he poured each a cup.

"Will there be anything else, your majesty?"

"No, thank you, Cedric. That will be all." Cedric left the room leaving the two alone to talk.

"Dr. Ross, it seems there has been some new information uncovered by Gretchen regarding the portal. Arius and she came to me this very afternoon to update me. I have been sorting it all out in my head and now want to talk to you about several solutions that have come to my attention. You may talk openly to me as we are alone and no one will hear. After we talk and I have heard from you, I will render a decision. It is important that you agree here and now to abide by that decision no matter what. Do I have your word on that?"

"You do, your majesty."

"Before we begin, I would like to apologize to you and your family. You did not ask to come here but were brought by our seeker, Gretchen, to diagnose and treat my illness and that was to be it. But as circumstances would have it, it became necessary to take me through the portal so that you could operate on me with modern equipment. No one knew then that you were no longer visitors to our kingdom. Having only gone through the portal twice, your memories, we have learned, would be more like dreams. But then there was the love that occurred between Justine and James, which was another complication. When James left to find her, we never imagined he would return with Justine and you, her family. That made the third time you and Justine entered the portal. This meant you would now have full memory of your time here if and when you returned to the future. You must understand that this presents a problem to the security of our kingdom and those around us if anyone on the outside learns of our existence. That is why I stated your family would remain and never leave again. But now, there is more we did not know about travelers and that is why I have asked you here. I will share what I have learned and will hear your thoughts. Then I will decide if my first ruling stands or if I should rescind it and propose something different."

"I will gladly have that discussion, your majesty. I am eager to learn what Gretchen has told you and to hear any suggestions you may have as to how all of this might be resolved."

King William and Dr. Ross talked for over an hour each making suggestions as to the fate of the Ross family. Dr. Ross brought up some things the King hadn't thought of. Tying up loose ends wasn't going to be an easy task, for not only did they need to consider the life they were to lead in Oxford, but there was the house and life they lived in America. The King was very surprised by what needed to be done by the family. King William was most appreciative of all Dr. Ross had shared and the collaboration between them. He dismissed Dr. Ross and explained he would contemplate what was learned and make a decision within two days. He explained he also needed to consult with Gretchen and Arius to make sure whatever he decided was possible. The two then got up from the table and stood across from each other.

"May I share what was discussed with my family, mainly Stephanie?"

"I want this conversation to remain between us for some of it may not be possible. I do not want to raise the hopes of someone only to have them disappointed."

"Good point. You have my word. This conversation will remain just between us."

"Thank you, Dr. Ross... Drew."

Dr. Ross smiled when he heard the king say his name for it signaled to him this conversation had been between two friends.

"I will eagerly await your decision, your majesty."

Dr. Ross respectfully bowed to the King and left the room.

All the calmness he had just felt in the garden was now gone, and the stress of this decision began to consume him. He wasn't sure what to do and needed to consult Gretchen and Arius before he could make any decision. It was getting late, and he was probably expected at dinner. It would be best if he put off any decisions until the next day. He would summon the family in the morning.

The King didn't sleep very well that night as all of the possible scenarios were swimming in his head. He knew there was the possibility that what he wanted to do might not work after he talked to Gretchen and Arius. But that didn't stop him from thinking.

Morning came and he found he had actually drifted off to sleep. The servants came and helped him get ready for the day.

"I will take my breakfast in the Throne Room. Have Cedric deliver it there. And tell Gretchen and Arius I need to see them straight away."

"Aye, your majesty." And the servants left the room.

When the King arrived at the Throne Room, Arius and Gretchen were already there and Cedric had delivered his breakfast as requested. The King made his way to the table and started to eat.

"Thank you for coming. Please, sit. I have some thoughts and concerns to share with you two regarding the fate of the Ross family. It is of utmost importance that we, collectively, come up with a solution today so that I may render a decision we all can live with and abide by."

"Aye, your majesty," Arius began, "we understand your dilemma and wish to help in any way we can."

"Aye, that we do," Gretchen added.

The three of them talked all morning presenting the pros and cons of each scenario suggested. One plan was finally agreed upon which they felt was the best solution for all involved. King William asked them to remain with him and together they would inform the Ross family of the decision. The King told a member of his guard to locate the family members as well as Dr. Lange and have them all meet with him. He also wanted the members of his own family to be there so they would all hear the decision from him and not someone else. Everyone would be on the same page at the same time. However, Catherine was not to be included in this meeting for she was an outsider and would always remain so.

One by one they arrived in the Throne Room. He asked the Queen to take her seat next to him and his children to sit in the chairs in front of him to the right. He asked the Ross family to sit on the left side of the room. Arius and Gretchen stood next to the King's throne on the left. Once everyone had arrived, he cleared his throat and started.

"As we all know, what we knew previous to this day regarding the portal was not totally accurate. We were negligent in our duty to ensure we had all the facts before we put it to use. We did not know there were documents, notes, books, painstakingly kept by Merlin stored in the tower occupied by Arius. Gretchen is the one who discovered their existence and has since apprised me of the information contained therein. We still have much to learn from Merlin, and I look forward to the opportunity to share in that knowledge. But right now we have a pressing matter to discuss, that being the fate of the Ross family.

"Gretchen, Arius and I have been in conversation all morning and think we have a proposal all may live by. But it must be agreed upon with no exceptions. There will be consequences if the agreement is broken by anyone in the Ross family. I will divulge the plan and the consequences we have written up in this document. Then I will ask each member of the Ross family to sign the pledge and live by this document until the death of that family member. Now, without interruption from anyone, I will proceed."

King William set about explaining that the original ruling he made was void with this new one to take effect upon the signing of the document. He explained it was Gretchen who first presented this idea to him and later, after much thought and discussion with Dr. Ross, he agreed it was the best method to "tie up loose ends," as Merlin put it. He told them they would be able to return to Oxford for the next two years and finish what they had started when they originally moved to England. However, he stated that they would never be able to return to their home in Indiana. They would need to settle all their affairs without leaving England regarding the sale of the property in Indiana and anything else that needed their attention. As for Justine, she would be treated no differently than the rest of her family if she decided to return with them to Oxford. Then he stated they would be assigned a seeker to follow them wherever they went day or night. The seeker would have the ability to silence them if they mentioned anything about the portal or their time in Wiltshire. If that became a problem, meaning that person could not practice restraint in this matter, then the seeker would immediately return that person or persons to Wiltshire and whatever was left undone would remain so. This last part also pertained to Dr. Lange whose visits would now be accompanied as well. He told them that if a seeker had to return someone to Wiltshire, that would mean they had lost the trust of the King and would never be allowed to travel through the portal ever again.

Once King William finished, he waited for the reactions from either family. Finally Dr. Ross spoke up.

"King William, this is all new to my family as I did not share any of our conversations with them as requested. I would like the opportunity to discuss this with them before I agree to anything."

"Agreed. I will give you until tomorrow morning to render your decision."

"Thank you, your majesty. We will take our leave of you now as we have much to discuss."

CHAPTER 46

IN THEIR HANDS NOW

"Father, what if Justine decides to return with her family? I cannot be without her for two years. May I go with them if they leave?"

"No, you may not. You are now the heir to the throne since your brother is King of Dorset. You must remain here and be by my side so that you will learn what it is to be a King. You will not learn that if you live in Oxford with them. So, no. You will have to wait until they make their decision and then you will know what Justine has decided. Have patience, my son. That is a good quality in a King."

"I have patience, but not when it comes to Justine. But I will wait."

"Father, you mean Luke may be leaving us for two years?" Bethany whined. "You cannot understand what that means to Madison and me."

"More to you than me, sister," Madison replied. "But this means that after two years they will return to live here forever?

"Yes, my princesses. That is what the Ross family will be discussing. I ask that no one from our family approach them until tomorrow morning when they are to inform me of their decision."

"Aye, Father. We will try. I am with James, on pins and needles until tomorrow morning," Bethany sighed.

"Father, I may be in need of that silence spell. I do not plan to mention anything to Catherine, but what if I do? Since I will not be traveling through the portal and residing in Dorset, would the spell even work on me? And then there is the additional issue of when Catherine and I should depart for Dorchester. I do not think it prudent to leave Dorset without a ruler for very long."

"I agree, John. You have raised some valid points regarding the issue of now having Catherine in the family. I did not consider the possibility that you, more than anyone else, might be the one to expose our secret. Now I have grave concerns about sending you to live in Dorset. Gretchen...,"

"Aye, your majesty. I have heard what was said and I agree with you. I will look through the documents to ascertain if there is any information regarding this particular concern. I will return as soon as I know anything." Then Gretchen left.

"John, I want you both to prepare to leave by the end of the week as Catherine has already been gone for over two weeks now. Gretchen should know something by then and I hope we will be able to resolve this issue. Lord Chauncey and Victoria will accompany you. No one from outside the kingdom may be here if and when the Ross family departs. I will see to it that you have a small band of soldiers accompany you on your journey."

"Father, I am afraid that may be too long to wait. The journey alone will take the better part of a week. May I suggest another idea."

"You may."

"The trip would be much shorter if Arius were to change into a dragon and transport us there. We could leave and arrive on the same day. He has already been seen by many in Dorset so this would not be something new to them. Although, the last time they saw him was under very different circumstances. I would ask Sir Gregory, Lord Chauncey, and Victoria to leave now along with our belongings and they would arrive soon after we do."

Arius was about to speak up when the King spoke instead. "You would arrive much sooner if Arius were to take you, that is true. However, since being a dragon is new to him, I must consult Arius before I agree to your idea. And there is the matter of your healing. You are still recovering from your injuries. We will talk about it later," the King stated as he turned to look at Arius.

"May we ride the dragon, too, Father?" Bethany inquired. "Madison and I want to soar through the sky like James and John did."

"Arius is not one of your toys. I do not want him to regret having transformed in order to save the life of your brother. One day, it may be possible but not now. My family, you may not speak of what you have heard just now or of the idea the Ross family may be leaving. We have guests in this palace who are not to know any of this. You may not leave this room until you have promised me you will do as I have asked."

One by one they promised their father and King they would be silent on this matter. Then they left the room leaving King William, Gretchen and Arius alone.

"Arius, until our guests leave, our kingdom must continue to keep those things hidden we have acquired from the future. And Arius, you have heard from my son. What say you regarding his request? Will you carry the two of them back to Dorchester?"

"Sire, I have carried two on my back before so I know it is possible. But there is the problem of a saddle. The one I have created was suited only for one rider, and that was James. I will need to have a little time to invent one for two people but it can be done. I would gladly fly Prince, excuse me, King John where he needs to go. There remains the issue of me arriving as a dragon. The people of Dorchester did not see me in a positive way the last time I was there. It might be best if I land near there and have them ride on horseback the remainder of the way. I should be ready by tomorrow in the early afternoon."

"Thank you, Arius. I know if you are taking them, they will arrive safely. Your suggestion is a fair point and I agree with you. But how do we ensure that the horses will be where they are needed?"

"I will see to that, your majesty. It will be done."

"Very well. Once Gretchen has located the needed information, I need her to find a trustworthy seeker, other than herself, to accompany the group from Dorset. I want to be sure they carry no information with them regarding our secrets."

"I will let her know, your majesty," Arius replied. "I will also place a spell on them which will make them forget anything out of the ordinary they may have seen. But the idea of sending a seeker will help ensure there are no issues especially regarding the possibility of King John inadvertently disclosing anything."

"I am most grateful for you both. Your counsel in matters of the kingdom has truly been a blessing for me. Thank you."

"You are most welcome, your majesty, and I will inform Gretchen of your compliment. Now we must be about your business. I take my leave of you," Arius responded and he disappeared.

King William left the Throne room confident his proposal would be accepted by the Ross family and that John and Catherine would arrive safely in Dorchester thanks to Arius. There was still the concern their guests may have discovered one or more of their secrets. But he knew everyone had been very careful to ensure none had been divulged. He wondered if the 'silence' spell could work on someone in their own time but who lived in a different kingdom. He would have to wait to see if Gretchen located that information in Merlin's notes.

As he walked through the halls of the palace, he couldn't help but notice the quiet that engulfed the household. It seemed that no one was talking to anyone, not even within his own family. It was good they were following his orders. He decided it was best if he also kept to himself. He saw Cedric on his way to the kitchen carrying empty dishes.

"Cedric,"

"Your majesty."

"I see you are carrying dishes to the kitchen. Did anyone eat dinner in the Great Hall."

"No, your majesty, it was very strange, but all asked that dinner be served in the bedchambers. It was most unusual. It is so very quiet in the palace this evening."

"That was my doing but I did not expect for them to all retreat to their bedchambers for the evening. You may be serving breakfast there as well. It remains to be seen. With this family, every day has its surprises!"

"So true, your majesty. So true."

"I will follow the example of my family and eat in my bedchamber as well."

"I will bring your dinner straight away, your majesty."

King William proceeded up the stairs and down the hall to his bedchamber. It had been a long day and he was very glad he didn't encounter anyone in the halls. He opened the door, and sitting in a chair near the fireplace was his wife. She looked up as soon as she heard the door open.

"Marianne, I did not expect to find you here. Have you been waiting very long?"

"William, I want you to know how proud I am of you. You were not afraid to change your mind regarding the Ross family and their fate and present a new plan to them. I know the information you received about the portal is new, thanks to Gretchen, which enabled you to think differently about their eminent departure. Everyone in our family knows how important it is to allow the Ross family to decide on their own. You can hear a pin drop in this palace it is so quiet. It is also important to maintain our secrets and therefore not converse with our guests while we wait. I know John will not say anything to Catherine. But I fear that someday he will not be so guarded and may mention the portal by mistake. Let us hope that day never comes."

"Thank you, Marianne. Your words have been most welcome and mean much to me right now. I am glad you waited for me so you could deliver these words of encouragement. Gretchen is searching for an answer to the issue raised by John, and it is hoped she will know something soon." He heard a knock on the door. "Aye, who is there?"

"Cedric, your majesty. I have the dinner you requested."

"Oh, aye. Thank you. Bring it in and place it on the table."

Cedric entered with the King's dinner and placed it on the table as requested.

"Will there be anything else, your majesty."

"No, that will be all. Thank you, Cedric."

After Cedric closed the door, the King requested his wife remain while he ate. The two of them had the opportunity to spend time talking without interruption, which they hadn't had the chance to do for a long time.

CHAPTER 47

PREPARATIONS ARE MADE

The King and Queen got up the next morning not knowing what the day would bring. But the night had brought them closer than they had been for a long time and they felt relaxed and ready to meet the day head on. They dressed and proceeded to the Great Hall for breakfast. They both thought they would be the only ones there. However, when they rounded the corner, the whole family was there eating, talking and laughing as if nothing had happened.

"Good morning, family," King William announced. "So good to see everyone enjoying each other this early in the day."

"Father, we decided since we may not be able to eat together much longer that we should all be at breakfast this morning," James responded.

"That thought had not occurred to me and I am glad to see you all here. We must feast and enjoy this moment."

"Your majesty, I cannot help but wonder why the Ross family has not joined us," Catherine asked. "I would very much like to spend these last meals with them as well."

Not wanting to arouse suspicion in her, the King replied, "Thank you, Catherine, for that suggestion. I will have Cedric summon them at once."

Within about fifteen minutes, the members of the Ross family began to appear and take their seats at the table. Even though it was hard, James kept his distance from Justine as his father had asked. His patience was beginning to grow thin and he wanted desperately to know what the family had decided.

"Thank you for reminding us about breakfast, your majesty. It appears we were all sleeping in this morning," Dr. Ross responded trying to explain their absence.

"It was not I who requested your presence at breakfast. It was Catherine. She and John will be leaving soon for Dorset, and she wanted everyone here for what may be their last breakfast in Wiltshire."

At that point, Lord Chauncey and Victoria entered the room. "What is this I hear, that John and Catherine are to return to Dorchester soon?"

"You are leaving without me, sister?"

"In a way, we are. But you will be leaving soon as well. Maybe even today. We will explain while we eat this wonderful breakfast that has been prepared for us."

During breakfast, Catherine explained the plan as John had presented it to her. She and John could leave and return on the same day as they might be traveling on Arius, the dragon. Victoria and Lord Chauncey would be traveling in a carriage with Sir Gregory and would be at the castle by the end of the week. They would be escorted by a small band of knights from Wiltshire to assure their safe arrival.

"I think it is wise to return to Dorchester as soon as possible," Lord Chauncey insisted. "The people have been without a ruler for too long and need you both there. You must remember that your court is not aware of your marriage and may offer some resistance to this union. But they will come around in time. Sir Abbot will be there to assist you, and he is in command of the army if you find it necessary to assemble them."

"Thank you, Lord Chauncey. Your counsel is greatly appreciated as always," Catherine noted. "I do think arriving on a dragon may also be a deterrent to some who may question my seat on the throne."

Everyone laughed following that statement which lightened the mood at the table. The rest of the time at breakfast was spent in pleasant conversation with Queen Marianne recounting some of John's childhood to his new bride, embarrassing him to no end.

"I do not want to call an end to this wonderful breakfast, but it is time for John and Catherine to begin to gather their things together for I think it would be best if they depart today. Please remember, you are riding on the back of a dragon and must take only the essentials. Sir Gregory will deliver anything else by the end of the week."

"Understood, Father. I will make sure Catherine takes very little."

"Aye, my Lord. Whatever you say, my Lord!" Catherine stated sarcastically.

"Off, you two," Queen Marianne insisted. "We will see you soon."

Just then, Gretchen and Arius entered the Great Hall.

"Gretchen, Arius, I am glad to see you both. Do you have any news for us?"

"We do, your majesty." Gretchen replied. "May we speak in private? And Arius would like to meet with John before he makes preparations to leave. He would also like Dr. Ross to accompany him as well."

Gretchen and King William left the Great Hall together, walked into the parlor and closed the doors. Arius met John and Dr. Ross and led them to Dr. Lange's office.

"I have been up most of the night searching the pages regarding the portal for the information you needed and I have found it. Merlin wrote that hiding their secrets became a problem when the royalty of Wiltshire needed to visit other kingdoms or they came here. A spell was devised similar to the one used outside the portal that would keep them from mistakingly saying something they should not say about Wiltshire. Then, they were able to travel freely without the fear of any secrets being discovered. Arius has come across that spell and is ready to cast it on John."

"If we can do that right now, I would appreciate it. John and Catherine will be leaving this morning."

"Aye, I was not aware they would be departing today."

"Please inform Arius that he is to perform this spell as soon as possible."

"Aye, your majesty. He is doing that as we speak." Then Gretchen opened the door and left.

King William walked out into the Great Hall yelling for Cedric.

"I am here, your majesty."

"Cedric, please inform me when John is done with Arius. I must talk to him before they leave this morning. Then please tell my children and the Ross family that John and Catherine will be leaving sometime this morning and to be ready to go to the courtyard at a moment's notice."

"I will do so, your majesty."

King William left the Great Hall to find the Queen since she was not aware of any of this and needed to be told. He located her in the garden and explained what had just transpired and that John and Catherine were to leave soon.

"It is for the best, Marianne. The longer they linger here, the greater the chances of something being discovered. The Ross family is to deliver their decision sometime this morning and I would like John and Catherine to have left by then."

"But, so soon! I was hoping to have more time to say goodbye."

"It does not take long to say goodbye, it is the absence of them when they are gone that will hurt the most. And that will happen no matter when they leave."

"I will miss him dearly. Please allow me to linger in the garden a little longer and then I will join you in the courtyard when it is time for them to leave."

King William left the garden and needed to make sure all of his instructions had been followed. He located Cedric and was assured he had followed through on all the King had asked him to do and that John had indeed met with Arius. Cedric told him that John wanted his father to meet him in Dr. Lange's office. So, King William made his way to Dr. Lange's office hoping that John didn't have bad news for him about his injuries.

When he opened the door to the office, he saw John sitting on the doctor's table.

"John, is everything fine? Did something happen?" Then he noticed John's arm wasn't in the sling. "John, please answer me."

John got a huge smile on his face, hopped off the table, walked over to his father and gave him a big hug.

"John?" his father exclaimed. "But your injuries?"

"Father, I am healed! My bones are no longer broken!"

"But, how is this possible?"

"Your majesty, I came across a spell to heal broken bones while reading Merlin's manuscripts! I performed it on John and it worked! It can only be done once the bones are in their right place which was accomplished by the doctors. Now he can travel with no worries."

"I am as surprised as you are!" Dr. Ross responded. "But he's right. I checked, and the bones are as good as new!"

"This is more than I could have ever hoped for!" Then King William hugged his son tightly.

"Father, is that a tear I see in your eye?"

"No, no, just have something in it. We must go and inform the rest of the family of this great news. Oh, I almost forgot. Arius, did you also have a chance to perform the 'silence' spell on him?"

"Aye, your majesty. It has been done."

"It is time for us to go and let John surprise his bride with this good news and make preparations to leave. Now that everything has been accomplished, the only thing left is to meet everyone in the courtyard."

CHAPTER 48

JOHN AND CATHERINE
SAY GOODBYE

Everyone was summoned to the courtyard for the departure of the new King and Queen of Dorset. They were excited and sad at the same time. Soon John and Catherine appeared at the front door, and John ran over to his family. King William had already informed them of the spell Arius had cast, so they were very excited to see it for themselves. They all crowded around him, each in turn giving him a hug.

"I cannot believe how good you look, John!" James exclaimed. "You look as good as new! As if nothing ever happened!"

"I feel as good as new!" John replied. "Now I can hug my new bride and not worry about breaking any bones!" John looked around and did not see a dragon waiting in the middle of the courtyard. "Where is Arius?" John inquired.

He had no sooner asked the question when above them they heard the loud flapping of wings. Everyone backed up as Arius descended into the courtyard and touched down with a thud.

"I am here, your majesty, as requested. I have fashioned a saddle I think will enable the two to ride comfortably."

"Thank you, Arius. Just one request before you leave." Arius, the dragon, lowered his head so he could hear the King.

"You will be careful when flying my son and his bride back to Dorset. Now that he is healed, I don't want him to have any more broken bones."

"I will fly as smoothly as possible."

"That pleases me greatly! Thank you." King William looked around him to see if he could locate James. "Ah, there you are. James, would you demonstrate the technique you used to mount and dismount this dragon."

"I would be happy to do that. With the help of Arius, I was able to get on and off with ease. You will find that flying is an experience of a lifetime! I look forward to the time when Arius and I can again fly off into the clouds."

Then James showed John and Catherine the method he used to climb up on Arius' back and then slide off.

"There you go, brother. It is a rather easy process."

"Thank you for showing us how easily it can be done, James," his father shared. "Now it is time to say our goodbyes to King John and Queen Catherine. That is the first time I have used the titles given to you. It seems strange to have John be King of Dorset but they will have a just and fair King whom I am very proud to call my son." John hugged his father and then backed away.

"This is not forever," John insisted. "We will return to Wiltshire for visits, and you may travel to Dorset as well. Riding Arius would make the journey much quicker."

"I will miss you, John, I mean King John," Bethany babbled as she started to cry.

"Little sister, you may always call me John for I will always be your big brother." Then he stooped down and gave her a big hug. "And you, Miss Madison, will you miss me?"

"Every day!" and Madison began to cry, too.

John hugged his mother and then James. He walked over to Justine, and whispered in her ear, "You take good care of my brother. He loves you very much." Then he hugged her. Finally he shook hands with the rest of the Ross family. When he got to Dr. Ross, Dr. Ross gave him some last-minute instructions on how to take care of himself.

"Do not worry, Dr. Ross. I will take good care of him," Catherine assured him.

"Catherine, we must depart if we are to arrive before dark," John insisted.

John got on the dragon as James had instructed and then helped Catherine climb on. He had her sit on the saddle in front of him so he could hold her tightly. "Hold on to the strap Catherine, and do not let go. And I will hold on to you."

"I do not intend to, my husband."

Changing the subject, John affirmed, "In truth, this is very comfortable, Arius. Thank you for making it so."

"You are very welcome, King John. Now we must go. Hold on, you two."

With that, Arius spread his wings and ascended into the air above the courtyard.

"Ohhhh myyyyy goodness..." they heard Catherine scream as Arius took off.

Soon the dragon and its passengers were a small blip in the sky, and John and Catherine were gone.

No sooner had they disappeared when King William announced, "Now, we must prepare to send Sir Gregory and his band of travelers on their way,"

The King walked over to Sir George who had been standing nearby in case he was needed during the take off.

"Sir George, I need you to assemble the knights who are to escort Sir Gregory to Dorset. Also, tell Gretchen we are in need of the person she has chosen to accompany this group."

"Aye, your majesty. It will be done."

Within a half hour, the knights were assembled on horseback and Gretchen had appeared accompanied by a seeker named Joseph. However, the visitors from Dorset did not know he was a seeker for that was a term only used in Wiltshire.

Then the King addressed Sir Gregory. "This group of knights are to go with you on your journey to Dorchester. Once you are delivered and they find the kingdom to be receptive to the new King and Queen, they are to depart and return to Wiltshire. Joseph, however, will remain as right hand to King John and will decide if and when he will return to Wiltshire."

"Thank you, your majesty. We will ensure that Lady Victoria and Lord Chauncey arrive safely in Dorchester. I see a wagon has just pulled up behind the knights. Is it to travel with us as well?"

"Aye, I am afraid those are the items John and Catherine wanted to take with them but could not carry while riding a dragon."

"Understood, your majesty. We will see that the wagon arrives safely as well."

Lord Chauncey and Lady Victoria climbed into the carriage that had originally brought them to Wiltshire and Sir Gregory mounted his horse.

"We both want to thank you for your hospitality during our stay in Wiltshire," Lord Chauncey called out from the window on the carriage. "We are ready, Sir Gregory."

Sir Gregory signaled to the small band of travelers to move forward toward the front gate. Both families stood to the side and watched as they traversed the courtyard, went through the outer courtyard and on through the massive gates. Soon, they were all but specks in the distance and King William ordered the gates closed.

King William proceeded to walk to the palace with the Queen and everyone else followed close behind. Justine peered behind her and noticed James was not far away. He looked in her direction and she smiled at him. He smiled back and then looked away. No one talked all the way back to the palace. Once inside, the royal family went in one direction and the Ross family in another. However, Dr. Ross approached the King in the Main Hall.

"We have made our decision. May we share that with you now or should we wait until later."

"This is good news. Very good news indeed. We must discuss it now while it is fresh in your mind. You gather your family and meet me and my family in the Throne Room. I want everyone to hear what you are going to say, not just me."

"I will go get my family and will meet you soon."

"I will summon mine as well. I look forward to hearing from you."

CHAPTER 49

THE ROSS FAMILY DEPARTS

The Ross family entered the Throne Room simultaneously. Queen Marianne took her place beside her husband and the children stood to his right facing the Ross family.

"It is my understanding that you have come to announce your decision," King William began. "We are most eager to hear it. Please, tell us."

"We appreciate greatly the time you have spent on this matter. We are also very sorry our presence here has caused so many problems within your kingdom. It was never our intent. But at the same time, I think some good has come out of our being summoned here originally since you have now learned so much more about the portal and how it can be used. But I will not lie. We never in our wildest dreams thought that we would have to live out our days here in Wiltshire. That was an unforeseen consequence of Gretchen bringing me and my family here more than once. We have all come to grips with it now and are prepared to accept that fact. We are grateful for the opportunity you have offered to us to return to Oxford for the next two years..." At that moment, James looked over at Justine and held his breath. "... and we have decided we would like to do just that."

James dropped to his knees and looked down at the floor. Justine ran over to him knelt down in front of him, took his hand and whispered, "I am so sorry." James raised his head and as he did, she noticed he had tears in his eyes. "I told you I would never leave you and I meant it. But my parents have decided I need to finish high school. And they want me there to help get our affairs in order." He reached over and hugged her and then kissed her. They stood up together still holding hands.

"Prince James, you didn't let me finish. Stephanie, Luke and I will definitely be in Oxford for the next two years. We have informed Justine we may renegotiate at the end of a year. It is important we all finish what we came there to do. At the same time, we will work to get our affairs in order so we are ready at the end of the two years to make the move to Wiltshire. The one caveat to all of this is that we will be able to travel back and forth if needed. It is important we return to Oxford as a family. Justine will travel with us but intends to return to Wiltshire as often as she can during her school breaks. We feel Justine is still too young to get married and ask that James and she wait at least a year before they are wed. Then, they will have a whole lifetime to be together. If it is decided at the end of the first year that she will be returning to Wiltshire for good, we will tell people she has decided to return to the United States in order to finish her last year of high school. Also, we do realize a seeker will be with each of us, invisible I'm assuming, the whole two years. We also promise to never reveal any information at any time to anyone about our time here or about Wiltshire and the portal. If any one of us breaks that promise, we are aware that person will be immediately returned to Wiltshire. But that is not expected to happen. We will sign your document stating all of this and want to leave tomorrow.

We can't let anymore time pass between the time we left and the time we will return. Right now, we're afraid there will be too many questions as it is."

"Tomorrow? You are leaving tomorrow?" James asked Justine.

"Yes, it isn't something I wanted to do but I understand the point my dad made. People will be asking a lot of questions about where we have been for these many weeks and the more time we let pass the harder it will be to explain our disappearance. I hope to be able to return in a month."

"One month will be like an eternity! But how often will you be able to return?"

"I will return as often as I can. Once we are married, we will never again be parted."

"James and Justine, has your conversation ended? I would like to respond to Dr. Ross."

"Aye, Father. I am sorry for the disruption."

"I thank you for the promises you have made, and we will be sorry to lose you and your family for two years but understand the choice you have made. Now we must have the document to sign and the seekers who are to accompany you. We will wait to set the date for the wedding as you have requested."

"If I may, I would like to suggest a date for the wedding," Dr. Ross mentioned.

"Suggest away."

"Well, your majesty, there are breaks in the college calendar that would make it easier for us to attend depending on when the wedding takes place. But whether it is within a year or after two years when the whole family is to return for good, Stephanie and I would like to suggest a wedding at Christmas."

"Thank you for the suggestion. I think I will leave this decision up to James and Justine with the Queen also having her say in the matter."

"I think a wedding celebration at Christmas would be absolutely beautiful," the Queen insisted. "We have plenty of time to prepare, and John and Catherine would be able to join us then."

"That sounds wonderful, Queen Marianne. I would love a Christmas wedding," Justine admitted.

"Then Christmas it is. Now that that is settled, we must know who the seekers will be, and we need the document to sign. Once done, you are free to leave at any time. I will ask Gretchen to draw up the document for your signatures. The seekers will be ready to leave with you tomorrow morning. You may sign the document any time prior to your departure. Now I ask that everyone be in the Great Hall this evening where we will have our last feast together and say our goodbyes."

The Ross Family spent part of the day gathering their belongings and packing the bags they had brought with them. It didn't take very long since they had originally only packed for a weekend. Each one spent the rest of the day walking around the palace and the garden for the last time and visiting with the royal family.

Dinner was announced that evening, and they all gathered in the Great Hall. It was bitter sweet for the Ross family had come to love the members of the Pendragon family and would miss them dearly. It helped to know they would be returning for visits during the next two years and could look forward to the upcoming wedding set for Christmastime.

Everyone had a wonderful dinner that evening. There was some crying and a lot of laughs as they reminisced and said their goodbyes. Finally, the meal ended and everyone got up from the table.

"I will miss you, Luke," Bethany cried, and she ran over to him and hugged him.

"I will miss you, too. Take care of my sister for me whenever she returns, will you?"

"Aye, I will be most happy to do that."

"I will miss our morning walks, Stephanie," Queen Marianne shared. "I always looked forward to those. So many good conversations were had."

"I will miss that as well, your majesty, Marianne. But we can resume those when we are back in two years or when we come to visit."

King William walked over to Dr. Ross, "I will miss your counsel, Drew. You are most wise and always tell me the truth, which may not always be what I want to hear. I owe you my life, and for that I will forever be in your debt."

"Thank you, William. I have actually enjoyed our time here. It is a very interesting place to be living. I look forward to coming back for visits and then finally residing here."

"I am thankful you do not resent us for leading you here over a year ago. Without you, I would not be alive today. You will be missed."

Dr. Ross bowed to the King and then left the Great Hall followed by Stephanie and Luke. Justine remained behind to stay with James for a little longer.

"Come," James said as he grabbed Justine's hand. "We must go sit in the garden for a while for that is our special place now."

She put her arm in his, and together they walked through the door and out into the garden. The fragrance of the flowers surrounded them as they strolled down the path.

"I won't be gone long, only a month."

"One month is too long for me. I do not want you to leave, but I understand why it has to be this way even though I do not like it. Promise me you will be back."

"Of course, I will be back. I love you and want to be with you always."

"But, promise me," he turned and looked at her very seriously. "Promise me."

"I promise! I will come back. It would have to be something very serious that would keep me from returning to you."

"Then you must be very careful for I cannot be there to protect you. Nothing will keep us from being together."

"I will, I promise! I won't even leave the house if that calms your fears."

"That is a very good plan. I like that idea."

"Besides, I will have a seeker with me at all times. The seeker will look after me."

"That is true. I will ask Gretchen to be that seeker. She will make sure no harm comes to you."

"I would love it if Gretchen were to accompany me."

"Then, it shall be done. Now, let us go sit on the bench in the Gazebo together."

They walked over to the gazebo and sat down, he with his arm around her and she with her head on his shoulder. Neither of them talked for a while just enjoying the warmth of each other's body. Finally, Justine spoke up.

"I would like to lie next to you and watch the stars like we did the night of the wedding. Then I would like to watch the sun come up over the castle walls and be together until the very last moment I need to leave."

"My thoughts as well! I had hoped you would say that and left some blankets out here in the garden. The ground was cold last time we lay together. I will get them."

James found the blankets and placed them on a soft spot on the ground. Then both of them lay down and stared at the night sky. Justine turned on her side, placed her head on his chest and whispered, "I want you, too."

James raised his head and then sat up. "Are you sure?" he asked somewhat excitedly.

Justine knew she was protected and wanted this more than anything, especially since she was to leave the next morning and would not see him for at least a month. "I'm sure," she replied quietly.

The sun started to rise in the east and as it came up over the castle walls, sunbeams streamed across the garden and into Justine's face. She opened her eyes slowly for she did not want last night to be a dream. She looked next to her and there lay James, still asleep. He looked so peaceful she didn't want to wake him. She carefully lifted his arm, put her head on his chest and then placed his arm around her. She knew this was how she wanted it to be forever. She just lay there listening to his heart beat in his chest and her head rose and fell with each slow breath he took. He started to stir and opened his eyes. She felt both his arms wrap around her.

"Good morning. How are you this morning, my love?"

"I am wonderful. I didn't know love could feel like this. I can't explain how I felt last night. I've never felt anything like it, but I know I want to feel it again!"

"We will. We have our whole life to enjoy each other. But right now, I am afraid we need to get dressed for you will certainly be missed if we do not appear in the palace soon."

"Oh my gosh! My family! We're leaving this morning."

"I will help you dress."

"Nope. I mean no thank you. I know what will happen if I let you help me. I think it would be best if I dress myself."

"If you need my help, let me know."

"I will."

Justine walked over to a nearby bush and put on her clothes, the ones she was wearing when they first arrived.

"There, back to my old self."

James just stood there and stared at her. She wasn't dressed in 16th century clothing anymore, she now looked like the girl he first met that day in her bedroom. He knew the moment he saw her then that she was the one he would marry.

"Has anyone told you how beautiful you are?"

"Not since last night."

"Well, you are. I would not lie. As I look at you now, I remember the day we first met. I walked in the room and there you were. That moment I knew I would be yours forever."

She ran to him and kissed him. "And you, mine," she said as they stared at each other.

In the distance, she could hear someone calling her name and telling her to come inside. She grabbed James and held on to him tightly. "I don't want to go. I wish you could come with us, but I know your father said no."

"We will be together soon, only four weeks from now. That is not long compared to the lifetime we will have together. Hold my hand, and we will walk into the palace together."

The two walked back through the garden and into the palace. They found everyone standing in the main hall. Her mother walked over to her and extended her hand. Justine looked up at James and then took her mother's hand. They walked together to where Luke and her dad were standing. They were joined by three seekers. Then Justine noticed Gretchen was standing next to her. She turned and hugged her. "Gretchen, will you be coming with us?"

"That I will, Justine. I am to watch over you while you are gone and to see you safely back to Prince James."

"I'm so glad it's you that will be with me. I feel safe already!"

"I do not know where Arius is. He should have delivered John and Catherine to Dorchester by last night which means he should have returned by now," Gretchen said concerned.

No sooner had the words come out of her mouth when Arius appeared in front of her. "I have finally returned and King John and Queen Catherine are safe in Dorchester. However, upon my arrival back here, I had a vision of everyone standing in the hall so I came to investigate. What is happening?"

"We are leaving, Arius," Justine replied.

"Leaving? I cannot leave for an overnight without something happening around here. I suppose you need me to transport you to the portal."

"That we do, Arius. That we do," Gretchen repeated.

"Well then, I need everyone to gather in a circle and hold hands."

"We will see you again Ross family. Be safe and return to us whenever it is possible," King William told them. "Blessings on you all."

Justine turned to look at James and mouthed the words, "Goodbye, my love."

Next thing she knew they were all standing in front of the portal.

"Before you disappear, Arius, I want to thank you for all you have done for us," Dr. Ross stated. "You and Gretchen were instrumental in convincing the King to grant us this two-year leave before we are to settle in Wiltshire. We are all very grateful for that. So, even though we say good bye now, it won't be long before we return.

"Please know the Ross family will be missed," Arius affirmed.

Then Justine spoke up. "I would ask that you watch over Prince James for me, please. Keep him safe," Justine requested.

"I will do just that. Now I take my leave of you. You are in Gretchen's good hands now." And then he disappeared.

Gretchen turned to address the small band of travelers and, as before, explained the procedure for their departure. Once on the other side, they would all be invisible until she was sure no one had seen them come through. This was all very familiar to Justine now, and she looked forward to repeating this often in the next two years. What they were going to find on the other side she didn't know. She just knew she had to keep her mind focused on James and her return trip.

Gretchen pointed to the portal, and one by one each person walked through until no one in the group remained in Wiltshire.

And so begins another adventure.

ABOUT THE AUTHOR

As a young girl, reading was not one of my favorite past times. I would much rather sit and watch a movie than read a book. But this changed when I became a teacher. I loved to read the books my students were reading and looked forward to the conversations we would have about the characters. I also realized how much I enjoyed teaching my students to write. Because of this, I decided that one day I would write my own book but didn't realize how long it would take me to put those words on paper. Now that I have retired, I have finally accomplished the goal I set for myself. <u>Unexpected Return</u> is the sequel to <u>Unexpected Detour</u> and I hope you enjoy reading both.

Pam Knowles resides in Carmel, Indiana, USA. She is married and the proud parent of three children and Nana to six grandchildren.

Ingram Content Group UK Ltd.
Milton Keynes UK
UKHW042020090323
418309UK00001B/150